THE FLIGHT ENIGMA

MAGNOLIA BLUFF CRIME CHRONICLES

Breakfield and Burkey

Published by

ICABOD Press

ISBN: 978-1-946858-88-7 (paperback)
ISBN: 978-1-946858-89-4 (e-book)

Library of Congress Control Number: 2025913580
Interior and eBook design: F + P Graphic Design, FPGD.com

First Edition
Printed in the United States

MYSTERY | CRIME | SUSPENSE

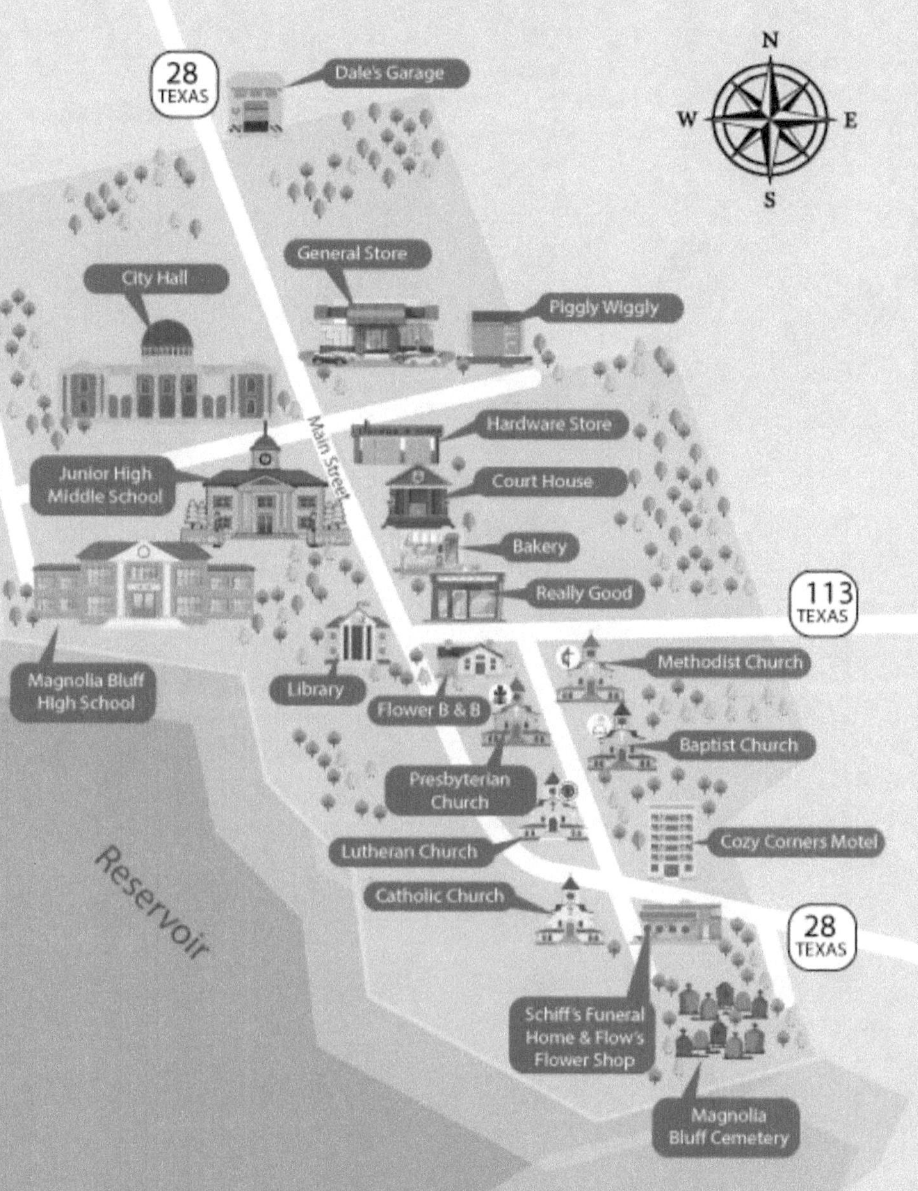
28 TEXAS
Dale's Garage
N
W E
S
General Store
City Hall
Piggly Wiggly
Hardware Store
Main Street
Junior High Middle School
Court House
Bakery
Really Good
113 TEXAS
Magnolia Bluff High School
Library
Methodist Church
Flower B & B
Baptist Church
Presbyterian Church
Lutheran Church
Cozy Corners Motel
Reservoir
Catholic Church
28 TEXAS
Schiff's Funeral Home & Flow's Flower Shop
Magnolia Bluff Cemetery
Magnolia Bluff

CHAPTER 1

The Ambush

CURRENT DAY

Mike completed his pre-flight check and then topped off the Cessna's fuel tanks. It took extra time, but he had learned the criticality of safety and never scrimped when flying. He recalled Juan Senior's training: "If the plane breaks down in the air, you can't just get out and walk."

He climbed into the cockpit, took another hearty swig of his special coffee brew, and complained, "Rats, cold already. I'll nuke it at Burnet Muni. It's too good to waste."

Mike fitted the headset and fastened his seat belt. He pressed the brakes firmly and started the engine. He wanted it to warm up before taxiing to the runway's north end. He spoke about his takeoff intentions to the chief, who was monitoring the radio of the private airstrip, and received a thumbs-up. Scanning the field, he decided it was clear that no one was approaching. He pushed the throttle forward, positioning for takeoff. Seconds later, the plane roared down the runway and easily climbed to his desired altitude, heading on course to Magnolia Bluff, Texas.

Forty minutes into the short flight, Mike's eyes couldn't distinguish the blurred numbers on the instruments. He blinked, wiping his eyes with the handkerchief, yet still unable to focus, but unwilling to admit he had a problem. Sweat beaded up on

1

his brow, rushing down his face to his chin, and then pooling in his lap. He took a calming breath and concentrated on staying on the correct heading. A few minutes later, he noticed that the yoke was not responding, despite his physical efforts to steer.

Mike felt a wave of dizziness. His gut tightened as stomach contents rose in the back of his throat. He swallowed several times, then held his breath for a long minute while focusing on the horizon. Praying to get the lightheadedness under control, he muttered, "Ash, honey, I won't crash because I got sick. I'm… what the hell?" He checked gauges, sensing the loss in altitude. "What the hell! The plane is set for landing. I've never seen this overgrown terrain on my approach to Burnet before." Panicking, he pulled back on the stick, but the aircraft continued its descent. "Why is nothing working?"

The plane barely cleared the tree line before it bounced hard on the field. The engine whine decreased to landing speed. Shocked, Mike's right hand grabbed the handle of his briefcase. His body jerked behind the seatbelt the moment the front wheel fumbled in a deep depression. Time seemed to halt the instant the Cessna dropped its nose into the soil. He was stunned when the upended plane didn't cartwheel. The abrupt stop caused Mike's head to hit the window. Dazed, he tried to comprehend the landing. His head throbbed, making him close his eyes and rest. Fighting to stay awake, he saw the ground from the front window and felt the straps of the restraints press painfully into his shoulders. He unexpectedly saw or imagined the passenger door open. Hoping for a rescue team, he grew worried when dark hands groped for something under the dashboard. The angles of everything looked wrong. Unable to move, he squinted, trying to identify the object the hands held before they vanished. The sounds of a struggle or fight outside flooded his brain, making his head ache even more. Mike fought to release his door. It abruptly released, but sounded wrong. His brain screamed to rest.

Then he recognized a familiar voice shouting. "Mike, Mike, are you alright? Can you talk? It's JJ."

"JJ, hide my briefcase," he insisted before darkness overcame his last thoughts.

A New Assignment

JJ grinned, seeing the caller ID. He quickly answered, "Hey. Mike, how's it going?"

"Work's crazy busy. I'm finalizing the specs for the radar sensing redirect we discussed for my F-35. I keep hitting a wall with the combined distance and direction variables needed to meet my safety specifications. I've added a new SOW for you to help verify the software and increase security on access to the program."

JJ enjoyed his work with Lockheed Martin, making this call a pleasant surprise. "Let me escalate this call to a meeting with video so you can show me." When the video engaged, he noticed deeper worry lines on his friend's face compared to the last time they had spoken. "There we are. You look a bit tired, buddy. Is this problem keeping you up at night?"

Pressing his fingers to his temple, Mike sighed. "Ashley's fed up with me and looking for a new place to live. She says I don't give her enough attention. She placed her wedding ring on the kitchen counter with a terse note. Almost five years. I can't believe she's calling it quits. She's my one and only."

"Wow. I'm shocked. Jo and I like her. Your home in the Pecan Plantation area reflects elements of you both." He arched an eyebrow and questioned, "Did you forget an important date like the anniversary of your meeting, your first kiss, or something like that? Women keep track of those types of details." JJ tapped his chin and looked Mike square in the eye. "You didn't stand her up at a restaurant again, did you?"

Mike laughed. "No. I've been working late nights to get this improvement ready for testing. She's angry at me for not being around." He took a sip from the disposable cup and sighed. "I recall we discussed all my faults before we agreed to build our home in Pecan. I'm fine with giving her the house, I don't want to live in it without her. She's made a lot of friends in the area. I'll find another place to hang my clothes. A simple apartment will suffice. I don't need much."

"You need a life, man." JJ's mind wandered back to their college days. He recalled the two of them, roughly the same age and height, when they exited the Fort Worth testing facility into the May afternoon sun. They sauntered to the parking lot, wiggling their fingers, then twisted their bodies to unkink after two-plus hours of sitting.

JJ sensed the relief coursing through his body fifteen years ago after finishing the exam with his best friend.

Then he said, "Whew! I'm glad the test is over. It was killer comprehensive. How do you think you did?"

He watched Mike shove his longish blonde hair behind his ear and roll his eyes. "I'm not sure. Some of the questions seemed ambiguous. I thought your dad was reviewing the smallest details to annoy us, but now I'm so glad he did."

"Mike, what did you think about those extra credit questions? They were tough."

"JJ, I figured it was worth the effort. I chose the one with the red telephone on the desk. Make a call to start World War III and report the socio-political effects."

"Yeah, I saw that one. What was your answer?"

Mike kept a straight face as he delivered a deadpanned response. "I stated I would call my wife and tell her to go on a diet because her derriere was getting way too wide. I added, honey, when I watched you walk away in your vacuum-packed workout pants, I thought your bottom looked like two Volkswagens trying to pass each other on a hill."

Laughing uproariously, JJ finally snorted a response. "I could see that observation starting a major war."

Mike punched his friend in the shoulder. "I added a few other gently finessed issues to round out the socio-political effects of relationships. Which one did you do?"

"I chose the one about the five hundred riot-crazed aborigines storming the room, whom I needed to calm down using any ancient language besides Latin or Greek. I created a meme library as a language tool mimicking Egyptian Hieroglyphics to help calm them down. The pictographs I built looked like they would do the trick." He pulled a piece of note paper used for scribbling during the test and showed it to Mike. "I made an extra copy with the proctor's permission. I can use them in my intern position with the computer sciences department at ETH Zürich."

"Good thinking, man. You're always repurposing stuff. I'm glad you got into their computer science program. It's supposed to be the best in the world."

"Mister socio-political details guy. Geez. Have you decided to accept your MIT or Georgia Tech scholarship yet?" he asked, finger-combing his untamed raven-black hair.

"I haven't. I prefer Georgia Tech because I'd also like to play ball. However, my dad wants me to focus on my studies rather than sports. Massachusetts gets too much snow for this Texas boy. How about you? When do you return to Europe for your higher education?"

"Not for a couple of weeks. Dad wants to do some motorcycle riding and camping. Mom and my twin Gracie are doing a girls' shopping spree, so Dad voted for the male bonding thing."

Mike checked his watch. "We need to move it, buddy, and get to the field. Our check rides are scheduled soon. We'll be pushing it to make it on time, going the speed limit."

JJ jumped into the driver's side because the top was down on his gray Porsche 911. When he turned the key, the engine purred to life. Mike methodically opened the door and sat on the other side, tightening his seatbelt.

"Our dads said they'd meet us at the field to take us for a celebration dinner. What if we don't pass everything?"

JJ laughed as he shifted and spun out of the parking lot, leaving a bit of rubber on the way to the airfield. "Mr. Hayes, when have you ever failed a test? Two full-ride college offers, and you're worried?"

"Yep. That's my middle name to make me try harder."

"Ah, finally. I've discovered the chink in your armor."

Skidding into the private airfield parking lot, JJ parked beside the men, eyeing his maneuver.

Juan, an older version of JJ with strands of white sparkling in his mane, checked his watch. "Three minutes to spare. I was unsure if this car was the best idea, but it does help you stay on time. Gordon, what sort of car did you get Mike?"

"A practical pick-up truck. After all, we are Texans, my friend." The older man adjusted his Stetson, tilting it back, revealing close-cropped, graying blonde hair."

Juan gestured toward the two planes with a man standing by each. "Complete your check rides, then we can go eat. I'm famished. I should have the other test results by then, too."

Gordon grinned, wiggling the fingers of his right hand for emphasis. "Get it done, boys. You've spent a year of hard study and practice. I know you will both pass at the top of the class."

The memory receded. JJ felt lucky to have maintained a relationship with his best friend. He worried about how the possible breakup would impact Mike's productivity. "Heck, you don't drink often, never gamble, or do drugs. Do you want me to see if Jo knows anything? Maybe she can help find out the whys so you two can patch things up? She has a knack for helping folks and being empathetic."

Mike pursed his lips and nodded. "That would be great. I love Ashley, but I'm clueless when it comes to romance. I wish I were as good with Ashley as you are with Jo. You both seem to have a secret wordless language." He glanced at his watch. "Enough on me for now. Let's get back to the new work order I sent you to leverage the parameters I want included in the radar-masking capabilities of the F-35. We incorporated its viability with your former contract. I need this change to call it complete. It's critical to the pilots' lives."

JJ opened the new assignment and quickly scanned it. "I see where you're going, and it makes sense. Please send the analytics to date to our shared Dropbox. I can begin work on it after I sign the contract and receive confirmation. Your projects go to the top of the queue every time. Is there anything else?"

Faced with the image on the screen, JJ saw the seriousness reflected in his friend's expression.

"Actually, yes, but I can't prove it yet." He frowned. "It'll have to wait because I have another meeting. Do you have time in the morning for another call?"

"Certainly. Pick your time and send me a bridge. Looking forward to it."

CHAPTER 3

I Want to Stay and Play

Mike was about to launch his conference call with JJ when he spotted his IT technician, Kamal, leaning into his office. Appreciating the man's ability to move like a cat with his wiry build, he said, "You're practicing your ninja moves today. What's up?"

"Hey, Mike. I've had to shut down your network access. Your email account appears hacked. Our policy states we must disable your login ID and remove any access until a review is completed. The secure Dropbox was also disabled. Someone or something has you in their sights. Our alpha-numeric phrased user IDs are not keeping you cloaked. Whatever you're working on, someone wants to see. Sorry, man. We're running forensics on the accounts to verify nothing was taken."

Tired and frustrated, Mike wiped his face with his hands. "Without a valid login, Kamal, I can't use our corporate communications system to join a conference bridge I created. What am I supposed to do?"

Kamal grinned, his white teeth shining through, as his expresso-colored eyes tried to convey empathy. "Call the attendees from your cell phone and instruct them to stand down until you send a new meeting request. Don't forget you may not use your mobile device to hold or join a conference call about your project, because it's not secure."

"Yeah, I know. I follow the rules so I don't have to wear an orange jumpsuit in a maximum-security prison. How long before I get a new user ID and password?"

"Mike, forensics will need to clear the old stuff before issuing you a new credential. Right now, you're off the clock."

"Kamal, did I tell you that I don't like this? I've got deadlines to meet. Will my corporate PC be impounded too?"

Hanging his head, his long ponytail cascading over his right shoulder, Kamal quietly offered, "I've already locked it down with a remote kill program. At this point, it's nothing more than a square paperweight with no USB port."

Mike sarcastically stated, "That's right. Guilty until proven innocent. I might as well go home, since this place is depressing and there's nothing to do. Mind if I take my PC with me so when everyone gets over their cranial-rectal inversion problem under control, I can get back to work without coming to the office?"

"Mike, I don't make the rules here. I also don't see anything wrong with you taking a dead PC home in anticipation of them reenabling your work account." He turned away from the doorway, then slapped his head with his hand. Looking over his shoulder, he said, "I almost forgot. Your hyper-charged mocha coffee latte infused with dandelion extract is at the front desk in the reception area."

"Humph." Mike picked up personal items and his corporate laptop, stuffing them into his briefcase. "At least there's one thing going right. You do someone a good turn, and it's paid back tenfold. Thanks. I'll get it on the way out."

Mike's call went to voicemail, which deepened his frustration. "JJ, this is Mike. My circumstances changed. We won't be having that call I asked for. Don't bother to call me back. I've been excommunicated from work for an unknown period. According to the security team, it will take some time to resume. Ciao for now."

A few minutes later, Mike's phone chirped with a text message from JJ:

> Cool. A timely vacation. Take Ashley away for a few days
> to patch things up. Fly to Magnolia Bluff
> and spend a few days with us. The girls will have fun.

Mike flinched. JJ meant well. He returned a text.

> Great idea. I'll see if I can talk her into it.
> We had a big bruhaha last night.

Mike laughed as he read the response.

> Bring your laptop. We'll talk through some ideas
> rattling around in my head.

CHAPTER 4

Too Much, yet Not Enough

Mike and Ashley built their house in the exclusive Pecan Plantation area near Granbury, Texas. He loved to fly his Cessna 182 to work. The convenience of walking out the door at the end of his day to take off from Air Force Plant 4, a government-owned, contractor-operated aerospace facility in Fort Worth, was easy. His passion was working at Lockheed Martin, home to the F-16 and F-35 military aircraft he helped design.

Air Force Plant 4 is adjacent to the Naval Air Station Joint Reserve Base in Fort Worth, formerly called Carswell Air Force Base. Mike and many of his coworkers loved not fighting the gridlock of commuter traffic. Instead of a hug and kiss, he'd left without a word this morning.

Ashley curled her feet under her legs as she sat on the living room's cream and green leafy-designed velvet couch, which she considered the room's centerpiece. Long blonde hair flowed over her shoulders after framing her youthful oval face with glowing, flawless, sun-kissed skin. This morning, only her swollen, red-rimmed blue eyes reflected her sleepless night.

Looking around her favorite room, which she and Mike created, she admired the supple leather chairs selected to match the various colors of the eight-foot sofa. End tables were scattered to allow beverage glasses to be accessible to any occupant. The plush area rug felt like walking on a cloud, so she often kicked her shoes off before entering this relaxing room. She loved the framed photographs they'd selected from their various travel destinations. These usually became perfect conversation starters when they entertained.

Half-smiling, Ashley's gaze locked onto the large expanse of windows, bookended by the sage silk ceiling-to-floor drapes. They showed the beautiful gardens she loved piddling in most mornings. She delighted in the numerous magnificent blooms on the Purple Queen and Jamaican White Bougainvillea, which thrived in the full sun, attracting busy hummingbirds, flitting dragonflies, and various butterflies during the day. At night, the white lights added a romantic ambiance.

Unable to find a viable solution, she was overcome by a fresh onslaught of fear and desperation, resulting in another round of unchecked tears and sobs. Gripping a throw pillow to her midriff, she wondered why she ever thought her secret could be kept forever. She slapped the couch cushion in frustration. Mike was the one who solved complex problems, yet he was the only person she couldn't tell. Last night, pushing him away seemed like her only option. With a sigh, she decided to shake it off and get more coffee. In the kitchen, she filled her cup and switched off the pot, plodding toward the master bedroom when she heard a noise. Tilting her head, she decided it sounded like careful footsteps.

Raised in Texas before meeting Mike at Georgia Tech, Ashley recalled her dad explaining the use of handguns while she honed her skills to become a skilled shot. Dad taught his only child to investigate suspicious activities with a suitably loaded revolver. Early on, with his guided training, she learned that women should squeeze off two rounds before shouting, 'Halt, who goes there,' just in case. Consequently, no teen ever came to her childhood house without announcing their arrival.

Ashley moved cautiously towards the bedroom. At the doorway, she saw the intruder with his back to her.

"Relax, Ash. I'm grabbing a few things to take with me. I know you're tired of me, but please don't shoot me in the back."

Ashley drew a ragged breath, lowering her pistol. "You know better than to sneak around, especially when you should be at work. Why didn't you text me?"

Mike slowly turned around so she could see his face. He cocked his head as if studying her.

Ashley croaked, "I'm sorry, I was furious last night." She offered a hopeful smile. "Honestly, I want to figure out how to make us work. I'm worried you've found someone else who isn't as cranky as me?"

"I could ask you the same thing," Mike quietly offered. "There's no one for me but you."

Ashley hiccupped, swiping new tears with the back of her left hand. "Liar! Your mistress is your work. I'm so tired of fighting to get your attention that I'll…"

Mike threw up his hands in defeat. "Don't bother finishing the sentence. I'm not up for another round of arguing, darling." Mike gathered a few polo shirts and underwear, stuffing them into his large gym bag.

Ashley looked down to see his ever-present briefcase, where his precious PC resided. She didn't want him to leave or end their relationship, but the only way out didn't feel like a real option. She wondered if her anger was justified. "I never thought you'd prefer work to our happiness. I thought it would be different after our first bad patch. You said things would be better."

Mike fatalistically chuckled as he shook his head. "I guess the old saying is true: Women go into relationships thinking they can change the guy. Men always expect things to be the same, but the girl changes. You know…"

Ashley watched in disbelief as Mike weaved and staggered before catching himself on the heavy oak bureau.

"Mike, what's wrong?" she asked in alarm, rushing to his side.

"Nothing a little R&R wouldn't fix. If anything does happen to me, you get everything. Next time around, find yourself a better guy." His eyes fluttered shut.

Ashley helped him to the bed and eased him down. Her college football star running back was only human. "You need to rest. We'll talk later. You're not going anywhere." She felt his head. No fever. His breathing indicated he was succumbing to sleep. She pulled off his shoes. "See what the job is doing to you?" she softly grumbled.

Opening his eyes slightly, he said, "See how the job you hate helped build a home for us?"

"Yes, for US! Why are you home so early?"

He mumbled. "Someone hacked my login."

"That sounds serious. Who would do that?"

"I have no idea. Do you want to fly over to see Jo and JJ later in Magnolia Bluff?"

She chewed her lip a bit. "That might be fun, if we don't argue."

Not opening his eyes, he reached over and patted her hand. "I don't want to fight with you. I'm so tired. My eyes nearly crossed as I landed at the airfield. Driving home, my mind wandered. I don't feel so good."

"You rest. I'll consider visiting our friends while I fix dinner." Pulling the covers over him, she pocketed his truck keys and left him to rest.

Confused by Mike's mid-morning admission, Ashley wandered back to the kitchen to figure out tonight's menu. He didn't complain about his stomach being upset.

Her cell vibrated in her pocket, jostling the truck keys. Grabbing them, she dropped them in the silverware drawer, knowing Mike wouldn't dream of looking there. Not ready to talk with any of her friends, she almost disregarded the call before recognizing the caller ID. With forced movements, she slid the bar to answer.

The gruff, nearly robotic voice stated, "What did you find out when he arrived home in the middle of the morning?"

Ashley struggled to keep fear from her voice, looking outside to see if she could spot her nemesis. "Why don't you ask him? He's not giving me any details of his work. I told you he rarely does."

"You know what's at stake. Find out his next move."

"He said he's off the clock because of a security breach. He can't work on anything for the company." Mentally grappling for a tidbit to share to get the jerk off her back, she continued, "He said we might want to visit friends in Magnolia Bluff, taking the Cessna he named after me. It's less than an hour by air."

"Do these friends have names?"

"JJ and Jo Rodreguiz. Why do you want to know?"

"That is none of your concern. Don't forget, we're watching you and your brilliant partner. We'll stay in touch."

Ashley stared at the phone, terrified to her core.

CHAPTER 5

Next Steps, but Where to Go?

Mike tossed and turned, replaying the newest arguments with his bride in his dreams. Feeling at odds, he rubbed a pain in his chest before finally coming fully awake. Oblivious to the warm, earthy tones of their comfortable master bedroom, he staggered into the bathroom, shocked at his reflection. The pallor of his skin was awful. He pulled out the thermometer and took his temperature. The tone indicated no fever. Perhaps he was hungry from skipping breakfast this morning. Stripping, he added his dirty clothes to the laundry chute before showering. Scrubbing off, he felt better than when he awoke. He dressed in shorts and a coral polo shirt, then slipped into sandals, suddenly famished.

Pausing at the doorway to their state-of-the-art kitchen, he watched Ashley busily chopping veggies next to the sink before tossing them into an adjacent pot. Mike cleared his throat to avoid startling her and said, "Hey, thanks for the covers. I was zonked."

"You looked awful. Honestly, Mike, I was worried when you said your driving wasn't the usual easy trip. Do you need to try to get to your doctor this afternoon? Maybe something's running around?" Turning, her eyes surveyed him, head to toe. "You appear refreshed. Glad the rest helped."

"I feel better after taking a shower. I didn't eat this morning. I don't think the latte I grabbed when I left work sat too well on my empty stomach."

She snorted, "A latte, no kidding?"

"Yep, with dandelion extract no less. Quite tasty, almost sweet."

"Grab some iced tea. My veggie pasta concoction should be ready soon."

"Okay. I love your Italian meals. Thanks."

Smiling, she turned back to the stove. A buzzer sounded. Removing the toasted garlic bread from the oven, she added it to a basket lined with a thick napkin to keep it warm. Minutes later, she plated some delicious-smelling pasta and placed it on the table.

He added a napkin to his lap and inhaled. "The combination smells and looks delectable, Ash."

"Thanks. I thought you might like to eat early. I apologize for arguing last night. And I'm sorry you had issues at work this morning." Hoping against all odds that her problem might have resolved itself, she asked, "Did you lose your job because of the hacker?"

"No. The security change is an inconvenience while they investigate the cause. I have nothing to worry about. The security team will get it sorted."

"I hope that's what you want. I thought about your asking me to go with you to Magnolia Bluff. I'd like to see Jo and get a change of scenery. Do you think you're okay to fly?"

Shoveling another forkful of pasta into his mouth and adding a satisfied groan, he said, "I think this meal and being with you was exactly what I needed."

"I'll clean up after we finish and go pack. How many days do you think?"

He grinned, thinking of how this might be a reset for the two of them. He said, "Three. Enjoy your food. I'll put things away and start the dishwasher while you go pack. I packed my duffle bag before, so I'm ready." He reached over and gently squeezed her hand, gazing into her bottomless blue eyes, recalling how much her baby blues charmed him when they first met.

"Deal." She finished her last bite and stood, taking her plate to the sink. Opening the drawer to the silverware, she extracted his keys and set them on the counter.

"That's where you hide them?"

"Not anymore," she grinned and winked.

CHAPTER 6

Start Over

Mike and Ashley joked as they reengaged, getting their bags muscled into the pickup. Blue skies and warm August sun made this escape on a late Thursday afternoon a delightful change of pace. He couldn't help but notice Ashley's shapely, long legs in tan short-shorts with her lightweight top sliding up, exposing her trim waistline. "I hope you added sunscreen to protect your gorgeous skin. I'm happy to help apply it everywhere," he added, waggling his eyebrows in appreciation.

Giggling, she patted his bicep. "Thanks, Mike. It's good to know I can get your sunscreen application expertise while we're at their pool. I'm glad we get a long weekend." She looked at the passenger seat and frowned. "Oops, sorry, I forgot my purse. Be right back."

Mike added a quick fanny pat as she turned before darting toward the house. "Lock the doors, please, and set the alarm," he called. He noticed her arm rise with an okay sign on her fingers as she hurried inside. He finished making sure their possessions were secured.

Mike stood by the passenger door as Ashley sashayed back, purse looped over her shoulder and a canvas bag in hand. "I brought a couple of bottles of water for the flight."

"Perfect. I texted JJ that we were leaving soon. I don't know if he wanted to pick us up or let us take a Lyft for the ten-minute ride to their place." His cell rang. Thinking it was JJ, he grabbed it, hoping there wasn't a problem.

He released an exasperated sigh. "Honey, I have to take this work call. Hop in."

Ashley looked annoyed while securing her seatbelt. He gently closed her door, stroking her cheek with his thumb through the open window, and walked to the other side.

"It's Mike. What's up? Did you clean up this mess so I can return to work Monday?"

He paused at the rear of the pickup, listening. Mike barked, "I'm not coming back for my latte. Give it to someone else, or pour it out. I need you to text me when it's a good time to return to my office."

Baffled by the unexpected call, he disconnected, rubbing his face, working to rein in his temper. He patted Ashley's knee as he slid into the driver's seat, noticing her worried expression.

"We're leaving to visit with friends for a well-deserved weekend," he proclaimed. "This phone stays in silent mode. I need to do better as your husband. Our journey begins with me taking a positive first step." He grinned, started the truck, and headed toward the private airfield.

Minutes later, Mike pulled into a space next to the Cessna. He transferred their bags to the plane's interior. He performed a quick preflight check and verified the airport staff had topped off the gas. "Babe, I'm going to park inside the hangar. You get settled in. Text JJ and Jo that we'll be wheels up in fifteen. No one else is flying on a weekday at this time of day, so we're in luck."

"I'm on it." She grinned in response.

Ashley grabbed her cell to send the message to Jo when she was interrupted by an incoming text.

> Good. You're traveling together. He loaded the briefcase.
> Get that combination. Time's not on your side.

Realizing they were being watched was scary. She wanted to look around, but fear made her focus on completing the message to Jo. After hitting send, she prayed for a way out of this mess. Mike wouldn't give her the combo. They'd joked about it more than once. It was the one place she couldn't access.

Mike's whistling preceded his return. He climbed in, rubbing his hands together, seeming satisfied. "I filed the flight plan stating we're headed to the Burnet Municipal Airport."

He used practiced motions to take off, quickly climbing to cruising altitude. During the flight, he pointed out landmarks with comments for Ashley as running commentary and to verify he was on course.

Still distracted by the annoying text, she absentmindedly nodded. Eighty minutes later, Mike communicated with the ground crew as he descended to Burnet Municipal Airport, or Kate Craddock Field as it was also known. Magnolia Bluff wasn't large enough to support a city-owned public-use airport. When private pilots needed a quick trip to Magnolia Bluff, they used this airstrip.

Circling to land, Mike joked, "Good, no one landing or taking off. You know it's at times like this when I turn on the external speakers to play Wagner's *Ride of the Valkyries*, but since this is a civilian facility, I'll skip it," he smirked. "I think I see JJ's Porsche on the ground. Can you verify it?"

She peered at the ground, anxiety rising in her chest as she thought about how much time she didn't have. "Yep, they're both waiting."

CHAPTER 7

Stop Me if You've Already Heard This...

Ashley's thoughts were interrupted by a change in Mike's tone.

"Honey, we're going to have a smooth landing. There's no traffic." Mike became hyper-focused on his landing process, touching down like a butterfly atop a flower.

The Cessna taxied toward the private tarmac parking area. She pasted on a smile, seeing JJ and Jo wave from their SUV. The moment the propeller stopped, Mike activated the doors' auto release and bounded out of the plane like a nine-year-old rushing to the playground. She wondered if they could have been childhood friends, or if his son would have that energy.

Feeling nervous about being scrutinized by Jo, Ashley slowly exited. She mentally made a checklist of her expected greeting behavior to avoid unnecessary questioning. JJ and Mike did the guy hug, slapping one another on the back. Mike delivered a brotherly hug when he kissed Jo's cheek.

"Ashley." Jo hugged her friend. "I'm glad you joined the party."

"I didn't want to miss a chance for some girl time," Ash replied as she eyed her friend from head to toe. "How is it you always look perfect?" she asked.

"That's what I tell her daily," JJ said, before adding a hug. "You don't look so bad either. Mike, you're one lucky man."

Mike reached in to extract the bags, handing them to JJ as he replied, "I'm lucky. Heck, I felt weird after I got home from my early release from work today. She made me rest and then made the best lunch." He patted his stomach and grinned.

JJ grabbed the two bags and frowned before he asked, "And you flew anyway?"

"Buddy, I was fine after a nap. I felt dizzy on the flight back from work, but I landed without issue. Driving from the hangar to home, my vision blurred."

Ashley interjected, "I checked him for a fever after he said he had a headache. It was normal, but he was tired. Mike hadn't eaten breakfast but drank a dandelion latte when he arrived at work. When he's focused on a problem, nothing else matters."

Jo laughed. "JJ's the same way." She looped her arm around Ashley's as they headed for the car. JJ began a series of questions regarding Mike's earlier issue, so she let the guys lead the way. Leaning over, she softly asked, "Are you alright? You look a bit stressed or distracted."

"I'm fine," promised Ash. "A few nights of unbroken sleep are what I need. You're glowing. I don't think it's only due to a warm August in Texas."

Jo giggled. "I'm a bit excited about possibly elevated hormone levels."

Ashley stopped in mid-stride and turned to face her friend. "Are you saying you might have your long-awaited wish come true?"

"Shhh!" She moved forward at a slower pace. "I haven't told JJ yet. I have scheduled a doctor's appointment in three weeks. Due to my history of random cycles, they wanted to wait a while before scheduling a checkup unless I performed a test kit. I haven't done a self-test for fear that JJ will discover it. He's way too observant." She giggled. "I knew you'd keep my secret."

Wanting to feel excited, Ash pulled her arm closer. "You can tell me anything. I've seen the same glow on others with that condition." Unwilling to divulge more, she tried to add a light note to the exchange. "You'll know the perfect time to let him know." As they approached the car, Ash whispered, "Well, shoot, I guess margaritas are off the menu."

Jo chuckled, "They've been off my menu forever. I can't afford the calories and keep my job. But I do know how to make great ones." She hip-bumped her pal. "Mocktails, too. What's keeping you up at night?"

As they reached the car, Ashley deferred. "I'd rather listen to the boys, badgering and poking at each other while we're in the car. Besides, having a casual conversation with them is hard, as they often engage in lengthy discussions about tech and their views on advanced sciences."

Jo nodded in agreement.

Mike hollered from the open door, "Let's go, ladies. JJ wants to discuss quantum computing as a solution for the next generation of AI. He promises a quiz on it later."

Everyone laughed. Ashley stared at Mike's briefcase, her mind filling with worry.

Jo escorted Ash to their room when they unloaded the car, where the guys had deposited the bags.

"Welcome to your home away from home. I'm glad you could make it."

"Your color schemes are so bright and cheerful. I love this room, Jo. Thank you for having us."

"I'm delighted to have time with my friend. We both know that JJ and Mike will sequester themselves in the office to discuss

Mike's latest problem. JJ has been animated since he received the contract yesterday."

Ashley quickly opened the bags and divided the contents into the drawers, the closet, and the adjoining bathroom countertop. "Mike will be on cloud nine. He's on leave due to a security issue. I hope JJ can help with that so Mike can meet his project schedule."

"It won't be for lack of trying, I'm sure. You are one of the fastest organizers I've ever seen. How about we grab a couple of iced teas, and I'll show you the changes outside. My garden is growing so fast. The pool is also ready if you'd like to use it."

Once outside with glasses in hand, Jo gently pried. "What's going on? We've been friends long enough for me to know when something isn't right. I can be a good sounding board."

She shook her head and said, "Mike and I are battling a bad patch. He's failing at life-work balance. We wouldn't have come if he hadn't been told to leave this morning. They disabled his corporate access. In a huff, he said. *'Let's head to Magnolia Bluff for a visit.'* I think he would have come alone if he'd felt better. At least the color is back in his cheeks. It's started fine, but I feel like this is only a short-term reprieve. As soon as this problem with his plane is solved, he'll get another project and put me on the back burner. We've had a good run. Yet we lost the in-love portion of our relationship. We're not like you two."

Jo tried to placate. "I'm sure it's not as bad as that, Ashley. When our men are together, they're in their element. Instead of playing with trucks, they play with computers and jet fighters. JJ is so cute when he tries to tell me what he is working on. I smile, nod, and say, *'Yes, dear.'*"

Ashley snapped, "If it were only that simple." Then she added apologetically, "I'm sorry, I've several things to sort out. I didn't mean to shout at you. How about we create a fun dinner?

I love cooking in your kitchen. You have all the latest gadgets. You can get off your feet, just in case." She added a wink.

Jo chuckled as they headed into the house.

Capture the Moment

JJ spotted the flash on the contour screen, indicating someone entered the side door through the pergola. He grinned as he saw the girls' heads together, thick as thieves in their discussion. His office provided views of the property's exterior. Mike was impressed earlier by the views from the external cameras.

Repositioning himself in leather gaming chairs, he pointed to the screen, which Mike acknowledged, before JJ continued his summary. "The cloaking solution you're working on, RADAR Hallucination for Cloaking and Targeting (RadHalCaT), aims to generate enemy radar hallucinations to cloak your fighters and disrupt the targeting capabilities of incoming missiles aimed at the aircraft. Mike, the premise is brilliant. I think it is doable with a few modifications to the coding." JJ swirled the red merlot, taking a small sip. "I'm digging this project."

Mike sipped his beer, his face twisting into a scowl. "I was all set to discuss my stumbling block with you this morning. Then the IT team informed me that my login credentials to any corporate system, including my laptop, had been disabled. Every time I think about the slimeball hackers that triggered this situation, I get mad all over again."

JJ raised an eyebrow as he took a deep breath. "Do you want me to get your laptop running again? I've had some practice in this area of IT."

Mike set his beer on the coaster of the desk. Hoisting his briefcase onto his lap, he spun the tumblers to align the correct numeric values, allowing the latches to release. He pulled out his computer and power cable before setting the case aside. "Sure, give it a try. I was hoping you might find a trace of how they hacked me."

Both men were so engrossed in breaking into Mike's computer that they hardly moved when the girls entered the office.

Jo confided, "Look at these two having so much fun. We should get some snaps of them, but JJ doesn't allow any photos in his inner sanctum."

Ashley didn't reply but deftly grabbed her cell phone, enabling camera access with a press of the symbol. She moved her fingers to draw the image of the briefcase on the floor. Moving closer, she took several photos. Slipping her device back into her pocket, she blushed as Jo shook her head slightly.

JJ asked, "What did you spot on the floor, Ashley?"

Pulling out her phone, she opened it and scrolled through her pictures. "I thought it was a spider on Mike's briefcase, but it was a trick of the shadows," she replied without missing a beat.

"As long as you don't take photos of my office setup, I'm good." JJ leaned over and kissed Jo's cheek. "Mike and I will be working on this for a while. Did you need something, sweetie?"

"No, we were just checking on you. Would you like dinner outside by the pool, maybe in an hour? Ashley wanted to make some of her mouthwatering chicken fajitas. I thought I'd add a cobb salad on the side."

Mike interjected, "My girl does some awesome fajitas."

"Sounds great to me," JJ said. "Perhaps some sangria as an option?"

"As you wish," Jo said, adding a sweeping bow. "Let's leave them to it, Ash."

JJ watched them leave, smiling. "They are great together, aren't they?"

"Yep. You told Jo we needed a bit of help, right?"

"I did. She'll discover things you or I would never even think of. Give it time." JJ reached into his backpack, stenciled with bold white writing 'Bag of Tricks', and withdrew a USB device.

Mike snickered, "Your remote drive isn't going to find a receptacle on my laptop. What's your next idea, bright boy?"

JJ grinned. "Ah, you know better than to jump to conclusions with me. I need my special program stored on her to install it remotely from my computer. I plan to intercept the boot sequence of your machine using a wireless Bluetooth connection and drop the machine into maintenance mode. Once it does that, I'll tell it to boot from my machine so we can access your files." He gently bumped Mike's shoulder. "The good news is that it will automatically revert to Lockheed IT specs when I'm finished, so your tech people won't get their panties in a wad. They will remove the kill program when you've been cleared, unaware we bypassed it."

JJ stopped his activities to peer quizzically at his friend. "You're not going to tell anyone I did this, right?"

"Oh, push-tush." Mike crossed his heart and raised one hand. "I never did this. I know no one smart enough to defeat our stellar defense contractor team's security lockdown."

Within minutes, JJ successfully booted the machine, mirrored the screen to the center monitor, and slid it in front of Mike. "Here, you drive. Let's figure out what's wrong with your RadHalCaT solution."

CHAPTER 9

More Brilliant and Alluring

Ashley and Jo frowned at the non-committal grunts received when Jo announced, "Dinner is ready outside, fellows."

They marched back to the kitchen to retrieve the pitcher of sangria for the guys and the frozen mocktail concoction Ashley created.

"Mike thinks frozen drinks are designed for chicks. Nothing in here a soon-to-be mom shouldn't enjoy, and I like it too." Ashley raised her glass. A light bell tone sounded when the glasses met.

They headed out to the table in the shade by the pool. Ashley's eyes popped wide. "Wow! I love how you set the table in bold colors like your rooms. Even the flowers match the oranges, reds, and yellows of your linens and plates."

"Thank you. We both enjoy being surrounded by bright shades. If the guys aren't out here in ten minutes, we begin without them. I'm hungry," insisted Jo.

Ashley chuckled. "Agreed. I think they often get distracted when they dig into something interesting. Mike's the same when Georgia Tech football is on the big screen. I'll only glance at the score and admire his excitement during the three wasted hours. I crack up when he tries to coach the one-way video feed going the wrong way."

Jo smirked. "I hear that. I keep pizza and wine on a table by JJ's chair when the soccer World Cup finals are on, with Brazil in the playoffs. I keep my mouth covered when he insists on lecturing the poor goalie, who ignores the comments. Once, we were in a Brazilian bar during the playoffs. The wait service was impossibly poor. After we finally ate, we couldn't find anyone to pay our bill. JJ finally yelled that Brazil's team isn't as good as it was last week. That certainly garnered some attention. We paid the bill that was immediately presented." Jo sipped her frozen drink, licking her lips. "Weren't you a hotshot cheerleader for the Yellow Jackets? Wasn't that how you and Mike met? I'd think you'd have the team's interest at heart after cheering them."

Ashley frowned at the mention of her college cheerleading years. She felt Jo watching her closely and worried that she would continue to push this subject. Her emotions threatened to bubble out. Taking a sip, she nodded. "Yes, that's where we met. It sure was a different lifetime, before I took the internship program abroad for a full semester before summer break at the beginning of my sophomore year." Without looking at her friend, she concluded, "We reconnected the year he graduated with honors."

"Lucky you. How great for you to have the opportunity to travel for an internship program. Was it awesome? I often wish I had a traditional college education."

"My college life wasn't what I expected. I was naïve and too trusting in hindsight. It caused me to make some tough choices."

"Oh. How would you have done things differently?"

Ashley started to explain when JJ and Mike rushed outdoors and slid into their seats.

"Sweetie, did we make it within the ten-minute window?" JJ asked, looking almost ashamed.

"Yes, but barely. You can fill your glasses from the pitcher. Ash and I have the frozen variety, if you'd rather have that," said Jo with a grin.

"I think this pitcher will suit us perfectly."

Mike raised his glass in agreement.

Ashley howled. She uncovered the guacamole, condiments, sour cream, lettuce, and charro beans. Jo passed the warm tortillas, followed by protein choices. Everyone dug in. Light banter filled the warm air of friends gathering.

Following the delicious meal, the men returned to JJ's office. JJ wanted to make headway toward resolving Mike's impasse in solving the technical issues of RadHalCaT.

"I'd like your opinion on where the roadblock is located, Mike."

"Let me map it out for you." Mike picked up the electronic pen and drew on the screen while he spoke. "I want this program to distort the returning signals to enemy air, ground radar, or missiles. Ideally, it would physically target at least a dozen yards from reality. The goal is to deceive the source with false positive targets, making the hallucination appear perfect. Then the enemy will send armaments to the wrong location. Our aircraft must be invulnerable to land or aircraft-based radar." Rubbing his hair, he added, "I have nightmares about what happens if this isn't in place."

JJ tapped his chin, considering the steps needed to reach the desired goal. "To consistently achieve that result, we'd need to have the onboard systems consume the encrypted radar signals, understand the signal header information, reply with the correct encrypted response, generate a random but legitimate location, and respond to the interrogator in real-time, or within nanoseconds."

Taking a sip from his glass, he paused for a few beats, then asked, "Are you planning to use an onboard AI-enhanced supercomputer to handle the process? I didn't see one in the aircraft's technical specifications."

"I put two graphical processing units onboard. I believe that resolves a significant portion of the required controlled data exchanges." Mike pointed to the information flow diagram. "I can't be one-hundred-percent certain that the return signal will contain a valid handshake for acceptance. Currently, my modeling is accepted half the time. Those are unacceptable odds for the pilot and the aircraft's survival. The hallucination must be perfect every time, with a success rate of at least ninety-nine-percent. I've achieved a one-hundred-percent victory with unencrypted standard radar signals. The question is, how can we take it to the next level with accurately encrypted codes in the header ID?"

JJ studied the screen for a few minutes. Taking another sip, he sensed the formation of a possibility at the edges of his mind he'd not yet considered. "How much do you trust me?"

Mike recoiled and scrunched his face. "I'm showing you next-generation stealth code that will be implemented in the F-35 and potentially used in the upcoming F-47 aircraft. I'm facing decades in prison if this falls into the wrong hands. Why do you think you have an ironclad contract with my organization? And, after all our years, why would you ask?"

"Because we are friends and I don't want you compromised." JJ sucked in a breath, then highlighted an area of data on the big screen. "May I copy this section of code to my machine? I have some resources that should help me do extensive modeling to defeat this problem. I know what you need done. As the prime contractor for this assignment, it's incumbent upon me to provide you with answers. They won't happen overnight."

Mike groaned. "Of course." He threw out his hand. "Take it. But if you ever ask if I trust you again, I'll make you get the drinks for both of us."

"Does that mean it's your turn now?" JJ grinned, handing his glass to Mike.

When Mike returned with the refills, JJ heard the girls laughing before the door closed.

Mike said, "Your lovely, charming wife suggested we wrap it up for the evening in the next thirty minutes for a dip in the pool."

"Sounds good," JJ said, setting a timer to display on the monitor. "I've learned to take her recommendations to heart. We've been at it for hours. A break and rest until morning wouldn't hurt."

Mike sipped his beverage and then looked serious. "How do you and Jo do it?" You work as hard, if not harder, than I do. Yet every time I see you together, I catch myself wanting to remind you to get a room, based on your playful behavior. I wonder if we need counseling."

"Perhaps it's time to seek help and ask one another. As for Jo and me, I couldn't begin to explain why we put one another first. I know we try to talk about everything."

Mike sighed and nodded.

CHAPTER 10

Wanting to Tell, But Afraid

Jo woke early, melancholy washing over her. The weekend had gone too quickly, like all getaways do. She set up a simple breakfast buffet on the bar, unsurprised that Mike and Ashley had everything ready to head to the Burnet airport for a quick flight home. JJ helped Mike load up. Jo went to check and ensure that Ashley wasn't trying to dust and vacuum the bedroom or scrub the bathroom.

Jo leaned against the doorjamb and noticed Ashley fiddling with her phone, as if making up her mind about something. Finally, she asked, "Hey, what's wrong? I've seen you fiddle with that phone since the spider photos were taken. Then I see anxiety cross your face before you slip it into a pocket." She folded her arms. "Are you trying to decide between Mike and another guy?"

All the blood drained from Ashley's face. She swallowed and coughed, which made Jo more suspicious.

"No, well, yeah, kind of. I've been trying to get Mike to go with me to a marriage counselor. He doesn't want to talk about anything personal until his current pet project is finished. I've gone a couple of times alone. My counselor says we need to attend as a couple. He did say I could text anytime, day or night, if I need to talk. I've kept it to just texting until I can get my husband on board."

Jo advanced toward her friend and delivered a comforting hug. The moment broke when Mike said from the hallway as his footsteps sounded. "Come on, babe, time's a-wasting. I don't want to wait any longer. I might be called to return to work. Monday mornings are busy at the Pecan airfield. We'll visit again soon."

"Be right there." She grabbed a tissue to blow her nose before dashing past Jo.

Jo wasn't convinced by Ash's excuse but quickly followed, locking up the house on her way out.

Jo and JJ dropped their friends at the airfield entrance. They sat in the Porsche SUV and watched the Cessna taxi to the runway's north end to take advantage of the prevailing south wind. When Mike made a slight wing wave, they laughed and gestured goodbye with raised arms.

Tapping the steering wheel, JJ said, "Honey, Mike believes their relationship has problems. He wondered if they should consider marriage counseling. He told me he was slightly jealous of our relationship. If he believed there was a problem, I said they should tackle it head-on together."

Jo listened intently and shook her head. "Ashley told me she has a counselor but thinks Mike won't commit to going until this project is fixed. Something else is off, though. I sense she's hiding something. Whatever it is torments her, and she doesn't want Mike to know. I provided her with opportunities to open up and share with me what was bothering her. I couldn't find out. Sorry."

"It's not your fault. Your instincts are usually spot-on, honey. Let's try to stay in touch with them. I don't want to smother them. It is their problem. Still, I thought they were terrific together when I met her. Mike loves her."

"Yes, I agree. I know you've been buddies for a long time. I do like having her as a friend. I'll keep in touch."

CHAPTER 11

ICABOD, bring in the SPONGE

Jo stood at the kitchen island, watching JJ in his office through the open door. From her vantage point, he seemed deep in a conversation with someone. She tapped on the counter enough to get JJ's attention. He turned toward the noise. Jo pointed to her coffee cup, then back to him with a small smile and raised eyebrows. He nodded and gave her a thumbs-up signal.

Several minutes later, she carried the fragrant double cup of espresso, made with fresh coffee beans ground to perfection, to his office. She noticed he was engaged in the three-dimensional platform he called Gigazon. He'd developed it for immersive, realistic virtual meetings. It made attendees feel together in a room, regardless of the physical distance. JJ invited her to a virtual meeting when her modeling assignment extended an extra week. Sensations were uncanny in the environment.

JJ kissed her cheek as he accepted the cup.

"Good morning, Jo." The avatar image ICABOD projected reminded her of a rocket scientist bent over data objects. The screens were filled with massive amounts of information.

Wiggling her fingers, she replied, "Good morning, ICABOD. Sorry if I interrupted your conversation."

"You, madam, are never an interruption, especially when you bring espresso to JJ. He works better with organic vigor hourly in the morning."

"True that," said JJ, following a sip. "And my bride prepares it perfectly." He patted her hand. "Thank you, sweetheart. You're welcome to stay if you wish."

Jo grinned. She liked that he didn't mind her learning and loved watching him. "Tempting, but I need to go tend the garden. I'll be back within the hour to refresh your café."

JJ faced the center screen. "I've uploaded the software code to our most secure area of your data drives. I've also included a detailed description of the issue. I wanted to review a few additional things I think are needed." His hand swiped through some of the data objects, bringing a group of them to the forefront. "First, I wanted to discuss the problem with you to ensure my logic is correct. Second, I don't want anyone in the R-Group or CATS team to access this area because of the security protocol requirements of the Lockheed Martin contract. It has nothing to do with my level of trust in the team. You and I are the only members with access. Please confirm?"

"Yes, JJ. I appreciate your confidence. I have analyzed the upload and am ready. In summary, Lockheed Martin wants to equip its fifth and sixth generations of fighter aircraft with technology that will cause hostile radar signals to malfunction in a specified manner when targeting the stealth fighters. Do I correctly understand the scope of the problem?"

"Yes, ICABOD. Mike has gotten the program to work when no ID-header information is present. The hostile powers saw their radar problems early on and implemented a unique identifier in the radar header to verify the authenticity of the signal. Each radar blast has a unique identifier, so reading it only once becomes inadequate."

"I agree, sir. We must constantly interrogate the radar signals to ensure we can return a believable authentication with a misdirected location signal. Reviewing the years of software support I have delivered to the R-Group, I isolated a program we can adapt to accomplish this goal. My creator, Dr. Quip, your uncle, and I created the SPONGE program to meet similar requirements. SPONGE code, or *Software Purposely Omniscient Needed for Generic Evasion,* can ingest the radar headers, looking for a sequence change. Then we direct it to echo the signal with the wrong geo coordinates. It is a straightforward operation that is rapidly processed. The code is intelligent enough to detect when an algorithm is being used. We can mathematically modify the headers with minor modifications rather than merely incrementing the identifier by one."

JJ clucked his tongue. "SPONGE code, huh? Do I need permission to use it, or would my uncle be satisfied with my repurposing his program?"

"I am certain your uncle would be delighted. Would you like me to begin developing the test and verification program to demonstrate the reliability of the SPONGE code in absorbing the issues of your project? Hee, hee!"

JJ shook with laughter. "I'd forgotten you learned humor, ICABOD." He collected his mirth. "Yes, please. My process documentation illustrates the test sequences of ground-to-air, air-to-air, and low-Earth-orbit (LEO)-to air attacks. If we can show a reliability factor of 99.9% in our tests, I believe we can fulfill this contract."

"I will proceed now and contact you as soon as we are ready to run the simulations."

CHAPTER 12

Reality Check

Mike circled once around the Pecan Plantation private airstrip before landing to the south into the wind. While taxiing to their normal tie-down location, he noticed Ashley's fidgeting. "Babe, what's up? You weren't worried I would make a poor landing, were you?"

He noticed she took a breath before their eyes met. "Mike, our weekend away was refreshing. I'm dreading when you turn on your work phone. I'm afraid I'll lose you again, and we'll return to square one."

"Seriously?" Mike was instantly agitated. "I need to finish this project, you know that. We had a delightful weekend. I enjoyed our time together. However, I need to check in for work to review the schedule. JJ is well-positioned to help resolve the project's final issue. Once that's under control, the stress load will be off my neck." He rubbed his hair, reset his ball cap, and powered off the plane before adding, "I want us to work on our relationship, just like you do. Hon, give me a little time to get my corporate job under control. Please?"

Ashley was staring blankly out the windows of the Cessna when her phone vibrated from inside her purse. He decided not to try to learn who she was texting and locked the yoke. Then he exited, secured the plane with the tie-downs, and opened his door to grab the bags. Ashley plucked the phone from her purse and stared at the screen, a deep frown forming on her lips. Her fingers wavered over the screen. She tapped a few keys, hit send, and slipped the phone back into her purse.

She squeaked loudly as Mike opened her door. Tears were in her eyes as she reached for his face. Schooling her features into composure, she said, "Sorry, honey. I was daydreaming, and you startled me."

Confused and not entirely buying her comment, Mike decided to take the high road. He asked, "Uh, do we need to shop for food, or are we good?"

"Can we stop for some wine? I think we're completely out."

"As you wish."

CHAPTER 13

Sleight of Hand

Mal-chin wiped his ruddy, chapped hands on the towel looped into his grimy apron, stiffening at the sight of the incoming caller on his mobile device's screen. He brushed back the wayward strands of greasy black hair under his snood. His associate shrugged in his matching black T-shirt, exposing a slight build with sinuous muscle structure.

He nodded toward the pans on the stove. "Stir sa food, Jun."

Picking up the spoon from the edge of the steamy pot, Jun attended to the task without saying a word.

At the beginning of the fourth ringtone, Mal-chin blinked his dark, almond-shaped eyes and answered, engaging the speaker. "*Ah-nyung-ha-seh-yo, sah?*"

"Mal-chin, have you started to provide the limited special?" the gruff, almost mechanical voice demanded. "I've invested a great deal in your venture. I expect results. I've provided the components and the directions to make the special brew. You must follow through."

"Sah, as a hand, of a hand, of a leader, we are constantly scrutinized, and strive to provide good value to our customers. We appreciate your support. Your request is being fulfilled, though it takes time when the customer doesn't visit daily."

The response reflected anger. "I've given you only the most meaningless tasks to fulfil. I've digitally raided banks and governments of crypto and secret defense plans from the assault platform in Pyongyang. I have worked to make global connections. You will ensure the task is carried out according to the daily schedule. Make it a special delivery if necessary."

"Sah, we do not have time to add demeaning work as an errand boy. I would—"

"You're not permitted to say what you like or don't like. You and Jun owe me. Unless you want me to reveal your true status to the proper authorities," the voice scolded.

Mal-chin flinched and noticed Jun balked momentarily at the rebuke from a man who held their lives in his hands.

"My Chinese connection calls me daily, reminding me of my commitment. You help me get the code; I will deliver it to those who can free your families back in your home country from those who use economic sanctions as a noose. With all you have at stake, I thought honor to your families was paramount. Yet you're moaning about your pride? You're eating regularly, which is an improvement over your prior job. Stop wasting time and give me results."

Mal-chin looked at Jun, who nodded. "Using your auto programming routines, we received the combination to the briefcase from the *maechunbu* a few minutes ago. It belongs to the person you identified as the head project engineer manager. Inside is the portable computer containing all the engineering design specifications."

Slightly appeased, the voice replied, "Good. I can arrange to access the device to extract the needed plans." A long sigh sounded. "This is more in line with my expectations," the speaker calmly replied. "Confirm that you use our military-grade voice encryption algorithm so no eavesdropper can capture our conversation."

"Confirmed, suh. Since this raises a red flag about American 5G networks, we need new burner phones by tomorrow. I need the app pre-loaded to mask my voice when I run your outreach program to call the target."

"Agreed. Use the Lazarus Group crypto funds you can access. Advise me immediately of any number changes. Call when you've secured Mr. Hayes' new stealth solution details."

Kamal placed his order, then leaned his hip against the counter. Mike Hayes had introduced him to this place because he loved stopping in for breakfast and lunch a few times a week. Kamal agreed that the food choices were better than those in the office cafeteria. The two men who ran the shop provided good value for the price. He was pleased when they greeted him by name, as if they were friends, though they rarely smiled. Being an immigrant from India who worked to become a naturalized citizen of the United States, he understood the value of hard work.

"You guys are like me. You work hard to advance to the next level in your careers, after arriving in this country," he offered congenially. "You're fortunate to have your own coffee business. I get a weekly paycheck, but you're creating excellent customer value. Everyone at work enjoys what you serve. My family in India has a small business, yet they wanted me to work in America. I bet someone will walk into this delicious shop one day, asking to buy a franchise from you. When that happens, perhaps I can become your IT tech expert for your empire. Are you both working to become citizens of this fine country?"

The two men looked and nodded with their standard stoic Asian expressions. Mal-chin set the bag of food and drink on the counter before saying, "Kamal, you're going to be late returning to work. Please take Mr. Hayes' coffee. You said he was out of town for a few days on Friday. He's probably going through withdrawals without his double mocha latte infused with dandelion extract. We owe him so much for helping to promote our business."

Kamal checked his digital watch. Afraid he'd return to work too late, he reached for his beverage and Mike's coffee. Securing the drinks, he grabbed the bag and moved briskly to the door. "Someday you'll need to tell me how you earned his favor. With his dedication to his job, he's usually oblivious to taking breaks. These big designer coffees aren't cheap."

"Since you mention he works long hours, we can deliver one this afternoon to the front desk. Can we leave it in your name to hand to him?"

"Sure, if you also bring a few of your fresh afternoon *yakgwa*."

"Yes, suh. Thank you."

Upon returning to the office, he cleared security, and Kamal delivered Mike's coffee.

Mike accepted the beverage. "Thanks."

Kamal edged Mike to the side to wait for the group of pilots heading for the testing center to pass. "On my way in today, I spotted Hank DeSoto at the Wing It Café. He appeared to be meeting with a group of Asians. I hope he's doing well."

Mike snorted. "Really? The guy was sloppy with his work. He possessed no sense of loyalty."

"He was great with programming and finding security gaps," Kamal insisted. "You're right, though, he did take shortcuts that weren't best practices. We got along well while he was here."

"You do know the guy had sticky fingers when it came to copying programs, right? He was dismissed with cause. I'd stay clear of him if I were you, Kamal."

"Thank you, Mike, I hadn't realized that. I was new to the security department when he was here," explained Kamal.

Mike took another sip and anxiously asked, "What about my…"

Kamal chuckled. "I figured you'd ask. Last night, I verified your status, and then I reinstated your access. You're good. Security welcomes you back to work, Mr. Hayes."

Mike beamed. He took another hearty swig of the latte before disappearing toward his office.

Kamal shook his head, entering the secured IT workspace.

Learn to Stand Down

Jo felt queasy this morning when she first awoke. She didn't think it was like the morning sickness she'd read about. However, she refused to feel negative that she might be wrong. Squeezing a couple of apples, oranges, strawberries, and a lime through the juicer emitted a fruity scent. Pouring two glasses, she put them into the freezer for a rapid chill. While mixing the eggs for a quiche, she thought about sharing the possible news with JJ. She mentally kicked herself, recalling the last time her cycles paused, resulting in them both being upset for weeks.

Doctor Truly Peters had said, "Jo, you work hard with your daily exercise routines and calorie counting to stay in shape for your job. Sometimes your body skips cycles. I'll run additional tests, but I suspect everything is fine. Eat right, don't worry. You'll get pregnant at the right time."

She recalled how supportive JJ had been then and every day since. He'd convinced her that it allowed them more time for practice, which he volunteered for anytime, anywhere. "Sweetheart," he'd held her close and murmured in her ear. "I love you enjoying your job. I will love you when you carry our babies. The tests said we're both good, so stop worrying."

She sighed and straightened, determined to be patient. "I can wait until after the doctor's appointment. I'm glad Doctor Truly timed it with my annual physical. JJ won't be suspicious when I go alone," she mumbled. She slid the yellow mixture into the oven and plugged in the pot. Leaning her hip against the counter, she watched JJ work through the open door to his office.

When he stood at his desk drumming on his keyboard, she imagined him to the side of an orchestra playing the bass. JJ pantomimed his emotions first, raking his hands through his hair in frustration before he clapped his forehead as if he was struck with an epiphany. He'd hop from one foot to the other, waiting for the results to appear on one of the massive, mounted screens. His voice floated in the air when he did a conference call. She was certain ICABOD was on the receiving end, helping to work through a glitch. Almost on cue, he shot a fist into the air triumphantly, shouted a loud, "Yes!" then said, "Can you update the documentation for that portion?"

"Completed, JJ," ICABOD replied.

He'd been working nonstop on Mike's job order since Sunday. Grabbing the juice from the freezer, she decided it was time to take a small break. Jo couldn't help but chuckle when JJ turned at her approach. His furrowed brow melted away, leaving a smile on his face.

Handing him the juice, she raised her glass for a morning toast. "Does this mean the show is over?"

JJ clicked her glass, took a sip, then fidgeted with a telltale tinge of red rising from his neck. "You've been watching me the whole time?"

"Honey, your projects appear frustrating at times. I enjoy your fist thrown in the air or hearing, *Eureka, I'm finished*. Then we can do something together when I'm in town."

"Babe, sorry to spend so much time working. I try to get up early and let you rest. You've looked a bit tired since the weekend." Taking an additional sip, he grinned. "This batch is the best yet. I needed this in between my coffee, thanks."

"Glad you like it," she said. "Can you take a break soon?"

"I wanted to finish this to reduce the pressure on Mike. He wants to wrap it up so he can focus on his relationship. Lockheed lifted his work restrictions, so I can show him the results." Grinning like a Cheshire Cat, he added, "I am convinced I found the key element to make his dream for this project a success!"

Gently caressing his jawline while studying his features, Jo agreed, "Sometimes the best inspirations happen if you disengage and focus your attention on something else for a while."

"Sweetheart, do I detect amorous alternatives in my future?" He wiggled his eyebrows.

Jo laughed. "Certainly. But right now, I need your help turning the soil in my garden." With a wink, she added, "But we'll need to get cleaned up afterwards. Then I'll let you lotion my back, or I can give you a rubdown. What time is your call with Mike scheduled for?"

He took her hand and kissed it, then turned toward the keyboard, rapidly typing a message. "I hope a couple of hours will work for your soil project. I'll fix dinner tonight, too!"

"We're having quiche tonight. It's cooking now, but we can reheat it later if you rather have stir-fry."

Grabbing her hand, he said, "Let's do this."

JJ joined the video call with Mike a few minutes early, taking a delicious bite of his steaming wedge of quiche. Jo laughed when he tried to sneak a piece. "I'm just testing it to make certain it's good." The late morning midday diversion with Jo was playing in his memory. From the camera feed, he noticed she was picking vegetables from their garden to support her nomination for him to make stir-fry for dinner if he wanted.

With an exaggerated wipe of his mouth and a hearty swallow, JJ stated, "That hit the spot. The quiche Jo fixed is addictive." Noticing Mike's frown as he eyed the plate, he added, "Ready for some good news, buddy, even if I can't share the rest of this snack?"

Beads of sweat had formed on his friend's brow. Wiping it off with a napkin, Mike replaced the frown with a poor attempt at a grin. He straightened. "Repeating my dad's mantra at the end of a long day, I'm bright-eyed, bushy-tailed, and ready for some magic. Whatcha got?"

Seeing his friend's pallor, JJ's enthusiasm for his program discoveries was derailed. "Mike, what's wrong? You look like two hundred twenty pounds of condemned oatmeal. Should you even be at work? We can postpone this call until tomorrow."

Circling his neck, Mike stared straight into his camera. "Not you, too? Ashley's been badgering me to go to the doctor since Monday afternoon. I'm worried about this project. The stress of my self-imposed deadline and concern over my personal life is tying up my guts. It seems to come and go. I don't want to go to my family physician to hear him remind me to lose some weight, not work so many hours, and stick to a daily workout. The sooner I have a solution, the sooner I can rest. You said good news." Mike inclined his head expectantly. "Let's hear it, buddy."

"I've structured a program to force the target direction finders to vary from three to seven percent. My test cases are coming back ninety-eight percent positive. I know, you said one hundred percent bulletproof. Therefore, I added the human ability to modify the target location fractionally in real time. You might like to add routine logic into the whole program for an end-to-end run. I will continue to tweak it to see if I can get the last two-percent to give you choices. Unless you say the issues are immaterial to the overall program with a variation enablement."

A weak smile nearly lit up Mike's face. "Fascinating. I can't wait to test it. Could you bring it here to test it jointly in the formal facility? I was told you're due for a new photo ID update with our contract manager. Until this gut thing eases, I've grounded myself." He chuckled, "Or to put it bluntly, Ashley has hidden the keys to the plane until I stop getting dizzy walking around the house."

JJ raised an eyebrow, worried. "Dizzy? You missed mentioning that before. Perhaps a trip to the doctor would be smart."

"I don't eat regularly, which is causing both issues. Please give me a break. You and your charming bride could drive up tomorrow, then stay at the house for the weekend. Quid pro quo. We can work on Friday at the office to implement your program and thoroughly test it. I'll let you fly my plane to the office. You can help reassure Ashley. Heck, hearing we have a possible solution makes me feel better."

"You're the project officer. Jo will enjoy the chance to poke around Granbury with your sweetheart."

Mike tried to hide a grimace by taking a breath. "Ash will be delighted. See you guys tomorrow. Thank you. Drive safely."

CHAPTER 15

Wicked Webs We Weave

The walk to the parking lot eased the gut cramps. "I guess extra exercise would help," Mike grumbled. The air felt like a mini sweat lodge as the steam rushed out of the truck's door when it was opened. Even the custom window shade that matched the redfire pearl metallic exterior hadn't helped. He remotely started the vehicle, which triggered the air conditioning to blast into action. The leather seats made this beast feel like a luxury ride when he slipped into the driver's seat. An hour-plus drive in traffic to home replaced his positive attitude as he protested the assortment of poor motorists until he cleared the security gates at Pecan.

He turned onto his private drive. Aiming toward the side of the house, he stomped the brakes. The pickup responded nosing forward in a bow at the end of the driveway. He growled, slamming the gear shift into park, then turned off the engine. He steadied himself on the ground, collected his briefcase and empty latte cup from the holder. Annoyed at a slight wave of dizziness, he paused against the back fender. Mike wiped beads of sweat from his brow. "Hot day. Buddy, you are so close, don't blow it. Ashley can't see any issue, or you won't get the keys to your wings back. If I face another rush hour traffic mess on the ground, I'm gonna…" He kicked at the pebble stones with the toe of his boots. "Yeah, do what? Let's go charm her." He mopped his brow, then slid the soggy bandana into his back pocket. Putting a smile on his face, he entered the house looking for the woman he loved.

He tossed the cup into the trash and set his briefcase on the counter inside the doorway to the rest of the rooms. His pulse quickened as he admired the picture she painted in his mind, envisioning her dancing with him in that delightful summer outfit. He admired her form at the sink, surrounded by various vegetables next to the cutting board and knife, as she fumbled with her phone. "Honey, I'm home. I've got good news and better news."

Moving close, he nuzzled her neck; she flinched, setting down the cell.

"Babe, what's wrong? I didn't scare you, did I?" He chuckled before he added, "I spotted the knife next to the potatoes, so I figured you wouldn't stab me. Those shorts still suit your long legs and fit like a glove."

She shrugged and turned with an even expression. "Thanks." Her lips turned up a hair as she quickly added, "I'm fine. I have a lot on my mind. What's your news?"

"JJ believes he has the breakthrough code I need to complete my project. If it's okay with you, he and Jo will arrive tomorrow for the weekend. JJ and I will fly to the office to begin testing acceptance. I thought you and Jo might have fun, perhaps going to town for lunch and shopping."

Several emotions skipped across Ashley's face. "Mike, the place is a wreck. I don't know if this is a good time."

He looked around at the spotless kitchen, knowing that she never left the place messy unless it was holiday decorating time. "JJ will come alone to do the testing if I ask. I thought you'd like more time with Jo."

Ashley shuffled her feet. "I do love spending time with Jo. We always have fun." She looked at him. "You haven't been feeling well. We're snapping a lot at each other. They don't need to witness that." She pushed some hair behind her ear and looked at him with a forlorn expression.

He gently placed his hands on her shoulders and looked into her eyes. "I thought you were ready for me to get this stinky project finished. Isn't that what you want?"

"Yes. I also want to know what's wrong with you. You have beads of sweat on your brow. I'm not giving you the Cessna keys based on how you've been feeling, because I'm scared something will happen. I'll have to get groceries. Jo eats much lighter than I do. With JJ here, you'll be at the computers all night."

"I'll go back to the store now if you want, or order online for morning delivery. Please don't make excuses for missing time with friends we enjoy. I want the Cessna keys, but I agree with your concerns. I feel better today, but I promise to let JJ fly us to and from the office. I don't want to waste time in rush hour traffic. It's awful, honey." He took his hand and crossed his heart. "I will not stay up all night with him on the computer. I promise not to come home too late from work. Life work balance, right?" He glanced at his watch. "I arrived home tonight before supper, even with the awful drivers."

"Yes, but you aren't taking care of yourself like I asked." She burst into tears and leaned into him.

Patting her back, he offered, "I can uninvite Jo, if that's what you want. I'll put JJ in a hotel because we're uh…renovating. Does that help?"

Ashley pulled back and wiped her eyes with the back of her hands. "No, don't do that. I do like them. It was just…so sudden. I'll call Jo after dinner. It's all good. Let me finish making our meal."

Feeling his endurance waning, Mike smiled feebly and nodded before heading toward their bedroom to change.

Jo saw the incoming number and grinned. "Hey, Ashley, I'm glad you called. I understand we're headed to your place for a long weekend. I'm excited."

"Oh, good. I was worried that you might not want to come. I'm hoping we can do some shopping. One of the ladies in Pecan is sponsoring a craft fair on Friday with local artisans, which we might attend."

"That sounds fabulous. If you'd like some fresh peppers and tomatoes, I have plenty. Would you like me to bring a few?"

"I never turn down fresh food. I need to confide in you when you're here. I don't want to discuss this on the phone, but I've made some mistakes that I can't fix. Mike hasn't felt well in a few days, so I'm extra worried. He's been getting dizzy spells and intestinal issues. I want him to see the doctor. Do you think you can ask JJ to suggest he get a check-up?"

Jo chuckled. "Sure. But you need to convince Mike to tell JJ he needs to disengage from his work more often. They will learn someday that neither we nor food are short pitstops in their endless work race for universal dominance."

Ashley hooted for a long minute. "We do have the same problem. How did you and I land two such work mutants? Is that why some females have another male stashed somewhere to fill the gaps?"

"I, for one, do not have another male stashed," Jo snarled. "We have jobs and important roles in our relationships. I love JJ as much as you love Mike. I see it when you look at him. I do make sure my man is properly distracted as often as possible.

Even on photo shoots, I still send him notes, updates, and spicy tidbits to ensure I'm not forgotten when I'm away."

"I'm sorry. You're right, Jo. That didn't come out the way I wanted. I shouldn't have…let's talk when you get here. We're going to have a great time running around town."

Surprised at the shift in conversation, Jo wanted to understand the cryptic comment. "Great. I'll bring veggies. We'll talk up a storm and laugh. Girl time rules."

Jo ended the call, hoping she could get to the bottom of what Ashley was hiding. "I guess I finally have a definition of how someone behaves when wrapped around the axle about something. Maybe it's a Texas thing."

CHAPTER 16

But Seriously

Pleased that his darling Jo had assembled their bags by the side door efficiently, JJ said, "Honey, thanks for packing everything. After loading them, I'll start the car, turning on the air."

She looked up from her favorite purple insulated bag, which was being packed with snacks for their trip. "Can you place the cooler on the backseat? I've added some fresh veggies from the garden as a thank-you gift for hosting us. You might want to add a couple of bottles of wine, too."

"Sure, great idea." JJ walked up next to her, wanting to kiss her, but she was focused on assembling the snack bags, seemingly lost in thought. He shrugged and focused on his chores.

Once he finished adding two bottles of wine to the cooler, he decided to load it first. Outside, he hoisted the heavier Igloo into the backseat. Then he turned on the car, delighted that the air responded with a tremendous blast of cool air. He returned inside, grabbed the duffle bags, and piled them into the back seat on the passenger side. Looking forward to a road trip where they could chat and laugh, he returned to the kitchen. Jo leaned against the counter. Her willowy figure took his breath away, like always.

"You look lovely, honey. Are you ready?"

"Yes, the snacks are ready. I checked that everything is turned off. Are you taking any computers along? I didn't see your backpack."

JJ smacked his leg. "Thanks. I was so focused on getting on the road, I left it in my office."

She pointed to the chair. "I found it when I was doing my checks."

He pulled her into a hug. "You got me. Let's get on the road."

Jo stared out her side window after he navigated to the main highway. He grew concerned as she was unusually quiet, not even commenting on the cows, horses, or goats in the fields browned by the August sun.

"Jo, what is going on in your pretty head? Where is your newsworthy commentary on the roadside scenery? Did I do something to annoy you? I thought this would be a relaxing trip."

She turned and reached for his hand, giving it a slight squeeze. "My conversation with Ashley last evening is playing in my head. It ran through my dreams, causing me not to rest as well as I prefer. I woke feeling tired and a little cranky." Pulling back her hand, she added, "I think something is wrong with Ashley. First, she complains about Mike's health and expresses her concern. Then she jumps into a tirade about how lonely women need a secret male to make up for relationship deficiencies. Lately, she runs the gamut of emotions from A to Z in a single conversation. When talking to her, I'm like a game show host dealing with an over-the-top contestant with secrets she wants to but can't share."

"Your intuition is usually spot on. How do you plan to find out what she's not saying?"

"Mike was your buddy way before you and I met. When you introduced us, I thought they were nice people I would enjoy as friends. I built Ashley up as a possible confidant, whom I like a lot. But you know, I worry about being around people who aren't honest. I'm trying to rationalize our friends' issues. We aren't making this trip to play counselors or supervise a couple of teenagers." She glared in a way he hadn't experienced and firmly stated, "I also don't want to be a useless bystander waiting for the wheels to fall off their lives."

JJ sat up and considered his wording carefully, realizing he'd stepped over the line. "I'm sorry for my flippant remark. I want to help because I care for our friends like you do. I can offer a sympathetic ear. If their domestic issues spill over onto us, we will pack up and find a nice hotel."

"That's fair, honey."

"I must deliver the contracted software code. On the educational side, I also get to watch high-end military-grade testing and craft program changes as needed. The winning benefit for me is a nice weekend near a pretty town we like."

Her fingers curled around his hand. "Ashley told me she needs to speak with me about a mistake she's made but can't fix. I intend to be there to see if I can help her. Thank you for agreeing that we can leave if the weekend stay starts going downhill at a gallop."

"Perfect."

"We're good. How about a snack?"

"Absolutely. I saw some of the goodies you included," he said with a devilish smile.

She handed him two snack bags of his favorites and added a water bottle to the cup holder. She took a sip of water and leaned back in her seat. They silently traveled the rest of the way.

JJ carried the cooler while Jo slung the duffle bags over her shoulder and knocked. Mike welcomed them with hugs. JJ thought his skin reminded him of drywall joint compound. Mike showed them to their room.

"You settle in. I'll be in my office, JJ, when you're finished. We have a little time before firing up the barbecue."

Making quick work of unpacking, Jo leaned in for a quick hug, signaling all was well. He sighed and carried the Igloo while Jo led the way to the kitchen.

"I'm going to set this on the counter and then find Mike, okay?"

"Yep. I'll put away the produce and see if I can help with the meal prep."

Jo turned to JJ wide-eyed after she spotted Ashley wiping away tears in the kitchen, holding her phone. Her hand signals told him to skedaddle. He overheard Jo rush to her friend. "Ashley, are you alright?"

JJ, laptop in hand, wandered into Mike's home office to work, or at least plan their approach before dinner. "Hey, man, we can do a little project scoping now if you like, before you fire up the barbecue. Or we can kick back with a glass or two of wine before we ramble to the grill. Your choice."

His friend twisted around in his chair, blinking his eyes to try to focus.

"Hey, are you okay? You look pale. Are you dizzy?"

Mike tried to straighten in response. "I'm fine. I'd rather relax a bit and enjoy your company. Glad you made it in time for dinner. The thick steaks may require extra cooking time to achieve the desired color. Ash and I like ours a little pink. You prefer medium well, as I recall. Jo frequently requests chicken, with her diligent calorie counting, so we selected a plump breast, seasoned with a pepper-lime baste." Placing his hands on the arms of the chair, he said, "Let's get 'er fired up."

Mike stood, wobbling. He faltered, banging against the edge of the desk. JJ quietly stepped in to steady his friend. When his balance was re-established, they headed for the kitchen to verify their intentions with the ladies. Neither woman was present. JJ noted the counters were cleared of any prep work.

Mike appeared confused and shook his head before retrieving the meat from the refrigerator, handing the plates to JJ, and leaning on the edge of the counter. "I wonder if they're outside. We may have to text them to see what else they want grilled?"

"I will. I have this platter; do we need any sauces or seasonings?"

"Nope, I have all dry spices on the shelves and extra sauces in the outside fridge-freezer."

JJ noticed Mike discreetly grabbing handholds as he made his way to the grilling area. There was no pep in his step, but he figured further questioning would annoy his friend. Mike lifted the lid to the Blackstone, turned on the propane, and started it. Then he dropped the tongs. "I guess I need to slow down some," Mike said with a lopsided grin.

JJ placed the meat platters on the prep table. He noticed Mike maneuvered to the closest stool, one hand gripping its side.

"I haven't seen a Blackstone in action," commented JJ. "How long have you had it?"

"Quite a while. It's much easier to clean. The even temperature controls make cooking a breeze, though I still use onion slices on the heated surface that permeates the meat to perfection." He punctuated the comment by bringing a hand to his lips for an exaggerated air kiss.

"I hope the girls show before we put on the meat. I can time the entire meal, but I need to get the whole scope of the menu."

"Do you want me to go hunt for them? I could pour us wine if you're thirsty."

"No, I'm sure they're gabbing up a storm. Ashley said earlier she couldn't wait to see Jo." He held up his hand, which was visibly quivering. "I'm feeling a bit shaky."

"Should we head to the clinic and get you checked out? I can take you."

Mike shook his head. "No, this will pass. I need more water. Can you grab one from the cooler?"

Concerned, JJ obliged and took one for himself, while keeping an eye on his friend.

Chugging half the bottle, Mike's color immediately improved.

"JJ, need your help covering for me tonight. Then I would like you to fly us to work tomorrow, so we can complete the testing. I need this program delivered. I'm haunted by pilots who won't return without this solution. Please?"

JJ tersely replied, "Something's not right. You're off balance, though your color's improved with the water. Did you eat today?"

"Some, earlier. I'm hungry." Carefully rising, he retrieved a cold snack tray from the small refrigerator and set it on the counter between them. He snagged a few pieces of cheese and said, "Help yourself. It'll tide us over."

"I'm not convinced. What else is bugging you?"

Mike shook his head almost with resolve. Leaning back, he stretched out his legs, popped the last bite into his mouth, and chewed. Moments later, his weary eyes faced JJ. "It goes back a while to when I first got involved in radar development. I've never wanted to share this with you because it hurts too much.

"I was two minutes late for the briefing by our Air Force Lieutenant Colonel, the project coordinator attached to our facility. When I tried to quietly secure my seat, my briefcase bumped the metal chair, which tottered on the concrete floor, causing a loud scraping noise. Everyone turned.

"I can hear the Colonel's annoyance as he remarked. *"Now that we are all here, I want to explain the project. I feel background color would be valuable to what I'm about to request. Let me begin by defining a call-sign in pilot speak.*

"Today's call-signs are still based on the same sources as in the early days of aviation — a derivative of a last name, physical fea-

tures, personalities, or pop culture. A colleague of mine stated that call-signs are usually intentional misspellings of common words to create an acronym referencing a story about the pilot. Most are based on a pilot's early successes or screw ups. The ones based on retelling the mistake, a young pilot tends to be ten-percent honest.

Everyone chuckled.

"This audio transcript I'm about to play," he emphasized, "has been declassified so I can use it as a teaching aid, but you may not record it to share with your buddies. It's personal, since I knew these brave men. Their call-signs are Goblin and Stork. They were a part of the 1991 response to Iraq's invasion of Kuwait. Following the nighttime raids, which eliminated most of the ground-to-air missile sites, all that remained were the mobile units. Goblin and Stork were part of the F-16 squadron tasked with eliminating this problem."

Mike's eyes filled as he whispered, "The colonel turned up the speakers and played the transmission exchange. I've remembered every word. This is what plays in my dreams, JJ."

This is sector control. We see heat plumes in your area.

This is Stork, I see them, sector control.

Goblin, climb up and bank right.
The bandit's on top of you.

Stork, I can't shake him.
My chaff dispenser is clogged or empty.

This is sector control.
The AWACs are picking up more heat plumes.

Stork, bandit got radar lock on me, can you—

This is sector control. Goblin, what's your status? Goblin?
Stork, do you see Goblin?

This is Stork. I'm on the heat plumes. Goblin is down.

Stork, did Goblin eject?

Negative, sector control. Goblin is down.

This is sector control.
Stork, more heat plumes, return to base.

Negative, sector control. Delivering ordnance
to all the registered radar missile sites.

This is sector control,
Stork, return to base with your ordnance.

This is sector control. Stork, do you copy?

Stork...

"When the audio ended, the room was eerily silent. We knew without a doubt the problem we needed to defeat. We need all our fighters to fly with immunity and deliver ordnance to terminate hostiles. We need our brave pilots and planes to achieve air superiority."

Mike swiped angrily at his tears. "During our training, we leverage one line from that recording when we fail. 'Stork, bandit got radar lock on me, can you…' It's why I must reach the one-hundred percent."

JJ clucked his tongue and reached an arm around his friend. "I wish you had told me sooner. I believe we can do it. Take a breath. I'll see if I can locate the girls."

Mike nodded, appearing a bit relieved to have shared his mental burden.

CHAPTER 17

Reason or Speed Bumps?

Ashley stared at Jo, waiting for a response. "Please don't tell JJ or Mike. I'm so scared." Picking up a pillow, she grabbed it around her middle. "I've only exchanged letters once a year with his mom. I promised to never interfere."

"I'll keep your secret, but I don't think Mike could hate you or be angry because you were wronged. You were just nineteen. Is this why you've never spoken to him about having children?"

"Not really. Mike wanted to wait until he reached a better job level because he thinks we'll be more secure."

"Okay, so you have talked about it together."

"Yes," she snuffled.

"I'm confused. What's upsetting you now about something that occurred when you were in college? It's what nearly seventeen or eighteen years ago."

"Someone has been texting me and threatening to expose my secret. I have no idea who this person is or how they learned about it."

"Ashley, we need to find out. JJ can help. I know he can."

Tears streamed down her cheeks. "No, please! He would think the worst of me and be compelled to tell his best friend." Frantically, she wiped her tears. "I never should have confided in you."

Jo's hand clasped hers. "I won't tell. I already promised. I do think we need to find the person threatening you. How are they contacting you, and how often?"

"Somehow they located my cell number and…"

"There you guys are," said JJ, making Ashley nearly jump out of her skin. "We've got the grill heating. Mike wants to know what else we're cooking besides the steaks and chicken."

Jo didn't miss a beat. "We've been solving world peace in here. Sorry. Ash, let's get the veggies. I'll help set up outdoors."

Ashley rose but wouldn't face JJ. "We should have brought it out sooner. It's ready to go."

She rushed toward the kitchen with Jo by her side. She knew being outdoors would strengthen her resolve.

Jo took her shower first, then slid under the sheets. She was unsure of conveying any portion of her discussion with Ashley to JJ, and she didn't want to break her promise. Gratefully, supper had been filled with lighthearted conversation and laughter. She hoped Ash would feel more confident by sharing more with her husband.

"Hi, beautiful," JJ murmured as he slipped into bed and wrapped his arms around her. "The steak filled the void in my stomach. How was your chicken?"

"Very moist. The grilled veggies in butter were even better. Mike seems to know exactly how to grill every type of food perfectly. He looked better, too."

"Agreed. He and I spoke about going to the office tomorrow to work on the testing. He told me why not fixing this problem was so important. I felt terrible learning the fear he's carried around for years. His intentions are to be commended."

He rolled onto his back, holding her hand but staring at the ceiling. He grinned slightly before he continued. "I get to fly his Cessna to the office. Very cool. Then, after updating my contract credentials, we will test my program to ensure it works. I'm excited to get a look at the inside operations."

"You sound ready to jump into the plane and go early."

"Nope, first I want to catch the sunrise with you, my love."

"I like waking up with you by my side. Sadly, I think Ash is hiding something more than what she shared, and I swore to keep as a friend's confidence, like a monkey on my wrench."

JJ rolled his head toward her. "Honey, are you quoting that famous lyric from Lonnie Lupnerder?" JJ then sang, ♫ "Can't have your monkey on my wrench. Unfair fun on an indecent fate. I've got to leave. Don't want this hate. I'll never let your monkey on my bench." ♫

Jo giggled. "Honey, you need more practice. Good night, sweetheart."

He kissed her sweetly. She closed her eyes, succumbing to sleep.

CHAPTER 18

Another day at the office

Close to seven, JJ ambled down the stairs for breakfast with his backpack in place. Hearing quiet banter mixed with an occasional laugh made him smile. Pausing at the doorway, he was delighted to see his friends cutting up with one another. Perhaps they had a good late-night talk.

"Good morning," JJ announced with a chuckle, spotting Mike patting Ash's fanny. Mike turned with a grin. Ash's face bloomed shades of red.

Sporting a mischievous smirk, Mike alleged, "I'm feeling well rested this morning, raring to go. Hope you slept well."

"I did. Jo will be here in a moment. She's looking forward to a shopping day and the pre-art show you mentioned during dinner, Ash."

"Me too," said Ashley. "We'll stick around the square near my art buddy's gallery. I'm hoping Jo will enjoy lunch at Christina's American Table. It's located on the square, offering some nice outdoor seating. We might hit some of the cute boutique shops, too!"

Jo chimed in on the conversation. "Sounds like my kind of place. Much better than big cities. Small-town Texas is why we built our home in Magnolia Bluff."

JJ pulled Jo to his side and kissed her cheek. "What time are we leaving, Mike? I'm thrilled to fly today. When I checked outside, the weather seemed perfect."

Mike glanced at his phone for the time and nodded. "We need to leave in five. The air is nearly windless with cloudless blue skies. Ashley fixed some fried egg sandwiches for breakfast; we can eat on the way." He held up a small bag. "You need to grab some juice or coffee before we go." He sidled up to Ashley and hip-bumped her. "Honey, can you please give JJ the keys?"

"You do look much better this morning. However, I feel better knowing he will take the wheel." She took the keys from her apron pocket and handed them to JJ.

"Heck, I'm going to let him drive the truck to the airfield and sit back relaxed. I'm anxious for the tests with the new programs JJ built." Mike handed his friend the keys.

"No problem. You have one sweet truck. I'm generally not a truck fan, as you know."

Kissing their women goodbye, they left from the back door. JJ climbed into the driver's side. "Mike, you look like a different person today. A stunning change."

"I do feel better. The good food, friendly conversation, and good night's rest seem to have helped. The lack of wine probably didn't hurt either. I thought about your program and believe we may have the best solution."

"I'm excited to experience the testing setup. I'll make real-time changes as needed." He buckled in and started the truck. The engine was powerful, but not so loud as to interrupt conversation. "Thanks for letting me drive. I may have to add a Ford like this to my collection. We have the older farm truck, but this beast is classy."

Mike cleared his throat. "I appreciate you listening to my fears last evening. I also apologized to Ashley for being so grumpy. I think we are on a better course."

"You two looked delighted this morning. Glad to bear witness to the change." He headed toward the airfield, excited to be flying this morning. Minutes later, he pulled up to the space adjacent to the Cessna's tie-downs.

"Let's do a quick flight check and head to the office. This is my idea of commuting," said Mike with a smile. "Even with your piloting, it beats the rush hour drivers."

"I never realized how hard your life was, man," JJ mocked. His shoulder flinched at the friendly punch.

"You should talk."

A scant thirty minutes after take-off, JJ landed and was directed to a spot at Lockheed Martin Aeronautics for commuter tie-down.

"Pull into that open slot," said Mike. "We'll stop at security to update your photo and badge before entering."

"Do I need to speak to the purchasing manager?"

"Yep, he's waiting inside with your paperwork. This shouldn't take long, but it will cause me to wait until lunch for my latte. The things we do for best buds."

"I can't wrap my head around you drinking those." JJ squinching his nose, imagining the taste. "I'm not sure I could. But a couple of expressos would be welcomed after those delicious breakfast sandwiches we had in flight."

"My woman does know how to cook," Mike said.

It only took fifteen minutes to complete paperwork and move through security.

"We need to hit my office before heading to the training center. I think you'll be impressed."

Rubbing his hands together, JJ replied, "I agree. I'm glad I've maintained my Top-Secret status. I'm tickled to see the operations center in action."

Mike felt acutely disappointed when the first three tests ran but resulted in the message playing. The failure percentage reduced each time. Mike completed a debrief after each simulation. When the fourth test was finished, JJ appeared crestfallen and immediately reviewed the code after the speaker in the observation room had played the message.

Stork, the bandit's got a radar lock on me. Can you…

Mike reviewed the data. It displayed ninety-seven-percent good quality. The type of radar signal that caused the problem was one of the latest available in the United States. The good news was that this capability was not in the hands of any known foreign power. "JJ, best numbers of success today. The good news is our latest radar technology tracked us."

"I uploaded the data you're reviewing. The deviation algorithm I used can be modified to overcome this. However, it will only match what is currently known. With your permission, sir, I would like to try the simulation again using the alternative I mentioned earlier: to give the pilot real-time access to pivot the range. If that works, I think it is necessary to incorporate it, no matter the final code structure."

Mike stepped to the side and conferred with one of the pilots, explaining the potential functionality this change would allow.

The pilot approached JJ with Mike on his heels.

"Can you show me how this would work, where I would see it, and what I must do to override the program?"

JJ nodded and positioned a clip of how this would look on the cockpit screen. He stepped through three scenarios, illustrating the available options and their corresponding response times.

"Wow!" the pilot commented. "I agree with what you suggested. This feature should be included, end of story," he insistently demanded tapping the back of one hand to the palm of the other. "The human factor and experience of the flyer could make the difference."

"Agreed," JJ said nodding. "The caution would be to not override the program unless there is no other choice. I'll update this change. You and the others see how it runs through the same scenarios to see if you can solve the last three percent."

The pilot rushed back to the other four doing the testing to brief them on the changes.

"Thanks, JJ. If it works, this helps fill a gap against future technology." Mike patted his friend's back as the program changes were uploaded. "Following this sequence, let's break for lunch. I want to take you to a quaint deli run by a pair of hardworking lads. The food is delicious."

"Do they have espresso?"

"Yep. Whenever you're ready to launch the program, please do it. The fellows in their cockpit modules appear antsy. I think they have wagers on this test."

JJ grinned and pressed go on the simulation. The giant screens illuminated with the pilot's view of the sortie. Land masses showed images of the geographic locations. Various ground-to-air missiles were observed being deflected, bypassed, or turned upon one another. During the forty-minute exercise, the program successfully outmaneuvered and downed four bogies. They also bypassed thirty FOX ONEs, twenty-five FOX TWOs, and seventeen FOX THREEs.

Mike grinned as cheers erupted from the pilots. He was further elated when no Stork message played. He rubbed his eyes with his handkerchief. "Take an hour and a half break for lunch, then we'll try your other modifications, JJ."

Mike clapped JJ on the back after the others left. "Let's get some food, man."

"I finished the other code change to address the radar we missed on the prior test. It will be ready to run when we come back.

CHAPTER 19

Shop 'til you drop.

Driving back to the house, Jo couldn't stop talking about their great time. "I enjoyed poking into every shop in the square. I could have stayed another couple of hours, but I think six plus hours of walking is enough, even with the delicious lunch at Christina's as a break. My feet want to be on a chaise lounge by the pool."

Ashley kept her eyes on the road but laughed. "I'll do you one better. My feet want to be in the pool, cooling off with my husband's promise of a foot rub."

"I can see that, too." Jo wanted to see if she could garner more information, but didn't want to dampen the fun. "I'm glad we could visit your friend's gallery. The talent of the local artisans is fabulous."

Ashley chuckled. "I think Maggie appreciated you letting her keep the nine items you purchased so the guests would get the full sensations from tomorrow's art event. Did you want to return for the full show tomorrow and meet all the artists?"

"Yes, and I want pictures with each of them. You also had your eye on a beautiful painting. Where are you thinking of putting it? Your home is so well decorated, I wondered what you'd want to displace."

"That's why I kept returning to it. I took a photo so I can get Mike's thoughts on it. It wasn't desperately expensive, but the colors would work in the living room, don't you think?"

"I do. I've had so much fun today. It started so nicely. It seemed like you and Mike had fun like you used to. Did you share stuff with him?"

"Not really," Ashley admitted. "I don't know how to approach it. It was before we ever dated." She stopped at the gates into Pecan and showed her ID to the guard. "Mike looked healthy when he woke. I couldn't help but wish we had that every day. Maybe you guys being here helped, or the dinner with everyone sharing stories, or he finally slept all night for a change."

"I'm glad. Did you want to finish telling me more about the person who contacted you?"

"Not yet. I want to try to handle it."

Jo noticed her friend's deflection. She decided to hold off for another time. "What are we fixing for supper?"

Ashley pulled to the end of the driveway and turned off the car. "Can we do pool first? It's only two-thirty."

"The guys aren't home, so yes, we can. I think one of your mocktail sangria delights would be wonderful."

"You're on." Ashley grinned as she opened the door. "I'll meet you at the pool. I'll have towels."

JJ opened the door for Mike. They returned to the test center just after two. "That was an interesting deli. The staff seems nice. They must like you, as evidenced by the extra latte they give you. I don't know how you drink that. Dandelions are supposed to have antioxidants, but that smells nasty."

"I'll admit your espresso smells richer. My latte has an almost sweet aftertaste. Plus, dandelions have vitamins and minerals. You wanted me to be health-conscious." After walking inside, he patted his stomach. "I wish you hadn't talked me into that Caesar

Salad with chicken, onions, and tomatoes. My gut's telling me that was way too healthy. I wanted the chili burger with fries and extra cheese. I get my health rush from dandelion lattes."

"You have no time for a nap this afternoon. We have three tests to run and victory until we celebrate."

JJ slipped into his seat and launched the program without the pilot option but with the expanded algorithm. Forty-five minutes later, the results showed success. He watched Mike review the stats and provided a positive debrief.

"You got it, a hundred-percent."

"Good. Can we try two more scenarios? I have requested the simulation to imitate the toughest action imaginable."

"Sure."

JJ breathed a sigh of relief when the modification worked. He felt confident that the program was top-notch and was being put through realistic paces.

Mike approached, leaned over, and said, "I'm getting a bit of a headache. Are you about finished with your magical program, which I am most grateful you crafted for me?"

"I'd like to test one last set of circumstances before we wrap it up." JJ checked the time. "It's four-ten; we should be done before five. Are you enjoying no more Stork?"

"I am indeed. I'll text the girls. One more time, my friend."

The final scenario ran flawlessly. The pilots in the back cheered. JJ and Mike were the last to leave. JJ was satisfied he had done the right thing as they walked toward the Cessna. A few moments of worry earlier in the day vanished when Mike congratulated him.

Mike lost his footing and bumped into JJ. "Sorry," he mumbled, as he took more deliberate steps.

"Are you feeling dizzy again?"

"No. My eyes feel a little out of focus. The simulation room with its immersive screens, I suspect. Nothing to worry about."

JJ wasn't convinced but didn't want a downer conversation to dampen the evening. "How about I try cooking something different on your Blackstone tonight?"

"Alright, I'll be by your side."

"Nowhere else I'd rather have you on that test drive. I make a mean stir-fry. Can you tolerate that?"

"Sure. Let me text Ash." The response returned in seconds.

> Stir-fry is fine. Cut the veggies, please.
> Chicken and steak are inside the refrigerator.
> Cooked white rice is also in a container.
> If you want to create fried rice. 😔
> Our tired feet are soaking in the pool.
> Jo says brownie points for foot rubs later.

JJ completed the pre-flight check and then buckled into the pilot seat. He started the engine. Mike turned his phone so JJ could read the response.

"We have our assignments. Are you feeling any better?"

"A bit, though I forgot my latte." He pulled out two waters and passed one to JJ. "This will have to do until we get home."

"Thanks. It's all good, man."

CHAPTER 20

Confidence Crisis

"I have perfected the spices I prefer when preparing stir-fry," JJ commented as he selected his items from the orderly shelves, including sesame oil, red pepper, star anise, Szechuan peppercorns, fennel, cinnamon, clove, soy sauce, and curry powder. Scrutinizing the pile of fresh veggies Mike was slicing, he said, "Those long, thin slices are perfect. Can you mince some fresh garlic cloves and crush a tablespoon of the fresh ginger, which I think was in the refrigerator?"

"No problem. I've always liked working with you," Mike said, finishing the last carrots with machine-like precision.

Several minutes later, as the guys focused on their tasks, JJ looked at the assembled food. "We seem to have all the ingredients ready." He added the items onto the two trays for easy transport outdoors. "I'll take the food and get it started." Frowning slightly, he said, "I almost forgot the eggs for the rice."

Mike grabbed three for his tray. "I'm on it. I'll lay out the settings. I enjoy traditional barbequing, but this will be way more fun. We need to have green tea with ice water on the side. I'm going to opt out of wine tonight. My headache is gone, and I don't want a repeat. Do you want wine or think the girls will?"

JJ chuckled, "I don't think we need it. You wouldn't happen to have fortune cookies, would you?"

"I didn't see any in the pantry. I don't recall Ashley serving them here. Do I need to run to the store?" Mike asked.

"No. Jo likes them when we go out. We have more than enough food here."

They assembled the items adjacent to the cooktop. Mike showed JJ how to start it and control the heat. Savory, spiced scents filled the air. JJ kept a close eye on each portion as he methodically prepared it. Ashley and Jo arranged the table, with the plates conveniently placed near the main chef.

JJ delivered each plate, then he took his seat. Based on the sounds emitted as each person tasted their food, stir-fry on the Blackstone was a winner.

"Great work, JJ." Three bites later, Mike complimented.

JJ waved his hand with a flourish. "It was a team effort."

"Yummy," commented the girls in unison.

Relishing the delectable meal, the four friends shared stories of their day. JJ wasn't surprised that Jo had purchased some artwork, which they agreed to pick up tomorrow afternoon. Mike appreciated the photo of the painting Ashley earmarked for the living room. The big news of the evening was the celebration that Mike's project was nearly finished.

JJ was relieved. Mike looked better than when they left the office. He said, "I need to add a few things required by our contract, which I can work on over the weekend and deliver Monday morning."

"Monday or Tuesday is fine, my friend. I think we are taking a day off for the art fest tomorrow with two of the prettiest women in the world." He reached over and covered Ashley's hand with his.

"I saw an ice cream store I'd like to try," said Jo.

"You know you won't finish a whole scoop," JJ added with a grin.

"That's why I'm waiting until tomorrow when you're with me. We can share a cup or cone. Your choice." She blew him a kiss, then patted her mouth with the napkin. "If you folks will excuse me, I'll be right back."

JJ admired his bride as she stood with her beautiful, graceful ease and started toward the kitchen door. Four steps down the path, she suddenly collapsed onto the stone walkway in a heap. Rushing to her side, JJ assessed her condition. Her skin was cool. She had no labored breathing, though she was unconscious. His concern escalated when he discovered a cut on the side of her head.

"Do you want to take her to your room?" Ashley came close and stood to his right. She touched Jo's head and felt for a pulse. "I can feel her heartbeat, but her breathing is more shallow than normal to me. I think a physician should check her."

"Where's the closest hospital?"

"Granbury's is less than twenty minutes. We can take the truck and make it in ten."

"Mike, are you good to drive?"

"Yep, I'm fine."

He tossed the keys to his Porsche to Ashley. "I hate to ask, but can you pack up our stuff and bring my car to the hospital? I want to be prepared for anything. She has a local doctor I can contact in Magnolia Bluff." JJ looked at his wife's serene face, more worried since she hadn't stirred.

"It won't take me long."

Mike hugged her quickly and rushed out to unlock the truck."

JJ scooped up Jo and secured her in the vehicle, cradling her head worried she wasn't coming around.

Minutes later, they arrived at the entrance to the ER.

"I need a gurney, she's unconscious," JJ said through the window.

Efficient staff carefully transferred Jo to the gurney and took vitals. JJ walked alongside, providing basic information on his wife. He explained the circumstances leading up to her fainting. The doctor asked a few additional questions before rushing her through the doors for evaluation.

A nurse thrust a clipboard into JJ's hands. "Sir, please, I need this data as soon as possible."

"I want to be by her side."

"I understand. The doctor and his team are evaluating her. He'll be out to see you as soon as possible. You can help by giving us specifics. Does she have a local doctor?"

"No, but I can provide you with the name of her Magnolia Bluff physician. I think she has a check-up scheduled for next week."

"Perfect. Put it all down and any insurance information too, please."

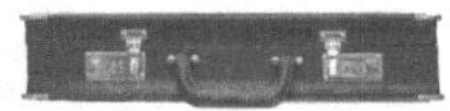

JJ completed the required paperwork. Then, unable to relax, he alternated between pacing the waiting room and sitting next to Mike. He slumped into the chair. "When do you think I'll get to see her?"

"They'll come get you when they know something. The staff is highly rated," assured Mike.

JJ looked up when Ashley entered. Mike rose to hug her.

"How is she?" Ashley asked with an anxious tone.

"They won't let me back to see her yet."

She patted his arm. "This hospital has a great reputation. She bumped her head on the rock along the path. I'm sorry."

"I don't know why she fainted, though. My mind is running through all the possibilities."

"I'm sure she'll be fine. We walked miles today. Both of us complained of sore feet." Ashley removed the backpack and gave it to JJ along with the car keys. "I thought you would rather have this with you than in the car. Everything is loaded and locked."

Rubbing his hands in frustration, he stood and began pacing again. Pausing in front of Mike, he said, "You guys can go. No reason to wait for who knows how long. When they release her, I'd feel more comfortable taking her home. I'll let you know what they tell me."

"We don't mind staying with you," said Mike.

"It's already late. You guys, head home and get some rest. I can work on the changes we need if I get bored."

Ashley tried to hide a yawn, followed by Mike.

"Like I said, you two go home and get to bed. I'll let you know if something changes."

Mike and Ashley reluctantly agreed, hugging him before they left.

Slumped into the chair, JJ tapped his foot, frustrated at waiting.

Twenty minutes later, the nurse approached. "Mr. Rodreguiz, the doctor would like to see you. Your wife's awake."

Relief washed over him as he stood, grabbed his backpack, and followed the woman.

When the curtain was pushed back, he took a breath. Her eyes were open, though it seemed she'd been crying as they were red. A bandage covered the cut. She had an IV attached with what looked like saline, not medicine. The other machine reflected standard vital signs.

"Mr. Rodreguiz, I'm Dr. Daniels. Your wife and baby are fine. I don't see the fall causing any negative impact…"

Though the doctor continued, JJ was dumbstruck by the baby comment and rushed to her side, taking her hand. "You're pregnant. Why didn't you tell me? Are you okay? Do I need to call a specialist?" His mind moved at Mach One with all the open questions.

"JJ, I'm fine. Dr. Daniels decided, based on my age, to run a pregnancy test before X-rays or anything else. The head bump isn't serious. I fainted because, sometimes, in the first trimester, it occurs due to hormonal changes. I thought I might be pregnant, but I hadn't taken a test because I planned on asking my doctor during my annual physical appointment. I didn't want to fail you like before." She smiled and rubbed her fingers on his hand.

"You never disappoint me. I'm glad you are." JJ turned toward the doctor. "Apologies, I didn't hear everything you were saying."

Laughing, the doctor said, "I figured. Your wife said you didn't know. My concern was the head. I don't feel she has a concussion, though I would like to hold her here for a few hours for observation. She's currently getting saline because her blood sugar is lower than I'd like."

"Whatever you say, doc. We were visiting friends, but when she's ready, I'd like to return to our home in Magnolia Bluff."

"No problem. The staff can bring you a blanket to rest," advised Dr. Daniels. "I abide by the four-hour rule to admit or discharge. I believe it will be the latter in this case. Congratulations."

JJ grinned. "Thanks." Then he leaned over and kissed Jo. "Ashley packed the car for us, so we can go home when you're released."

When they were alone, Jo looked at him and smiled. "We're going to have a baby, honey. I bet Lara will be disappointed."

JJ shook his head. "I bet she won't. Neither will Uncle Carlos. Your adopted parents love you, and they're related to me. It's a win all around. I'll text Mike that you're good, but keep our secret about the baby."

CHAPTER 21

A Warm Send Off

Saturday morning, the doctor released Jo. JJ rushed to get their vehicle to the exit door, anxiety clutching at his chest when he'd left her with the nurse and wheelchair. His mind listed all the ways he wouldn't let her out of his sight again. Pulling up close to the wheelchair, he hurried to open the passenger door.

"I've got you, honey," he said, holding her arm as she stood. Reaching around her, he grabbed the seatbelt. "I want you safe, so buckle up." He grinned and kissed her cheek.

Jo chuckled. "Thank you for the ride, ma'am. The staff here is great."

JJ slid into the driver's seat and pulled away from the entrance of the ER. "Do you want to go to Granbury or head home?"

"I'm tired from being up most of the night. I would rather head home than stop to rest at Mike and Ashley's. Are you up for the drive?"

JJ brushed his hand over his face. "I'm good to go, though I'd rather pick up a coffee. The hospital's free stuff was nice to have available, but…"

"I understand," she laughed. "Not espresso. Stop and get one. If they have any, an apple and a banana would be great."

He leaned over and kissed her again, then patted her leg. "If that's what you want, I'll find it."

Two miles down the road, he pulled into a Starbucks. The drive-through line was long, so he decided not to wait. He found a parking place where he could easily see the car while he waited for their order. "I'm going to go in. It'll be quicker. Why don't you phone Ashley and let her know we're heading home?"

She looked at him with an odd expression that he couldn't decipher. "Are you all right, honey?"

"I'm great, JJ. I'll call her. I'm not going to tell her about the baby yet. I want the follow-up doctor visit first."

"Perfect." He kissed her and opened the door to exit.

"Can you please grab me a tea as well? Love you."

"I love you, too. Be right back." He quickly entered the building, glancing back several times to see Jo on the phone. He placed the beverage order, adding fruit, a couple of yogurt cups, and two fresh breakfast sandwiches, figuring they needed options.

Focused on watching her out the window, especially when she waved and blew him a kiss after the call ended, he was startled when he heard, "Mister, did you want this order? I've called your name three times."

"Sorry," he said, turning. "I was daydreaming, I guess." Retrieving the bag of food and the beverage tray, he grinned. "Thank you, ma'am. Have a great day." He headed for their vehicle and handed the items through the window. "I think I have everything."

Jo peered into the bag. "It seems you do. The warm egg thingy in here smells yummy."

He got in, grabbed his espresso, and took a welcome drink. "Now this is coffee."

"Ashley promised to get photos of the artists for me and retrieve our purchases. I know she'll text pictures to me."

"Great. We can either have them ship your new treasures to us or we can pick them up when you're feeling better."

"Sweetheart, I'm feeling great. Stop worrying."

"The doctor said you could get lightheaded and maybe faint again. I will be right by your side until the second trimester."

He didn't miss her eye roll before she giggled, then bit into the banana as he pulled out of the parking lot and onto the highway.

Traffic was sparse, and they made good time. An hour down the road, Jo asked for a pit stop. He pulled into the first available option. Barreling around the SUV, he opened her door, holding her hand while she exited.

"This looks clean," he said as he walked beside her and reluctantly let her enter the proper door alone.

Minutes later, she appeared, tilting her head at his proximity. "Thanks, JJ. Let's go," she murmured, twitching her lips.

Enjoying the smooth ride and delightful conversation, they reached their house a little after noon.

JJ walked Jo inside. "You need to rest, sweetheart. I'll make you some tea."

Jo smiled. "JJ, I appreciate the tea, but I'm not a piece of porcelain. I'm fine."

"But, honey, I'm worried."

"I won't rush around. I'll eat more frequently to maintain a stable blood sugar level. And everything else the doctor recommended. If you keep hovering, we WILL have issues." She stood with her arms crossed.

JJ sighed, realizing she was right. "You can't be angry with me caring about you."

"I'm not. I appreciate your concern. But, REALLY, standing outside the bathroom door was a bit much." Unable to hold back the mirth bubbling inside, she giggled. He caught the chuckle and was nearly hysterically laughing along with her. Leaning in, she held him until the hilarity subsided. "I'm fine."

"Alright, I'll try not to worry," he agreed almost resignedly.

"I'll water the garden while you start on those program changes you mentioned. Mike will want an update."

"Sounds good. The doctor did say fresh air was good for you."

"I hope they get to the art show. They could use a bit of fun. Ashley would feel better if she opened up to Mike. I thought they were sweet together at dinner."

"Me too. Mike's trying to wrap up this project."

They prepared snacks in the kitchen for nibbling. Then parted to work on their respective chores.

CHAPTER 22

Business upended

Mike awoke with a smile. Kicking around the art exhibit in Granbury and a fun day with Ashley reminded him how much he loved her. Turning his head, he was surprised she wasn't still asleep. It was rare for her to beat him out of bed on a Monday morning. The alarm played a soft melody, alerting him to leave for work within an hour. Stretching, he ambled toward the bathroom to complete his morning rituals.

Cleaned up, he stood in front of the closet, trying to decide what to wear. He planned to put the final touches on the presentation of RadHalCaT, to the military liaison. "JJ's email response indicated the program should arrive by the end of today. He made the difference between success and failure. I owe him, big time."

Picking up his briefcase, he headed toward the kitchen to kiss his bride, hoping for a cup of coffee. Pleased with his project's status, he had a pep in his step. Taking the shortest route, he paused in the hallway, adjacent to the kitchen, when he overheard Ashley talking to someone.

"I've done everything you've asked. You have to keep your end of the bargain. Leave Brett alone. He's not part of our life..."

Mike frowned, growing irritated, and he continued to eavesdrop.

"I've told you everything." Her voice sounded hoarse, like she'd been crying. "His contractor was here Friday, and they celebrated success...I don't know the status..."

The call disconnected. He couldn't help reacting to Ashley's sobbing. He entered and saw her curled up on the chair with tears streaking her face. "What have you done? Who was on the phone?" Mike roared.

Her eyes widened, terrified. "I don't know, Mike. He threatened me. I couldn't tell…"

"Threatened you or paid for information?" Angry beyond belief, he couldn't decide what to do. "Did you call him?"

"No."

"When did you meet?"

"Never. He texted me a month ago. He knew things. He said he would hurt people if I didn't answer questions. I told him I didn't know anything."

"What did he want?"

"Your briefcase. He said you keep all the important data inside. I said I didn't know how to get it or the combination."

"But, Ashley, why didn't you just tell me?"

"I didn't want to bother you with a nuisance texter. I got concerned when I couldn't block the contact on my phone. Then the calls started."

Throwing up his hands, he paced. "What am I supposed to do now?" He glared at her. "Who's Brett?"

"Someone from before we met."

"You're hiding something, Ash. And now, you've compromised the security of my project." Resigned, mad, and confused. "I'm leaving for the office. I won't be home tonight."

It felt good to slam a couple of doors and drawers before he stomped to his truck. His fists clenched as his mind was unable to determine the best course of action. He muttered, "My success with this project could put the U.S. ahead in ways other military powers couldn't. I could finally fulfill my dream of saving lives. I can't believe she would betray me, but…" En route, he called

Kamal. "Good morning, Kamal," he said when the man answered. "This is Mike Hayes. If the security line is short, I plan to arrive at my office in twenty minutes. Do I have any issues with my machine or login credentials?"

"No, sir. Were you expecting a problem?"

Realizing his almost-blunder, he sighed and replied, "No. But I have an essential presentation to put together for our military leadership and didn't want anything to slow me down. Plus, I'd like you to set up a new Dropbox for JJ to forward some updated project data."

"Everything looks good. I'll set it up now and send you the access information. I was heading over to the deli. Did you want me to pick up a latte for you?"

"No, I'll stop there on my way in."

Landing promptly, he tied down his aircraft and jaunted to the deli, supercharged by the plan forming in his head.

Mai-chin greeted him and took his order, offering a breakfast sandwich, which Mike accepted with a slight smile. "Mr. Mike, you look happy today. Do you have a good week ahead?"

"I do. A project I've worked on for nearly a year is ending."

"I hope it is a positive end." He handed over the order.

When Mike tried to pay, the co-owner lowered his gaze. "It would be dishonorable to accept your money after all you have done for us. We are your grateful coffee-making team."

"Thank you. I have grown fond of this brew. I may make a trip later. If I do, I'll grab another cup to go."

"Thank you, Mr. Mike. You have given us much success. We hope for more in the future because of you."

Mike shook the man's hand. On the way to the office, he paused at a crosswalk. Watching the pedestrians in the area, he spotted Hank DeSoto having a conversation with a man on a bench in the square. Mike cocked his head. He considered striking up a conversation, but then dismissed the idea when the light changed. He hurried to the office to capture the idea that popped into his mind.

The presentation came together reasonably quickly, which pleased Mike. He tried to book a short meeting today with the bigwigs but discovered the first available time slot was on Wednesday. He took the spot, shrugging at the delay. Finishing his latte and breakfast, he decided to visit JJ. He knew JJ provided digital security support. He wanted advice on handling the Ashley wrinkle. He was at a total loss for steps to take. The whole discussion with her was bizarre and broke his heart. He booked his time out of office for the rest of today and tomorrow. He secured his laptop inside his briefcase, then took the short trip to the deli for a refill on his latte.

The propeller turned over after he slipped on his headset. Taking a hearty swig of coffee, he muttered, "This was supposed to be a great day. JJ has always been a good friend and sounding board."

Mike nosed the throttle forward and the plane taxied to the end of the runway, then rose into the blue skies.

Jo wrung her hands, fearing the modeling shoot was problematic. The production crew, focused on their tasks to make it a great shoot, seemed disturbed by the logistics of the location.

Destiny Fashions' owner, Lara Bernardes, and her adopted mother appeared. "Jo, honey, I've decided to use a new lead model this season."

Crushed, Jo tried to appear stoic until Lara walked away. Then she flopped onto a chair, thinking of ways to salvage her career. The production crew loaded equipment and then moved on as if she weren't there.

Jo called out to Lara, hoping to learn why there had been a change in the model lineup. Unable to gain Lara's attention, much less find the right words, she stood. Dizziness overcame her. Jo shot up in bed, gasping for air and moaning loudly.

JJ awoke with a start, putting his arms around Jo, waiting for the worries to recede. A few moments later, he whispered, "Same nightmare?"

Jo nodded as she took a ragged breath. "Oh, honey, what will I do if that's the reaction I get from Lara? Every night it's the same thing. I want her to be happy for us, but she is in business. I never imagined pregnancy would cost me my job, modeling as JoW for Destiny Fashions. I'm sure they'll think I'll get round and plump, then leave them in the lurch after I deliver. The models will knock themselves over jockeying for my position. Do you think Lara is angry that we built this house, so far from Brazil?"

"I don't think so. She thought it was lovely when she and Carlos visited." He rubbed her arm. "Honey, do you want me to say it's all puppies and rainbows, or would you prefer the cold realities I see with my analytical mind?"

Jo sniffled. "I'd like both, please."

With a slight chuckle, JJ said, "My Aunt Lara will start a maternity line with you as the star. She loves you more than the fans love you, which is saying a great deal. She and Uncle Carlos will dote on this baby. I love you."

"Wow, that was pretty good, honey. Maybe hormones are making my imagination go into overdrive."

"You'll get to do the fall shoot with hardly an extra pound to show. Let's work out the timelines after you get your physical, then we can break the news to the family."

"Sweetheart, I'm sorry to be fretting about something that seems to be in only my mind. Can we have an early breakfast, please?"

Grinning, JJ suggested, "How about we work out first?"

"In the gym or…?"

"Sometimes what you don't ask is delightfully enticing."

"I've learned from you, honey," she chuckled.

"I'll start some breakfast while you take your shower."

She completed her shower, feeling refreshed and even hungrier. JJ grumbled at his phone when she sat down to watch him cook. "Hi honey, sounds like you just found out that you must do something you don't want to do. Can I help, so long as it doesn't entail being a coding *choeda*?"

JJ smirked with a raised eyebrow. "Is that what I am, a coding *choeda*? Why can't you think of me as a dazzlingly derivative or, better still, a programming Parthenon, epic in stature?"

"I can do that. What's wrong?"

"According to his email, Mike's flying in to work on the finalized code with me. I called. I can't get him to answer, so he's in the air. This coding *choeda* needs to drive to the Burnet Airport."

Jo chuckled and sipped at the tea he'd set at her spot.

Her heart lurched, and their teasing ended at the sound of an airplane engine sputtering. Seconds later, she felt the floor vibrate under her feet. Horror streaked across JJ's eyes. The sounds of breaking metal echoed through the open window that moments ago had been delivering a gentle breeze. She reached for JJ's hand. Her breath caught, then their eyes met. They hollered "Mike!"

They rushed outdoors. Spotting smoke, Jo pointed, then headed toward the fence at the end of their property. Stunned, she and JJ stopped at their fence and stared into the open field at the upended aircraft.

JJ yelled, "Jo, call 911. I'll head over to get Mike out of the plane."

"You've reached Magnolia Bluff police department, please state your emergency."

"Hey, Robert, this is Jo Rodreguiz. A Cessna crash-landed in the open field behind our far fence line toward the reservoir. Send emergency equipment, please. We think the pilot is the only passenger."

"Yes, ma'am. I'll let Tommy know. Is there a fire?"

"Not yet. I think the fire department should be called as well. Please hurry. The brush is dry in August." She felt helpless watching JJ dash toward the wreck to check on the pilot.

Worried, she kept JJ in sight as he bounded over the fences toward the plane. He reached the aircraft at the same time two hooded individuals frantically raced up and tried to open the passenger door of the wreck.

She couldn't understand what JJ hollered before he leaped at the men, sending one into the upended aircraft. The man thumped off the metal and dropped onto the grass. JJ grazed the other man with a right hook. Staggering, the man grabbed a piece of equipment from inside the Cessna and sprinted toward the highway. The other one rose into a fighting stance.

Her grip on the phone tightened, seeing JJ's side kick miss the assailant. The sounds of heavy punches and shouted exchanges reached her ears. Elated, she jumped for joy the instant the pilot door dropped, knocking the hooded adversary to the ground. Moments later, the man regained his footing and raced in the same direction as the other assailant.

Dreading the worst, Jo tentatively edged her way toward the site, grateful the smoke was heading away from their house. She spotted Mike moving and sent a prayer toward heaven. JJ reached in, she presumed to release the seatbelt and extract his best friend.

She heard Mike weakly croak.

"JJ, they're after this." He held up the familiar briefcase Mike always carried. She reached to grab it so JJ could extract Mike with both hands. Mike vehemently begged, "Protect this!"

Then Mike lost consciousness.

JJ felt for a pulse and gave her a thumbs-up sign. "I'll stay with him and wait for the ambulance. Go secure this in my office, honey."

JJ's eyes filled with tears as he laid Mike on the ground. Heart swelled to near bursting; Jo hurried to the house.

CHAPTER 23

Give me the Details

JJ and Jo, along with Magnolia Bluff Police Chief Tommy Jager, watched the ambulance roar down the road towards Magnolia Bluff Hospital. The crash site contained a full complement of mechanics, aviation specialists, and investigators.

Chief Jager's tan Stetson suited his khaki uniform and polished boots. Removing his hat to wipe his brow and neck with his kerchief, Tommy resettled it, contemplating the best approach. He liked and respected JJ. However, the man and his pretty wife had a way of turning his world on end. Closing the distance, he mastered his serious, no-nonsense expression, then demanded, "Give it to me again, JJ. I'm trying to understand how you are involved in another mess. Your explanation makes no sense."

"Tommy, this isn't my fault," JJ insisted, maintaining eye contact. "I'm a subcontractor to Lockheed Martin. Mike Hayes is the program manager for my current top-secret assignment. He flew in to meet with me on a project we're in the process of finalizing. He's an excellent pilot whom I've known for years. There must be some mechanical issue that caused his landing here."

"You're telling me that instead of you doing your computer mumbo-jumbo to send him information digitally, he decided to fly here this morning?"

JJ took a breath. "My friendship with Mike goes back to when we were teens. We took our flying lessons together. He and his wife were having some issues that he may have wanted to discuss with me, but I'm not certain. He has been experiencing bouts of dizziness. When I met with him Friday, he seemed improved."

Cocking his head, Tommy questioned, "Had he gone to a doctor or been checked?"

"Not that I know of. Jo and I, along with his wife Ashley, tried to get him to do that, but like you, stubborn is his strong suit."

"Don't do that deflection thing. Step by step, I want you to go through the sequence of events again."

"Jo and I were contemplating breakfast when I received the message from Mike that he was on his way here. We heard noise outside, like a plane flying too low, then felt the vibration when it landed hard. We hurried outside and saw dust and debris in the air. I sprinted toward the crash, asking Jo to phone 911. Before I jumped my fence, I spotted two hooded men, shorter than you or me by five inches or so. They opened the passenger door. One removed something from inside and passed it to the other." JJ splayed his hands as he continued. "I thought they were trying to help. But they turned and lashed out. The ground in this field is so uneven and rocky that I had difficulty landing consistent hits. One took off with the item. It could have been computer equipment or some other electronic device. The second guy tried some moves that let me know he had martial arts experience, but as we fought, he ended up under the door when it unexpectedly opened on his head, forcing him to the ground. I thought he was out. When I heard groans inside the cockpit, I didn't bother to check the assailant; I went to help Mike."

Tommy rolled his eyes as he studied JJ. "An unscheduled, impromptu, faulty aircraft landing occurs minutes from the airport. Two hooded individuals accessed the plane ahead of you, even though it's near your property. How is that possible, unless..."

JJ finished the thought. "Unless they knew where the aircraft was supposed to land. Without surveying the field, it would be impossible to see the number of holes, rocks, and hidden tree limbs hiding in the tall grasses and sage."

Tommy realized he needed JJ's assistance. "I need your eyes to explain things inside the plane." He pointed toward the craft, where the emergency teams were wrapping and storing their equipment. He closed the distance on the wreck, hearing JJ's footsteps close behind. "Don't touch anything. What do you think those two wanted from the plane? You said one got away with a piece of gear. How would they know how close the aircraft would land to them? What did they need to pull out of the wreckage ahead of the rescue services?"

"Okay. You have some great questions, Chief. I don't know how many answers I can provide. Your team will have filmed everything, I suspect."

"I want your thoughts and perspective, JJ."

When they arrived at the open pilot door, JJ snapped photos of the interior and the instrument panel. Then he moved to the passenger side.

Before he elaborated on his thoughts, one of the county deputies hollered, "Chief, we've got a high-level official government call coming in on our radio, requesting to speak to the chief investigator. Do you want to take it, or should I tell them to go pound sand?"

Tommy clucked his tongue in annoyance and bellowed, "I'll be right there." He murmured to JJ, "I'll maintain a civil attitude until I know who they are and what they want. You can head home now. We'll discuss this further after I've spoken with the government. Please send me a copy of your pictures. Guess your friend is pretty important to get a government intervention so fast."

JJ pocketed his phone and nodded. "I'll be at the house."

Tommy watched JJ turn toward his property and take Jo's hand, heading around the fence line toward the front driveway.

Tommy grabbed the mic. "This is Chief of Police Tommy Jager. Who's requesting to speak with me on a police channel?"

A gruff voice boasted, "This is Major Johnson, head of Lockheed Martin security in Fort Worth. We understand that one of our staff members crash-landed his private plane in your jurisdiction. Can you confirm?"

"That's correct. We are piecing together the accident details. The pilot is on his way to the hospital. A witness identified the pilot as Mike Hayes."

"Chief Jager, you are instructed to post a guard on Mr. Hayes. No one may approach the aircraft until our people arrive later this afternoon. Details are to be maintained in the strictest confidence without authorization from us."

Irked by the condescending tone, Tommy stated, "Whoa, slow down, Major. I make the rules in this city. Unless you have federal security clearance, your orders are considered advice. I suggest—" The ringing of his cell phone interrupted his tirade. "Excuse me, Major. I have another call I need to take. Please hold on." He switched the radio to the non-transmit mode and then answered his cell phone. "Yes, sir?" Tommy nodded as he listened. He slowly closed his eyes and acknowledged, "Yes, sir, full cooperation with the feds. Understood."

Returning to the patched call to the cruiser, he pressed the mic key. "I'm back with you, Major Johnson. I've been instructed to provide full cooperation. We will comply with your stated requests." Grinding his teeth, Tommy fought to contain his annoyance. "Will there be anything else, Major Johnson?"

Johnson politely replied, "I'm glad you appreciate our position. We'll talk soon."

CHAPTER 24

New rules of engagement

Frowning, Tommy approached the deputy. "I need you to post a guard to work the eight p.m. to eight a.m. shift. Once the emergency team is finished, you can head out." He scribbled his cell number on a notepad, tore off the page, and handed it to the woman. "You pass this along to the next guard and ask them to call me on that number. I'm headed over to speak to the witnesses." He pointed to the home nestled behind the fence. "Thanks for your help."

Tommy picked his way through the rough terrain to his car. He got in, turned it on, and then drove through the entry gate of Rodreguiz's home to the parking area. He spotted JJ and Jo sitting at a shady spot in the Pergola. They looked toward him as his boots echoed on the concrete.

"Hey, I thought we could continue our conversation, if you don't mind."

"Sure, I haven't looked at the pictures yet," said JJ.

Jo smiled warmly. "May I get you some coffee and perhaps a cookie or sweet roll? It's been a tough morning."

"Thank you. Sounds good." He pulled off his hat and set it on the tabletop. Subconsciously fingering his hair, he said, "I haven't heard any updates on your friend yet. I'm sure someone will contact me after they've assessed his condition."

"Thank you. May I call his wife now and explain the situation?"

"You can, but she may already be aware. The call that interrupted us was from a major in charge of security at his work. They are aware of the crash. I suspect they picked it up from the transmission by the first responders of the tail number."

JJ nodded. "Mike had Ashley's name painted on the tail near the number, too. He was delighted when he showed it to her before he proposed. I want to call or have Jo call to let her know she can stay here."

"It will save me the trouble of trying to reach her. I was told to keep a tight lip regarding the aircraft's condition or any details until the security team arrives later today. Focus on her husband and his condition when you speak with Mrs. Hayes. I may need to question her later."

Jo met JJ as he entered through the side door to the kitchen. "Babe, have you called Ashley about this yet?"

"No." She arranged several cookies on a plate before setting it on a tray.

He noticed a small coffee carafe, cup, and sugar sitting beside a napkin and spoon. "Is that for Tommy?"

"Yes." Her eyes darted around as if to make sure they were alone. "The item is locked in the safe in your office. I assume you don't want to tell him it's here."

He gave her a quick hug. "You are so smart. I'll wait for you to take that to Tommy and return before I place the call. We can both speak to her. Tommy said the feds are involved and will be here later to lead the investigation."

Jo arched an eyebrow as she picked up the tray. "I noticed he was annoyed, with his jaw clenching, when he arrived. I don't know if there are enough cookies here, but I can add more later."

"Did Tommy growl at you for us being in another issue situation outside our control?"

JJ smirked. "Babe, we're probably the most aggravating acquaintances he has in his speed dial. Let's get Ashley on the phone, but prepare for impact."

Jo returned a few minutes later. "Tommy said he'd be back in a while, because the deputy called about some issue. I told him we were going to call Ashley. He asked if you could record it so he could get a sense of her before they meet."

"I can do that. Let's do it in my office, though." He turned on his charm and peered at her from under his lashes. "May I have some of those cookies, too?"

She laughed. "Yes, dear. I'll fix a plate we can share and be there in a sec."

JJ set up the call, ensuring his number was reflected as the calling number so she would pick up. When Jo appeared with the munchies, he placed the call.

"JJ, is everything all right with Jo?"

"Hey, Ashley," said Jo. "I'm good."

JJ cleared his throat. "Ash, we're calling about Mike."

"What about Mike? We fought. He went to work. I haven't heard from him. He's angry with me." She sniffled then added, "Rightfully so."

Jo and JJ looked at one another with concerned expressions, noticing her voice breaking at the end of that sentence.

"Ash, Mike flew here to work with JJ. He made an emergency landing in the open field behind our property. He's on his way to the hospital, sweetie."

She shrieked and broke into inconsolable sobbing.

"Ashley, honey, take a breath. His condition is being evaluated. He said a few words to JJ. Do you want me to come get you and drive you here? I can."

She inhaled deeply a couple of times before she demanded, "What about his briefcase? Do the police have it? Is it with him?"

Astonished at the unexpected question, JJ looked at Jo for an answer. She shook her head. "We focused on extracting him from the plane so the paramedics could work on him before transport. Why is that important?"

Sounding agitated, she barked, "JJ, he NEVER went anywhere without the damn thing. The only reason he would head to you would be the stupid project. It should have been with him. It means the world to him. It should have been with him."

JJ raised an eyebrow and wrote a note to Jo. "Is there anything about your girl time you haven't mentioned?"

Jo nodded, then wrote. "I promised not to tell, as she wanted to tell Mike. It's a mistake from her first year of college. I don't know how it applies."

He nodded and patted her back, understanding her honor toward her friend.

"I'm sure it will turn up. A team of investigators at the crash site is assessing the cause."

Ashley blew her nose. "I'm coming there as soon as I can get into the car. When I get there, we need to find his briefcase." JJ disconnected the call, stunned.

JJ looked up at Jo. "Not what I expected."

"Me either. I need some juice before I tell you what she told me. I wasn't keeping things from you, just respecting her wishes as her friend. I think we have a lot to figure out."

CHAPTER 25

Plans gone awry

The two Asian men hung their heads as the verbal torrent assaulted them. "This operation was perfectly choreographed to have the pilot pass out in flight, allowing you, my drone operators, to use the remote-control unit to stage a random crash landing. The vacant field was chosen to provide time for you to retrieve the unit from the plane and secure the briefcase with its PC. After duplicating the files, you were to smuggle the item back into the aircraft. No one would realize it was compromised or try to build countermeasures. The goal is to ensure China is ahead of the Americans in stealth technology."

The older man stated, "Suh—"

"Shut up!" the man bellowed from the phone's speaker. "One more attempt to apologize for bungling this operation, and I'll have you transferred to the regular North Korean army. I promise you'll be at the front line fighting for Russian supervisors against the Ukrainians."

Both men flinched involuntarily at the threat and replied in unison, "Yes, Suh."

Seething for several heartbeats, the man growled, "How will you correct this situation? I want your plan to secure the stealth specifications without drawing unwanted attention. His wife can be convinced to swear that the briefcase with its PC and the stealth tech was not in Hayes' possession when he left for work."

"There, Suh, we must assume that the interloper who unexpectedly arrived has the briefcase, or it is at the hospital. We know where the interloper came from, so we can stage a break-in to retrieve the needed materials," suggested the older man, glancing at his comrade for agreement.

"That's only half of the assignment," retorted the voice. "You must get it copied and returned with no one the wiser."

"We could deliver it to his wife and make her swear he failed to take it with him due to his illness. You still maintain control over her, correct?"

"I do."

Ashley muttered incoherently as she haphazardly packed for her trip to Magnolia Bluff. "I'm so mad but scared for him right now. I've packed and repacked this suitcase three times. I've got to finish explaining. Why didn't I make him listen?" Her emotions flared out of control. She slapped the suitcase shut, frustrated at herself.

A few minutes later, she had her belongings assembled and ready for departure. When she reached for the SUV keys, she found a note.

> I thought you should experience what it feels like
> to have your keys hidden. After your temper tantrum,
> call me for their location.

Stunned, Ashley melted into the nearest chair and sobbed uncontrollably. Several minutes later, she yelled, "Call me for the location of the keys, except I won't answer you." Her tears threatened until she blew her nose and shook her fist. "You better stay alive so I can explain everything, including Brett. I love you. I'm an idiot."

CHAPTER 26

Targeted and Uncooperative

JJ smiled at Jo, standing by while he launched a session in the Gigazon virtual conference with ICABOD. He quietly stated, "Babe, you're welcome to listen if you like. I will remind you not to share anything you hear with anyone, please."

Jo wrapped her arms around his waist and gave him a loving kiss. Breaking away with a sly smile, she explained, "I can't tell anyone what I don't hear."

JJ grinned as his mind flashed on their future with their baby. He quickly refocused on the avatar that appeared on screen. "ICABOD, I'm uploading all my photos of the Cessna 182's cockpit. The plane crashed nose-down in the field. I suspect that someone with a remote-control device somehow orchestrated the event. The investigative team has been crawling over the site, taking notes and gathering evidence."

"I can provide data on how remote control might affect that model and how it would be implemented," replied ICABOD. "How long after you heard the crash did it take you to get to the plane?"

"I'd put it at six or seven minutes. I stopped to gawk at the Cessna tail in the air, before hopping the fence to run for the aircraft, hollering for Jo to call 911. The uneven ground slowed me down."

"Yes, I have all those recordings automatically from your devices, which I monitor as standard operating procedure. You activated the conversation recording before you cleared the fence. Once you got close to the focal point of the incident, you saw two figures accessing the plane?"

"That's correct, ICABOD."

"Based on the distance from your home, JJ, it would be impossible to have beaten you to the crash scene without knowing the particulars in advance. These individuals had to be waiting in proximity. That suggests control, which is risky based on the terrain I have captured from the satellite links. It was planned. Your photos of the cockpit show cut wires hanging from under the dashboard. Something was removed, or Mr. Hayes would have noticed it before taking off."

"I thought that looked odd. Does it relate to analyzing how a remote control might have been used?"

"I am running through various scenarios and configurations in background mode, but the verified results will take time. You saw a hooded figure get away with what looked like a piece of gear."

"Correct. My brief fight with them ended when Mike managed to release his door. I only saw them running toward the south. I was more concerned with helping Mike. Even though he was dazed and confused, likely from being in and out of consciousness, he had the presence of mind to hand me his briefcase."

"JJ, preliminary projections are that they removed the remote-control appliance from behind the dashboard. I am analyzing the manufacturers of these devices to determine the likely options. Removing the item suggests that they wanted it to be perceived as an accident. Would the briefcase have been the target, or could Mike himself have been the objective ? He is a brilliant engineer, and we just filled the gap in his radar issue."

JJ acknowledged, "I agree it was a carefully orchestrated attack, but by whom?"

"You and I provided a critical link in stealth technology that could easily tip the balance in an armed air conflict. There is a high probability that foreign nationals learned of Mr. Hayes' work and decided to steal it."

JJ turned his head to look at the large safe that held the briefcase before turning back to the screen. "Then it seems I'm sitting on a ticking time bomb. If the assailants are smart enough to engineer this kind of theft, they might show up looking to complete their acquisition."

"They would be speculating that you have it. Though, they might believe it is with Mike."

"I've known how important the briefcase is to Mike since his college graduation. For his mental wellbeing, it's incumbent upon me to make sure he has it handy."

"Yes, JJ."

JJ's phone screen bloomed to life with the picture of Chief Jager. "Hi, Tommy, what's up?"

"You said Mike was a longtime friend, right? I want you at the hospital when he wakes. I want to question him, but he's slipping in and out of consciousness. Your voice might make the difference. Once the military security with federal support arrives, we will unlikely be allowed to get any info from him. Can you get here pronto?"

"Tommy, it isn't like you to pressure someone for information while they're in a traumatic condition. Why don't we wait until he—"

"There is more at stake here than I can discuss over the phone!" Tommy barked. "Down here now."

JJ sighed. "Yes, Chief, on our way."

Tommy added, "I need to know what Mr. Hayes had you working on that has everyone wrapped around the axle."

"What I am working on is classified," JJ freely admitted. "If this is what you want, I won't be able to answer questions. Frankly, neither should Mike. I'm under a government contract concerning the project. The feds will tell you the same thing. I know this is your jurisdiction, but my collaborative work with my contract officer is not for open discussion."

"Harumph. I'll see you soon when you visit Mr. Hayes."

CHAPTER 27

Silent but Deadly

JJ parked his SUV at the outskirts of the hospital lot. Grabbing the briefcase, he locked the vehicle, then headed into the main entrance. Stepping inside, he noticed the tiled floors and tan walls appeared almost new with a faint scent of cleaning products that tickled his nose. He appreciated the artwork, which depicted pictures with a Western motif. He liked one of a doctor dressed in late 1800s garb pulling tools of his trade from a black bag, with a patient dressed as a cowboy on the table.

The smiling, perky brunette information clerk greeted, "Good day, sir. How may I help you?"

"I am here to check on Mike Hayes. He was brought in through emergency, and I don't know if he has a room yet."

"The patient has been transferred to our third floor, sir. Police officers will be checking IDs for all visitors."

"Thank you, ma'am. Which way to the elevators, please?"

The clerk pointed to the left. "Head down the hallway and take the first left. The elevator is on the right."

"Thank you again," JJ said with a grin.

He swung the briefcase, walking nonchalantly toward the elevators. Pressing the button, he entered alone and selected the third floor.

When the doors opened, Tommy said, "It's about time you arrived. What took you so long?" He spotted the briefcase and appeared confused. "What do you have there?"

"Hey, Tommy. This is Mike's briefcase. He carries it with him everywhere. It will comfort him, like the security blanket a comic strip character once needed."

Tommy scowled but silently led JJ toward Mike's room. JJ greeted the attentive Deputy Mars, sitting on a chair beside the door.

"Nice duty, Deputy."

The woman grinned but said nothing.

When they entered, the doctor focused on his tablet, commenting to the nurse in a low tone what JJ presumed was the patient's data.

"Any change, Doctor Everett?" asked Tommy.

"Yes and no. According to the test results we have, I don't think the plane crash injuries were enough to result in his current state. Mr. Hayes sustained a bump on the head. His safety harness minimized the impact. We began regular tests. The technician called attention to a result she found by accident. Regular tests wouldn't have caught it, but she is very thorough."

"What was her discovery, doc?"

"Arsenic. Trace amounts often appear in blood tests of those consuming regular American diets. But the levels in Mr. Hayes are significant. We believe he may have blacked out during his flight. With the amounts in his blood, he likely would have experienced several symptoms such as dizziness, nausea, or extreme exhaustion, for days, maybe weeks. We're working to flush it from his system."

"I thought arsenic was fatal," said Tommy, looking at the patient to make sure he was breathing.

"Chief, that's true in large amounts," explained the physician. "Small amounts over time will help build immunity, but the body will hate you."

"Are you saying he was being poisoned?" JJ interjected, with possibilities snapping into place in his mind.

"That appears likely at this point, sir."

"I am a close friend of Mike's," JJ gestured to his friend. "For several weeks, he has complained of the symptoms you describe. I have witnessed his dizzy spells and seen him grab his stomach as if in pain. This diagnosis is interesting. Doctor Everett, how would you get someone to ingest it willingly?"

"Assuming the person isn't suicidal, one would use something to deliver it routinely, typically in the same quantity. Arsenic has no distinct smell, taste, or color. That makes it undetectable and a perfect silent and invisible poison."

Mike began to twitch and flail as he fought to regain consciousness. He suddenly opened his eyes.

JJ leaned in. "There you are, Mike. Had me worried. I figured you would want your briefcase with you."

He laid the item on Mike's torso. He slowly wrapped his arms around it. Mike brought the briefcase close, then slowly closed his eyes, returning to his unconscious state.

The doctor checked Mike's vitals and eyes, then turned toward Tommy. "It appears he has slipped back into a moderate coma. You both will need to leave so I can assess his current state. He's been in the range of minimally conscious to this point with his body trying to repair itself."

Tommy slapped his thigh in frustration. "JJ, I can't question him if he's not awake."

"I know," JJ replied with an even expression.

Getting Everything to Work

Drawing ragged breaths, Ashley wiped angrily at her tears, pacing a trough in the living room floor. "We fight because I'm trying to protect you. You want to appear tough and strong, so you ignore your health issues even when they persist. GRRR!" Ashley exclaimed, stomping her feet like a two-year-old having a tantrum, then continued yelling, "You put yourself at risk by flying your plane days after you hardly make it into the house before you collapse. Now, you're in a hospital in another city, where I can't rush to you because you hid my damn keys. Thanks for the lesson in irony."

She sobbed, pulling open and rifling through drawers for the third time in each room of their house, leaving a trail of fallen items in her wake. Finishing her search in the bathroom connected to their bedroom, she paused, looking at her reflection in the mirror. Disgusted with her appearance, she ran warm water onto a fresh washcloth and covered her face, inhaling deeply for several heartbeats.

"What a mess," she told herself with a finger shake at her image. "Come on, Ash, you can get through this for Mike. No one gets to hurt him or Brett." Wiping her face again with the warmed cloth, a plan formed in her mind. "All you need are keys, and you won't find them here. Call a locksmith, or..." She tapped her chin, then opened her eyes wide. "The dealership, of course. Walker loves us. I bet he can work up a set of keys and even deliver them to me."

Returning to the kitchen, she emptied her purse to locate the salesman's card and grabbed her phone to place the call.

"Granbury Auto, this is Walker, how may I help you?"

"Hi, Walker, this is Ashley Hayes. Mike and I purchased a pick-up from you several months ago."

"Yes, Ma'am, Ms. Hayes, how may I help you?"

"You also sold us my Lincoln Navigator last year."

"Yes, I did. Are you ready for a trade-in? I expect the new models to arrive any day. Yours was silver as I recall."

"That's correct, Walker. I might trade it in. Right now, I need to ask you for a set of keys for my Navigator. I can't find mine, and I have a family emergency. I didn't know what else to do but see if you could cut a new set of keys and deliver them to me."

"Creating a new key set takes a while, Ms. Hayes."

"Please, I'm desperate," Ashley begged, sensing tears threatening again.

"Ma'am, please hold on a minute."

Ashley haphazardly replaced the things scattered on the counter into her purse. She paced in a small circle, waiting for the man to return to the line for what seemed like forever.

"Ms. Hayes," Walker began, "Sorry to keep you waiting, ma'am. I'm sending Sam over with a contract for you to sign. He will bring your car to the dealership to make the keys, but I will let you take one of our vehicles as a loaner. It's not quite as nice as your Navigator, but it drives like a dream. He's gassing it up for you, then heading over. You haven't moved, have you?"

Grinning like a Cheshire Cat who lucked out and discovered a bowl of cream, she replied, "No, same address, Walker. Thank you."

"I told you we have the best service in Texas, and I meant it. I hope your family emergency resolves in your favor."

"Thank you so much. Save me one of the new models when they arrive."

She was heading down Highway 281 to Magnolia Bluff in less than two hours. At the halfway point, Ashley told the Expedition's integrated system to call Jo Rodreguiz.

Jo said, "Hi, Ashley, are you headed this way?"

"Finally, yes. My vehicle had a problem. I ended up getting a rental. Are you at the house or the hospital?"

"Ash, I'm home, but JJ is there. The police asked him to help with speaking to Mike. He isn't awake. Head here, please. We'll go together to see Mike. I'm stuck since JJ took our car."

"Okay, that makes it easier for me to navigate." Ashley adjusted the directions. "Has JJ spoken to Mike?"

"Briefly. He slipped back into a semi-coma after JJ delivered his briefcase."

"They found it! That's great." She sighed, her mind running a mile a minute, thinking of options. "I bet Mike was relieved. He gets antsy when he doesn't know where that thing is." After a few seconds of silence, Ashley asked, "Jo, are you still there? Am I in a bad cell zone?"

"I'm here. You cut out momentarily. I'll see you when you get here, sweetie."

After disconnecting, Ashley considered. Should I text the location of the briefcase? Will that eliminate the threat? It would be nice to get past this mess.

Jo punched in JJ's number. "JJ, Ashley's on her way to pick me up. You were right about the briefcase. That's all she's interested in. How's Mike?"

"Babe, he grabbed the briefcase like it was his favorite night-time stuffed animal. But he is resting. Doctor Everett asked us to leave. Tommy's mad he can't get any answers. I can head back."

"Ashley will want to see Mike at the very least today. I'm going to ask her to stay with us as long as he is in the hospital. One of us can be with her all the time."

"Sounds good. I'll see you soon, honey."

CHAPTER 29

I Can't Tell You

JJ pulled into his driveway seconds before Ashley's arrival. Relieved, Jo stepped out from the pergola. "Hi, Ashley. You made great time." She added a hug and peered into the backseat. "Did you bring a suitcase? I'm hoping you'll stay with us."

Ashley moved her sunglasses atop her head. "I'd appreciate it, Jo." Her eyes met JJ's. "Jo mentioned you were at the hospital. I'd like to see Mike. If you don't want to go now that JJ is back, point me in the right direction."

JJ reached an arm over Ashley's shoulders. "Doctor Everett said he wanted Mike to rest for a few hours before you visited. He was still reviewing test results. Let me grab your bag and take it to your room. Consider it your home away from home. We are your friends."

Ashley opened the back door for JJ. The single bag was heavier than he anticipated. He headed toward the kitchen door, pausing at the crunch of a vehicle on the drive. Turning, he spotted the police cruiser.

JJ said, "The Chief was at the hospital while I was there, hoping to speak to Mike, but he wasn't conscious long enough. I told him you were headed here. I'm sure he has questions you can help with."

The cruiser pulled to a stop. Tommy stepped out with a no-nonsense expression and carefully added his Stetson.

Ashley's breath caught. Her fingers fidgeted with the long strap of her purse. Jo gripped her friend's hand as Tommy approached.

Tilting his head at Jo, he extended his hand toward Ashley and said, "My name is Chief Jager. I'm the law in Magnolia Bluff. I'm sorry your husband is laid up in the hospital, but he is in good hands."

"I'd like to go see him, Chief."

"I appreciate your position, Mrs. Hayes. Doc said he wasn't ready for visitors, but he would let me know when your husband's status changed. In the meantime, I'd like to ask you some questions."

JJ volunteered, "Let's step inside where we can be more comfortable."

"What would everyone like to drink?" asked Jo with a smile as she herded Ashley indoors.

JJ took Ashley's bag to the room she would use and hurried back to the kitchen.

Tommy removed his hat, setting it aside. "Ma'am, I know this must be a difficult time for you. I need to learn more about your husband. JJ indicated Mike works for Lockheed in Fort Worth. What else can you tell me about his work?"

Ashley inhaled. She glanced at Tommy and then at the table where her fingers twisted around each other. "He works on fighter plane projects for our government and has mentioned working on radar. He doesn't speak much about his work to me because of the security aspects."

"That explains why I received a call from Major Johnson, who indicated he would oversee this incident investigation on your husband's crash."

Ashley's breathing increased; lines of anxiety formed across her brow. JJ thought she might say something, but the words didn't come from her open mouth.

Tommy's eyes darted between his and Jo's as if looking for intervention. Jo moved closer and patted Ashley's arm.

Ashley's eyes filled until the floodgates opened. Silent tears streamed down her face.

"Ash, here's what we know," began JJ. "I received an early morning email from Mike that he'd argued with you and was headed here to tie up some loose ends on his project. Nearly fifty minutes later, Jo and I heard a low-flying aircraft, then a loud noise. We rushed outdoors. His plane was augured in, nose-first, in the field adjacent to our property. There were thick plumes of dust, which I initially thought might indicate a fire. I ran to help, while Jo called 911. What did you two fight about?"

Ashley sniffled and then commented, "Jo said you found his briefcase. Is that true? Does he have it now? It's the only thing he truly cares about."

JJ gauged Tommy's reaction before he rocked back into his chair.

"Yes, ma'am," said Tommy. "I saw it in Mike's hands before he slipped back into a coma. What's so danged important about the briefcase?"

Ashley sobbed for a minute, then blew her nose on the tissue JJ offered. "It holds his computer and any project he is working on. I can't tell you why it's so important because he wouldn't tell me. Ask JJ here; they've been working together on it for weeks."

Tommy looked towards JJ, who frowned and shrugged.

At that moment, Tommy's cell phone rang. When he noticed the caller ID, he rose and rushed outside without an explanation.

Jo suggested, "Let's answer as many questions as possible before Tommy returns. Then you and I can go to the hospital and wait for the doctor's approval to see Mike."

Ashley nodded, appearing somewhat relieved.

Tommy stepped back inside with a frown. "Ashley, the call was from the federal investigators engaged by Lockheed. I must wait to speak with you or Mike because this individual will lead all the questioning. They are interested in Mike's briefcase and its contents."

Ashley stood. "I don't know about either of those things. Unless you plan to arrest me, I'm going to the hospital to check on my husband. Jo, you are welcome to join me," announced Ashley as she crossed her arms.

The sounds of vehicles traveling the long driveway from the entry gate to the property interrupted the conversation. Tommy grabbed his Stetson and went outdoors, with JJ right behind. Tommy affixed his enormous hat and stood tall. He glared at JJ, suggesting he would do the talking.

A tall, well-groomed man in a dark suit and sunglasses exited the vehicle after it was parked, clearly blocking the exit. He extended a hand to Tommy. "I'm Agent Andrews. Major Johnson will be arriving shortly. We'll be leading the investigation."

Tommy extended his hand. "Nice to meet you. I'm Chief Tommy Jager. I spoke to the major earlier. Mr. Hayes is under guard at the hospital. He was unconscious when I left. The doctor will page me with changes in the patient's condition." He turned and gestured to JJ. "I'd like to introduce you to JJ Rodreguiz. Mr. Rodreguiz and his wife live here. The crash site is on the other side of their fenced property line."

Agent Andrews gripped JJ's hand. "You're the head contractor on Mr. Hayes' project, correct?"

JJ replied, "I have a small portion of the contract. Plus, Mike and I have been friends since college. I can provide the names of other U.S. contracts where my company, the R-Group, and I are listed as contractors."

"No need," Andrews chuckled. "You have more gold stars than most generals in our national database. Your cybersecurity accomplishments are part of the introductory studies at the academy. Nice to put a face with a name."

Tommy swallowed and stifled a snort, realizing JJ was even better than he suspected. He filed the information away for a later discussion.

A black Lincoln pulled in and parked. Tommy watched a man exit, wearing dress blues bearing the rank insignia of major. He was surprised the uniform had no wrinkles. The powerfully built man was shorter than Tommy.

"I'm Major Johnson," he said with an icy tone. "I head up security at Lockheed Martin. I'm here to investigate a plane crash involving one of our high-value engineers. Thank you for joining, Andrews."

"Major, I want to introduce you to Chief Jager, whom you spoke with earlier."

The man extended a hand before Agent Andrews continued, "This gentleman is JJ Rodreguiz, a high-security clearance contractor, verified."

JJ stepped forward for the obligatory handshake. "My wife, Jo, is inside with Mr. Hayes' wife, Ashley. She wants to go to the hospital as soon as possible."

Major Johnson stated, "Let's go inside and get started. I can appreciate that Mrs. Hayes would like to see her husband."

The four men filed indoors. Jo had placed coffee, cold beverages, and a plate of cookies in the center of the dining room table to accommodate the discussions.

Major Johnson opened his digital notebook after the introductions and launched the audio recording feature. "I will ask you questions. With your first question, please provide your name and the relationship you have with Mr. Hayes. Following this practice allows me to capture a formal transcript for the investigation. I'll begin with you, Mr. Rodreguiz. Do you know why Mr. Hayes felt compelled to fly to you rather than have you come to the Fort Worth test facility?"

"My name is JJ Rodreguiz. My organization, R-Group, has contracted with Lockheed Martin multiple times to work on various projects. I planned to finalize the revisions on Mr. Hayes' radar project today. I had promised to deliver to our standard Dropbox. He emailed me, indicating he was flying in to discuss the project. I don't know the details he wanted to review."

"Thank you. Can you forward that email?" asked Agent Andrews.

"I can do that." JJ dashed to his office to retrieve his laptop and complete the request.

"When I drove through the entrance gate, I noticed your property has multiple cameras. Did you happen to capture the crash from any angle?"

JJ shook his head. "I positioned the cameras to point inside our property. The closest I get to the adjacent field is the fence line. Nothing showed when I checked them."

"If you don't mind sending us those videos, I would like my team to evaluate them," suggested Agent Andrews.

Major Johnson took a moment to study the email and turned toward Ashley. "Mrs. Hayes, I need to know what happened between you two this morning that would force your husband to fly here rather than ask Mr. Rodriguez to come to Fort Worth."

She swiped at the tears as she fought to contain her visible emotions. Ashley stuttered, "My name is Ashley Hayes. I am married to Mike Hayes. We live in a home we built in Pecan Plantation near Granbury. We fought this morning before he left for work, because he listened to one side of a private conversation I was having on the phone. I did not know he was heading to Magnolia Bluff."

"What were the details of the fight?"

Ashley blew her nose and took a breath. "Mike had been struggling with his health recently. He experienced dizziness in between bouts of stomach cramps. He passed out when he returned home from work early one day. The symptoms seemed to pass after a good meal and rest. I worried about him flying. I hid his airplane keys, but this morning he found them and stormed out."

"Who was your overheard conversation with, Mrs. Hayes?" asked Major Johnson.

"It was a personal discussion, irrelevant to Mike's accident," she replied.

He raised one eyebrow as if considering the pursuit of that line of questioning, then asked, "Did he have his briefcase and computer?"

Ashley loudly insisted, "He never goes anywhere without the damn thing. JJ told me he delivered it to Mike at the hospital."

Major Johnson thought about that and added a note to his digital pad. "Mr. Rodriguez, how did you come by the briefcase?"

JJ made eye contact. "When I got to the aircraft, Mike was coming around. He handed it to me before passing out."

"Did you open it to see what was inside?" Major Johnson asked.

Tommy almost grinned when he noticed how annoyed JJ was getting.

"I typically don't break into other people's property when a combination lock is in place."

"What were you two working on?"

"Major, my contracted project is confidential. In your position, you should already know that answer."

A new level of respect regarding JJ formed in Tommy's mind.

Major Johnson snorted, "Good answer, Mr. Rodreguiz. Chief, anything else we should cover?"

Tommy queried, "Do you need to see the crash site or photos taken of the cockpit? The aircraft was relocated to the Burnet airport and remains under guard in one of the vacant hangars."

"No, I'll let one of my people look at it. Let's get to the hospital and see if we can speak with Mr. Hayes."

JJ asked, "Gentlemen, any objections if we also go? I'm sure his wife would like an update directly from the doctor."

CHAPTER 30

The Procession

Outdoors, Tommy stated, "Ya'll can follow me to the hospital." With a pointed look at JJ he insisted, "You're with me."

"I'll take my rental," announced Ashley. "I may want to stay with my husband when the questioning is finished," she added.

"Ashley, why don't you let Jo take you in our Porsche?" said JJ. "She or I will stay with you as long as needed at the hospital. I would rather you not get behind the wheel of a car when you're upset. We're here to help you. Mike would want you safe."

Ashley nodded. Jo looped her arm around her friend's and guided them toward the carport. "I love driving this car, and it's so maneuverable."

"Good idea," agreed Tommy. "Gentlemen," he said, inclining his head to the men, "I'll message my guard and then ask the doctor to meet us."

Tommy extracted his hat and entered his vehicle. Pleased when JJ dutifully sat in the passenger seat, he notified his staff via radio of his plans. Then he called the hospital and left a message to alert the doctor of the pending visitors to Mike Hayes.

Pulling out of the long driveway, he glanced back at the cars behind him. Chuckling, he remarked, "This caravan could pass for a funeral procession."

JJ laughed, "Can I add the light and siren?"

Tommy smiled. "Lights, yes. No siren."

Making the turn onto the highway, Tommy asked, "JJ, why didn't you mention the two men you got into it with at the crash site to Agent Andrews?"

"They didn't ask me. Plus, something about this whole crash feels off to me. I'm afraid they already suspect Mike of trying to stage a fake crash to sell the top-secret program we have to foreign agents. His security was recently compromised when someone hacked his email account. He was reinstated. The testing we did at Lockheed was perfect. I recall Major Johnson sitting in the observatory area most of the day, watching each test scenario. He never came to congratulate Mike on his success. In my uh… analysis, I'm convinced Mike was being set up. With what the doctor said earlier, someone was poisoning him. I don't know who that might be. I don't want these federal agents screening you and me out of the information loop. I will answer questions directly, but won't volunteer any details outside the specific asks until we get more information."

Tommy shifted uneasily in his seat, wanting to trust this man he'd worked with previously. "Based on what they said about you, I'm fairly confident Mike had you working on a top-secret weapon needed by our military. Lockheed has created some remarkable fighters, which I've read about over the years. It seems to me his wife could be in a position to leak secrets and poison him."

"Why didn't you mention the arsenic poison found in Mike's system to Major Johnson?"

Tommy snorted. "I'm not the doctor. I could suggest that Ashley might have been in a position to compromise the secrets and poison her husband. She sure was stuck on the briefcase."

JJ nodded then countered, "I don't believe she could poison Mike. I have seen how much they care about one another. Jo and I know she's hiding a secret that has something to do with Mike's briefcase. Each time we've spoken to her since the incident, she's inquired about its whereabouts. Mike has kept that briefcase by his side since he received it as a gift from his dad. He keeps it locked unless he is working with the contents. We told Ashley I took it to the hospital. I want to see how she reacts when she spots it with Mike."

"How do we explain the arsenic, if it isn't her? Identifying who else would have access seems impossible for a guy who seems a workaholic by all accounts."

"Agreed. We must get Ashley to tell us why the briefcase is so important, then I'm hoping the other pieces of the puzzle will come together."

"I presume Jo is working on that angle."

"Yep. They're good friends. Ashley recently mentioned some secrets. Not enough details to take action or identify anyone else involved."

"My money's on your wife to find answers," admitted Tommy, turning left into the hospital parking lot, followed by the caravan.

Jo expertly inserted the Porsche behind Tommy's cruiser. "Ashley, we have complete privacy during our ride to the hospital. Now would be the perfect time to finish filling me in so I can help you. You're in a mess, girl."

Ashley wrung her hands in between dabbing at tears. "I know. Mike hates me. Early this morning, he heard my side of the conversation with the person who had been texting me threats. Taking everything out of context, he decided I compromised his project."

"Are you going to tell them?"

Jo saw her friend flinch out of the corner of her eye before Ashley shouted, "Tell 'em what? That I'm having a phone affair with someone threatening me? I'm only responding to questions, because I'm scared that they'll hurt my husband and the child I gave up for adoption after being given a date rape drug." She blew her nose. "Oh, Jo. Mike will disown me once he finds out what I've tried to hide to forget that awful year of being alone. If I had told him, he would have demanded details and probably killed the guy."

Astonished at the revelation, Jo reached across the seat and briefly squeezed her friend's hand. "Ash, I wish you had told me earlier. I'm sorry you've dealt with this by yourself for so long. Please let JJ and me help. It looks bad, but your flimsy excuses aren't helping you or Mike."

"JJ won't want to help me. He'll think I'm guilty."

"JJ will do everything he can to help you and Mike. If you aren't guilty, then let him help. He's one of the good guys. It's why I married him."

"I don't know. They want that briefcase. I sent them a modified combo picture to protect Mike. You saw me take the photo, which I then altered with Photoshop before sending it. Anything to keep them away from Brett and to protect Mike. When Mike started to get sick spells, I couldn't understand why. He refused to go to the doctor. I begged him. If I tell that to Major Johnson, Mike will be fired for taking unnecessary risks." She clenched her fists and pounded her legs. "I kept hitting walls. I failed as his wife."

"Ashley, you haven't failed, but keeping secrets must stop. Federal investigators will turn over every rock to find the truth and claim national security. I've watched JJ get to the truth with his resources faster than others. You heard his background at the house. He'll fight for you and Mike."

Ashley hiccupped, dabbing at her tears. "This mess is worse than anything I've done, outside of going to a frat party I never should have attended, cheerleader or not. I'm grateful the jerk graduated the year I spent abroad, making the hardest decision an eighteen-year-old should ever make."

Jo bit her lip, pulling into the parking lot behind Tommy. "I'm going to loop the parking lot. Dry your face and fluff your hair. It's time to suck it up. I'll speak to JJ. Focus on seeing Mike and don't shout at the investigators."

"Okay."

CHAPTER 31

Help or Harm; On the Way?

Following Tommy, the group took the elevator to the third floor. Sounds of footfalls echoed as the visitors headed toward Mike's room. Relief flowed through Tommy when he spotted Deputy Stuart at his post, alert to the crowd approaching. No one would get past this powerfully built, no-nonsense man in his late twenties, undetected.

Tommy asked, "Hey, Stuart, has anyone attempted to enter other than hospital personnel?"

Rising to his full six feet, Deputy Stuart eyed the crowd. He faced Tommy and replied, "No, sir. No one, except the head doctor, two nurses, and a technician in scrubs. The technician was an odd character whom I watched from the doorway as he changed the bedding. I confirmed nothing was removed after each person left."

"I called and left a message for the doctor to meet us here. When did you see him last?"

"About an hour ago, Chief."

A modest commotion at the far end of the hallway alerted Tommy to the approaching physician and nurse. Tommy relaxed when he recognized both individuals.

Deep concern reflected on Doctor Everett's face as he exchanged pleasantries, positioning his body at the door. "Ladies and gentlemen, the patient's room is not an auditorium. His condition is not conducive to extensive interrogation at this juncture. Mrs. Hayes will be permitted to visit her husband for a short while. My nurse and I will accompany her to answer any questions she may have regarding his current health. The rest of you will remain outside." He gestured to an area behind the group, "Or you're free to go to the waiting area where coffee and water are available."

Major Johnson interjected, "I need to speak with Mr. Hayes as soon as he is awake, doctor."

Doctor Everett replied, "Our monitoring equipment transmits various metrics which my nurse monitors when at her workstation. She also receives digital notifications while on the floor or with other patients of any significant changes. Mr. Hayes is still unconscious. When he awakens, my nurse will inform the patient that you would like to speak with him, Major. For now, Mrs. Hayes, you are...."

Agent Andrews interrupted, flashing his badge. "Doctor, the major and I are on official government business. It is a matter of national security for us to see Mr. Hayes. Kindly step aside so we can do our job."

Tommy nearly chuckled at the doctor's hardened features before he retorted, "My job is the patient first, so I have no plans to step aside. If we were in another place and time, your comment might be laughable, Agent. Tommy, escort these government officials to the waiting room until I or my nurse grants access."

Andrews snarled, "I'm going in." He shoved the doctor aside and quickly moved toward the door. His nose banged into the door that didn't budge.

Doctor Everett snorted. "Our security measures here are state of the art. We don't allow patients or unruly visitors full run of patient rooms."

Andrews slammed the heel of his palm on the doorjamb. Glaring at the doctor, he clenched his fists to his sides and stormed toward the waiting room. The others followed on his heels. Tommy remained next to his deputy, observing Mrs. Hayes, who was shaking. He tried to decide if it was due to anxiety, remorse, or guilt.

Tears filled her eyes, threatening to overflow. The nurse provided tissues. "Thank you, ma'am," she softly said.

The doctor observed the retreating backs and retrieved the remote key lock from his coat pocket. He escorted Ashley inside Mike's room, nodding to Tommy as the door closed.

The rosy glow of soft pink lighting gave an eerie appearance to the patient's bed covers. The area around the head of the bed was bordered by blinking lights and low sounds from the machines attached to monitor the patient.

"Mrs. Hayes, sorry for the dark accommodations, but with head injuries or neurological disorders, muted lighting makes it easier for patients to regain cognitive skills when they awake," soothed the physician.

Ashley nodded.

"As I stated, we have him on remote monitoring, but we physically check him every hour, looking for a change in condition. We are running a saline treatment to help flush the poison from his system."

Ashley gasped. "What do you mean by poison?"

"Mrs. Hayes, can you describe the symptoms you observed in your husband for the last week or so?"

"He complained of dizziness, loss of vision, and stomach cramps. One afternoon, he arrived tired, almost lethargic, and passed out in our bedroom, fortunately on the bed. He slept for nearly three hours. He refused to go to the doctor because he was so engrossed in the project he was working on. Our friends, the Rodreguiz's, also saw the issues, but Mike tossed it off to long hours and poor eating when he was working," explained Ashley.

"Mr. Rodreguiz, or JJ, as we know him in town, said the same thing when he delivered the briefcase."

Doctor Everett noticed a change as Ashley looked around her husband's bed. She asked, "His briefcase, where is it?"

"It's safe. However, I'm trying to understand why our tests showed more than ten times the normal trace amounts of arsenic in his body, while you're focused on his briefcase."

Ashley whipped her head around. "What are you saying, doctor? Do you think I poisoned my husband? I admit, we've been having some marital issues at home, but I would never do anything to hurt my husband," she vehemently replied. "He's a workaholic and doesn't always eat at home. For all I know, vending machines could be delivering the poison. He does enjoy potato chips way too much, so I rarely have them in the house to reduce his salt intake."

The doctor sighed and patted her arm. "Those officials you arrived with will look at Mike's medical records and ask you tough questions. Arsenic is no joke."

"Doctor, the only thoughts of arsenic I've ever had were from a college theatre production of Arsenic and Old Lace. That was almost two decades ago." She swallowed and fidgeted with her hands. "I'm going to be sick."

Using a firm but kind hand, the nurse guided Ashley to the in-room bathroom.

Minutes later, the door opened. The nurse helped Ashley to the visitor's chair and placed a cool, wet washcloth over her eyes.

Determining the wife was past her bout of nausea, the doctor kindly advised, "I'm going to brief the authorities in the waiting room that Mike's condition is unchanged. I recommend you talk to your husband, even though he won't likely respond. Talking to patients has been known to reach into the subconscious, providing healing effects."

CHAPTER 32

It's All Planned

"The briefcase was recovered and is with Hayes in his hospital room," stated the gruff, synthesized voice. "Failure is not an option for either of you in completing this task."

"Yes, Suh," responded one of the Asian men through the speaker on the mobile phone.

"Federal authorities were at the hospital waiting to interview Hayes, who is still unconscious. They are gone until morning. Hospital staff check on the patient every hour. Avoid them. Do not face the cameras. You are maintenance staff according to your badges. There is one local deputy on watch outside the patient's door.

"On your way to the hospital, stop at the coffee shop and purchase a large cup to go. A packet of white powder you will add to the brew, along with a chocolate cookie, will get delivered to your hotel door shortly after this call ends. You must deliver the steaming pick-me-up coffee, indicating it is from Chief Jager for the all-night shift. Within ten minutes of its consumption, the guard will be asleep. In ten minutes, one of you will use your analog signaling device to open the remote lock on Hayes' room."

One man confidently replied, "Suh, my partner will keep watch outside the room, while I go inside. I will use the combination you texted to open the briefcase. I will launch the remote boot program, which will override any security in place on the laptop.

Using the Bluetooth connection, I will download all the files you indicated, which will be transferred to you. Then I will power down the PC and return it to the briefcase, verifying it is locked. I will quietly depart."

"Correct. Any questions?"

"What if the combination sent to you does not work? Additionally, what if the remote start program does not get me into the secured laptop?"

Anger radiated in the digital voice, which grew louder. "You forgot to complain about defeating the remote door lock release. The answer is a simple analog signal technology that has been around for decades. The combination to the briefcase is a primitive tumbler sequence that can be defeated with the magnetic wand I sent to you. The remote boot was the most challenging until I stole the User ID and password from a member of the Lockheed security team using Near Field Communications while he was at the deli." Maniacal laughter ensued for a minute. "You also have the failsafe tranquilizer in the unlikely event Hayes wakes."

"Understood."

The voice barked, "Do not fail in this mission. Your futures depend upon it."

Both men replied in unison, "Yes, Suh."

Deputy Stevens stood and stretched, wishing he hadn't eaten the second burger during his dinner break. At least the bruhaha from the feds was over until tomorrow morning. Twisting his back again after sitting, he briefly closed his eyes while extending his neck side-to-side. Turning to the chair, he was surprised by a smiling, smallish man in hospital scrubs. He relaxed, spotting the technician's badge.

With a slight nod, the man held out a large covered tumbler. "Deputy, Chief Jager sent this coffee and a chocolate cookie to help you stay alert." The man grinned. "I think he has tasted the hospital brew, saying it is very weak."

"Perfect timing. Thank you," Stevens replied, taking a warming sip of the fragrant French roast. "I'll thank the chief tomorrow."

The technician turned and ambled toward the supply closet.

Stevens resumed his seat and inhaled the robust, earthy scent before enjoying another sip. Taking a large bite of the cookie, he rolled his eyes with pleasure. "This is delicious. I haven't seen these at the coffee shop, I'll have to ask Tommy where he gets them," he mumbled, then finished his snacks. Minutes later, he rested his head against the wall and stretched out his long legs.

Two hospital technicians slipped into the area, soundlessly rolling a cart of supplies and positioning it adjacent to the deputy. One man kept his head turned as if inventorying the provisions. The other man, identical in build, surveyed the area one more time before pressing the remote door release. He slipped inside, leaving his comrade to keep guard.

A smile crept onto his lips when he moved close to the sleeping patient and located the briefcase with Hayes' hand resting over it. The Asian gently lifted the arm and slid the case onto the portable tray on wheels.

Carefully, the man intently entered the code once on the combination lock. Since the latches failed to release, he reversed the numbers to no avail. Determined, he retrieved the magnetic device from his pocket and quickly reoriented the tumblers to the correct position. He swung open the cover, then abruptly stopped as his stomach clenched in agony. Astonished, he pulled out his cell phone to snap a photo, which he immediately texted to his contact. He pressed to call the recent number, while a sensation of shame washed over him.

"Are you done?" the gruff mechanical voice asked.

"Suh, I am in the room and opened the briefcase. The contents are two bricks and nothing else. You have the photo."

The voice roared, "It's a trap. Close the case. Get out of there."

CHAPTER 33

That's the Job

Tommy was seated in the waiting room, thumbing a worn copy of Texas Monthly from July. Photos of upcoming summer concerts and music festivals reminded him of the tickets he had set aside for the annual Kow Kick State Championship at Scheiner Park. Perhaps it would be fun to ask JJ and Jo to attend. He chuckled at the thought.

Agent Andrews and Major Johnson arrived together at eight, looking ready to fight a bear. JJ, Jo, and Ashley lagged five minutes behind. Ashley appeared frazzled with dark circles under her eyes.

Tommy stood. "Ladies and gentlemen, I asked the doctor for a status report. He said he would meet us here after completing his rounds. There is no private conference room available. No visitors are expected on this floor, except for those seeing Mr. Hayes."

Agent Andrews rolled his eyes and stated, "I'd like to get this going, Chief."

The major nodded.

Jo brightly asked, "Would everyone like some coffee or tea? I'm willing to make a run to the cafeteria. I know what Ashley, Tommy, and JJ like. Would you gentlemen prefer some organic espresso to launch your morning?" She tapped the orders into her cell. "Tommy, would you like a coffee delivered to your deputy on guard duty?"

Tommy replied, "Yeah, good idea, Jo."

Jo smiled and nodded.

JJ interjected, "I've had enough this morning, honey."

Ashley raised her eyes. "I don't care for anything, but I'll come along to help carry."

"I've got this, Ash. I want you to stay close in case Mike asks for you."

Tommy watched Jo head toward the stairs to the cafeteria.

Agent Andrews asked, "Mr. Rodreguiz, can you update us on the status of your portion of the project? Your contribution to the project is the most critical piece, as I understand it, and could require further acceptance testing."

JJ stared from Andrews to the major. "Agent Andrews, our acceptance testing was done under his watchful eye. We've completed it with multiple scenarios. All that remains is to submit the completed documentation, incorporating the modifications determined during the testing cycle. Major Johnson observed all the simulations, so I'm surprised that he hasn't briefed you."

Andrews studied JJ for a moment. "I want you to review the events leading up to the crash. I am prepared to ask Mr. Hayes all he recalls from the time he took off from Fort Worth."

Ashley's chair squeaked as she fidgeted to get comfortable. The section of hair she twisted was nearly knotted.

Andrews asked, "Mrs. Hayes, can you confirm Mr. Rodreguiz's statement?"

Startled, Ashley took a breath before she answered. "How would I know where the testing stood? Mike has never shared the details of his projects with me. Most of his engineering jargon doesn't make sense to me. Mike and JJ work with technology, as devoted workaholics, acclaimed as experts." Wrinkling her nose, she snorted. "You'll have to get details from them, not me." Ashley appeared relieved when Jo interrupted any further questions by returning with something for everyone.

"Thanks, honey," JJ said, taking the burrito and bottle of water from her hands.

Murmurs of thanks came from each person as she doled out the items.

The elevator doors by the waiting room opened, and the doctor appeared. "Good morning," he said. "I've been told that Mr. Hayes is awake and ready to visit. If you'll all follow me." Without waiting for a response, he turned and headed toward the patient's room.

Chief Tommy escorted Ashley as they followed the agent and the major.

Jo pulled JJ aside and whispered, "I delivered a coffee to the deputy on duty before coming here. He was worried, yet grateful. When he arrived earlier to relieve Deputy Stevens, he got worried as Stevens admitted he'd fallen asleep on duty and didn't want to tell Tommy. When I joked that I should have been delivering coffee to him as well, the deputy mentioned that someone had delivered coffee in Tommy's name late last evening."

JJ stopped and stared at her with a confused expression.

"I know, JJ. We both like Tommy, but he typically doesn't think about mundane things like getting a coffee for someone doing their job."

JJ nodded thoughtfully.

CHAPTER 34

The Gatekeeper

Tommy inclined his head as Doctor Everett approached.

He purposefully stopped before the door to Mike's room. Facing the group, he said, "I'm taking Mrs. Hayes first to allow them a short time together. Then, I'll permit you gentlemen to conduct your security-based interviews while I wait outside here."

Major Johnson bristled, but Agent Andrews exploded. "We're here to investigate a national security breach, not to molly-coddle someone's marital difficulties. Doctor, Major Johnson, and I need to enter immediately to interrogate Mr. Hayes. No one…"

Tommy motioned to his deputy, a former college linebacker. Both officials aligned. Neither smiled. He watched as Agent Andrews' face contorted, fearing he would spin out of control. He relaxed when Major Johnson laid a hand on the agent's shoulder, which seemed to hold him in silent check. Ashley soundlessly grabbed the fingers of his extended hand. Together with the doctor, they entered the patient's room. Biting back a grin, Tommy couldn't help but notice the scowl on the faces of the federal authorities. He made a mental note to thank Doc Everett later for the perfect orchestration of a united front.

Moments later, the door opened. Doctor Everett escorted a tearful Ashley through the doorway. Tears streamed down her cheeks as she raced to Jo, desperate to be consoled. Tommy followed, rejoining his deputy.

143

Doctor Everett shook his head slightly, watching the two women head to the waiting room. "Mr. Rodreguiz, Mike requested to speak with you." He motioned for JJ to enter.

Appearing surprised, JJ gingerly stepped past the deputy to enter the room. Doctor Everett kept to the side. "I'm here to help you, Mr. Hayes, not listen, or share anything you say."

Mike nodded then replied in a hoarse, raspy voice. "Thanks, Doc."

JJ approached the bed and leaned in, clutching his friend's hand. "Glad you're awake, buddy."

"JJ, I dreamt someone was here last night. The person moved and somehow got into my briefcase." Mike flipped up the lid of the case. "When I opened it this morning, this is what I found."

JJ's features appeared to suppress a smirk before he quipped, "Bricks. How nice. Are those for me?"

"Man, you and I both know what was supposed to be in here. They must have grabbed the real contents last night."

JJ patted his friend's shoulder. "Mike, Major Johnson is outside with Agent Andrews, whom I don't think you know. They've been desperate to speak with you. The local police, Chief Jager, is also outside and wants to review the details of your crash landing in the field behind my property. Do you recall anything about your landing?"

"Jumbled bits and pieces. Nothing clear yet. Were you there, as I think I recall seeing you?"

"I was. These officials want to catch the culprits," said JJ.

"I don't want to see Ashley. I told her that."

"I understand. I will take her and Jo to my house while you speak to the authorities. Can you do that, Mike?"

"I would prefer you stay, too."

JJ rested his hand on his friend's arm. "You need to answer their questions to the best of your knowledge. Think of how you considered socio-political relationships and their long-term effects when we took that crazy final that seemed to test our sanity, years ago."

Mike gave a scratchy chuckle and nodded.

"Doctor Everett, if you can stay with him while he speaks to the authorities to make certain they don't overstress my friend, I would be grateful."

"Of course. Mr. Hayes, are you up for some questioning?"

"I think so." He reached and took a sip of the water through the straw.

"I'm going to take our ladies home and do a bit of extra research," JJ explained. "I'll return when I have something to add." He squeezed his friend's shoulder and smiled at the doctor before he left the room.

Tommy stopped JJ in the hospital hallway and pulled him aside. "Tell Jo to take Ashley home. Your friend needs to help resolve the open issues he will hopefully recall. You need to add the pieces you didn't share because they failed to ask those specific questions."

"I assume you are going to fill in some of the information you've gained."

Each chuckled, rejoining the other gentlemen in time to see the doctor open the door and motion for them to enter.

Tommy gestured for Major Johnson and Agent Andrews to approach the patient's bed. They appeared relieved to find Mike sitting and sipping water. Tommy nudged JJ to join him at the foot of the bed.

JJ was about to start the discussion when Tommy interrupted, "I think the most helpful approach is for each of us to state, on the record, their firsthand knowledge. Doctor, I would appreciate it if you could start with Mr. Hayes' condition and the findings since his admission. When you are finished with that portion, you are welcome to check on your other patients as needed. I will alert the nurse if Mr. Hayes shows an undue strain."

Doctor Everett related his findings of significant arsenic levels in Mike's tests. Then he commented, "In addition to the serious threat of poisoning, his work role adds a layer of stress which a lack of sleep can exacerbate, leading to bouts of dizziness, nausea, and potential blackouts. At this juncture, he should not fly an airplane or even drive a vehicle until he obtains a certified medical release."

Mike closed his eyes briefly and shook his head. "I under-stand, Doc."

"Mr. Hayes," began Major Johnson, "apparently, you've been fighting the side effects of arsenic poisoning for weeks. Without knowing the root cause of your inconsistent side effects, why did you decide to fly to Magnolia Bluff?"

Mike took a breath, his eyes shifting toward JJ. "The morning when I decided to come here, I had heard Ashley's side of a phone conversation. The ongoing secretive stuff she's done over the last few weeks set me off. I messaged JJ that I was flying to Magnolia Bluff to finish the documentation on our project to present to my leadership." He turned toward Major Johnson. "I also wanted to speak with him about my suspicions concerning Ashley. He's a good listener and a long-time friend, which my employer is aware of. Some personal things are better done face-to-face."

Andrews interjected, "Are you admitting that regardless of how you felt physically, you took top secret project code on a private flight to have a heartfelt conversation with your old running buddy?"

Major Johnson motioned for Andrews to pause, then added, "We have heard that you refused the counsel of your wife and best friend to see a doctor after they witnessed some of your physical problems. Understandably, they were concerned for your health. Is that correct?"

Mike leveled his gaze at the major. "I'm stubborn when I am working on a project. My job is everything to me. I also dislike seeing doctors when I thought I was overtired, and I knew I was eating poorly." Looking toward Doctor Everett, Mike added, "No offense, Doc."

Doctor Everett replied, "Lots of people don't like seeing doctors. I get it. However, your condition might have been diagnosed sooner. In many ways, you are lucky to be alive."

Tommy asked, "What do you remember up to and including the crash?"

Mike stared ahead as if searching his memories. He took a small sip of water. "I remember the light-headedness and blurred vision. I fought with the yoke to stay airborne, but the plane kept going down, as if it possessed a mind of its own."

"Anything else?"

"I tried to maintain altitude until it bounced on the field. I bashed my head. It hurt. I think I recall seeing hands from the right side through the passenger door, fumbling with the dash panel, maybe behind or under it. Then I heard voices outside, but I couldn't see anything."

Tommy leveled his focus on JJ. "Do you have any firsthand information to add?"

JJ cleared his throat and flashed his gaze from one man to the other. "Jo and I knew Mike was heading here. I was somewhat annoyed by the short notice and the lack of an agenda. I was awake and getting dressed to go to the airport to meet his plane when we heard a low-level aircraft, feathering its engine to land. We ran outdoors, fearing it might be Mike. If so, he was in trouble. It took me almost six minutes to get to the crash, but two masked individuals were already there."

Agent Andrews appeared stunned. He challenged, "Wait a minute. You didn't mention this detail before. Two men were there before you arrived? If it took you six minutes, they had to be there in advance."

"Correct. I thought they were there to help, but one took off with some piece of equipment in his hand, while the other wanted to do a martial arts stage play. I positioned myself to fight when Mike's door popped open, nailing my opponent on the head. He bounced up immediately and took off."

Mike nodded, apparently recognizing the scene. "I'm glad I heard your voice, JJ. I told you to take my briefcase."

JJ sighed with his face visibly relaxing. "Yes, you did. I was relieved you spoke at all.

"Because of the men at the scene when I arrived, I did some research modeling the possibilities. On multiple occasions, using the known elements of time, distance, weather, and other factors, my program consistently delivered similar results. The plane must have been remotely controlled to crash in a location that provided enough time for the perpetrators to remove the electronics before the emergency response teams' arrival. I suspect they were going to steal Mike's briefcase, but I disrupted their plans."

Andrews' jaw dropped, followed by rapid blinking. "Knowing the contents of that briefcase, why the hell would you bring it to the hospital? Mike couldn't access it while unconscious."

"Bait," replied JJ, adding a smirk.

Mike spun the open briefcase around to show everyone.

The major chuckled at the agent's reaction, but said nothing while he sobered his expression.

Andrews shook his head, appearing confused. "Mr. Rodreguiz, you stated you didn't break into Mr. Hayes' case. So again, why would you leave it with an incapacitated hospital patient?"

JJ pressed his lips together and shrugged. "Agent Andrews, to be clear, I said I don't typically break into other people's property when it has a combination lock. However, I would also never knowingly permit a security leak. Mike and I joked years ago about the combination of his college graduation gift. Rest assured, Major, this is the only instance I have used my knowledge to open the case."

Tommy took a breath. "Last night, my deputy was given a knock-out drug by a smallish Asian man posing as a hospital technician. I have forwarded the security tapes provided by the hospital team to you and copied JJ. Based on the review of the videos, he believes that this technician, accompanied by a cohort, entered Mr. Hayes' room to steal the contents of the briefcase. The camera in the room shows the case being opened and a call being placed using a cell phone. Unfortunately, there is no audio in the patient rooms. The intruder knows the briefcase did not contain a laptop. JJ, we gotta presume they know the PC is under your control. They will undoubtedly tie you to the crash site. You and Jo are at risk."

JJ's phone played the instrumental for I Hear You Knocking. "Apologies, gentlemen. My mother loved that song. Anytime I asked for something my mom had no intention of letting me have, she'd dance around the kitchen singing the lyrics. It always made me laugh." JJ pressed several buttons. He observed the content, then handed his cell phone to Tommy, who played the short video, then passed it to Agent Andrews. "Not surprised, Tommy. They're right on time."

Tommy said, "JJ, you're with me. Did you alert Jo?"

"I did. I also secured the house. She knows what to do." JJ grinned. "Heck, she has her frying pan in-hand."

Tommy laughed. "Private joke. I'll tell you later, Agent. Let's go, JJ."

CHAPTER 35

It's Not About You

Jo pushed and pulled to assist Ashley into her SUV. Ashley behaved as if her feet weighed several hundred pounds, making her movement slow and unpredictable. She was barely able to connect the safety belt as Jo closed the passenger door. Rushing to the driver's door, she entered and headed the Porsche toward home.

Jo had just turned onto the main road home when Ashley began whimpering, "He hates me. Of all the things to go wrong, this one is the second worst. I've made a mess of the relationship with the man who holds my heart. Before this crash, I thought we had a chance. Oh, Jo, I've failed."

Focusing on the road but concerned, Jo glanced at her friend. "Second worst?"

Ashley drew a ragged breath and wiped her nose. "Yes. Worse are the texts with threats to hurt my son. Jo, I haven't seen my son in person ever. The nurses took him away right after he was born. Even so, he owns a piece of my heart. I can't explain it. I love Mike. I'm terrified of the threats made against him. This person, this voice, is threatening my son to gain information to crush my husband's career. I can't win. I have no options. The bastard doesn't give a damn about anything but information on Mike's project. I don't know how he found a way to target me, but he's winning. I'm losing my heart and my soul. I'm not having an affair with anyone, Jo. I swear."

"Ash, I'm confused. Where is your son? I thought he was adopted, and you didn't know him."

"I DON'T KNOW HIM," She shouted, then paused, dragging in a ragged breath. "I know where he is living. I believe his parents are good to him and provided a loving home. He's an only child of a couple who were unable to have children of their own. I selected them during the last trimester after reviewing dozens of possibilities. I was mortified by being raped. I was ill-equipped to raise a child. The father denied any responsibility and told me to get an abortion to deal with my problem. I couldn't do that. But I was too ashamed to allow this heartbeat that mimicked mine to be branded like I would be as a single mother."

"I'm so sorry. Are you sure Mike won't understand if you explain it to him?"

Ashley blew her nose again. "When I returned to college in Georgia, I earned a top spot on the cheer squad. I also ended up in a couple of elective classes with Mike. He was smart, had a great sense of humor, and even though the football fans idolized him, he wasn't full of himself. We did some study sessions, saw each other during every game, and started dating after a year. Contrary to all the rumors, he was not a pushy man. He seemed to want a friend and confidant more than sleepovers. I wanted to feel like a fresh co-ed again."

Jo reached over and squeezed her friend's hand. "What happened that you feel you can't tell him the whole story, including the threats? No one can help if you won't share."

"Right after Mike's graduation, he asked me to be his life partner. The announcement made headlines in Georgia. I followed him to Texas after he accepted the job with Lockheed. I was working on my final year, traveling back and forth to Texas during every possible break. On a late spring trip to see him, I decided to tell him everything, as the wedding was scheduled for two weeks after my graduation. During the Saturday dinner with his parents, the conversation turned to a woman who worked part-time for Mike's dad during her high school years and after entering community college. During her second year, she attended a fraternity party and became pregnant. Then the woman took a leave of absence for the last month of her pregnancy to choose the adoptive parents. Mike's mom was outspoken about the woman's behavior, suggesting she must have teased the boy to cause the problem. Mike said he'd never respect a woman who gave up her child. He said, with a hint of pride on his face, he wanted a family with me, when he knew he could provide well enough for me to stay at home with our babies. Until that moment, I didn't know he wanted children."

Jo pulled up to the stop sign, paralyzed. She turned toward her friend and lamented, "Oh, Ashley. You poor thing. You never told him your story. He doesn't know the trauma you experienced."

"Nope. And I was so enamored, I couldn't give him up. He was, and is, the love of my life. I would have walked over burning coals to say my vows. Hell, I'd stand on the same kind of flames now, if it meant neither he nor Brett is hurt."

"Did you ever hear from your son's father?"

"Not once. Never saw him either. He graduated the year I was away. Fine by me. I never cared to see him again."

Jo felt concern for Ashley's mental state. She gave a virtual kiss to the baby she carried, understanding the connection her friend felt to her child all too well. "Let's get home and have some tea. I always make better plans when drinking a piping cup."

"I wouldn't mind a plan if you promise no one gets hurt," replied Ashley. "I'm not certain what is going to happen next or what demands will be made."

Jo punched the code to enter through her gate. She pulled forward and watched behind her until the opening closed. "We need JJ to check out your phone for the calls and the texts. He is smart with technology. He can find a molehill in a mountain in nanoseconds."

Both ladies laughed while Jo parked her SUV.

Walking arm-in-arm into the pergola, Ashley said, "Mike is never going to forgive me for what he heard, no matter how much I explain. If he knows the truth about Brett, it will be worse. I need to leave before he gets released from the hospital so he can recover without the stress of my presence."

"He loves you. JJ told me, and I have seen it in his eyes. You're not going anywhere until we get this mess figured out. I have every confidence that JJ will help get to the bottom of who is blackmailing you."

"But, Jo."

"No buts." She fumbled with the key to enter through the side door and turned off the alarm. "We'll figure it out. JJ once admonished me to face my fears. Now I'm saying the same to you. Go wash your face while I boil some water and find something for us to eat. I'm hungry."

Ashley headed toward her bedroom, where Jo heard the water running. She popped a frozen pizza into the oven. Fifteen minutes later, Ashley slid onto the kitchen bar stool and took a sip of the fragrant tea. "Are you making pizza?"

"I am. Margherita with a cauliflower crust. It is delicious."

"Healthy, too, if I know you."

The timer buzzed. Opening the oven, Jo slid the crispy crust onto her titanium board. With practiced precision, she sliced small, even triangles. She selected two bright square plates from the shelf to her right. Just then, her cell phone chimed a memorable melody, indicating a text message from JJ.

> Babe, take cover in our safe room. The house is secure.
> Two guys are outside. Tommy and I are on the way.

"Ash, grab the pizza and plates. We're eating in our secret room inside the master bedroom. I'll grab the tea and wine for later." Jo chuckled. "I'm bringing my frying pan, just in case."

Ashley nervously called over her shoulder, "Are we cooking in your saferoom too?"

"No, I have a knack with this thing. I'll fill you in once we're inside."

The door closed as the alarm sirens blared. Gradually, their intensity increased. Jo was grateful for the soundproofing of the ten-foot square room. Ashley set their food on the table and arranged two stuffed chairs. The bold colors throughout the rest of the house carried over into this space.

"Looking good, Ash," she said, setting down the tray containing the tea and cups. "We are safe and secure in here. JJ has extra food if needed, but I stuffed two mini wine bottles in my pockets in case you wanted them."

"It's comfortable like the rest of your home, except no windows. Do we need to turn on the television to find out what's happening?" Ashley anxiously asked.

"Not really. JJ mentioned that unwanted visitors might show up. We have a state-of-the-art warning system, making this the safest room in the house." She snatched a piece of pizza and took a generous bite. "Yummy. You've got to taste this."

Confused, but famished, Ashley selected a piece and bit off the end. Her eyes closed, small noises of pleasure emanating from her throat. "Heavenly."

"I agree." Taking another bite, she pulled out her phone to send a text.

Honey, are you here yet? We are safe."

A few seconds later, she received a response.

> Tommy and I will be there shortly.
> We'll check everything and turn off the alarm. Sit tight.

"JJ and Tommy will be here soon. He said not to worry."

Ashley nodded and finished her last wedge of pizza seconds before the outer door opened. Jo grabbed her frying pan, hiding it behind her back. JJ appeared, and she hurried into his arms.

"Told Tommy you'd be armed," JJ said, pointing at her weapon.

Ashley flinched, then clutched her cell to her chest.

"Are you getting a call or text?" Jo pointedly asked.

Ashley refused to look at either of them. "A text," she mumbled.

"JJ, I hope you left Tommy in your office," Jo said.

He shook his head. "He's outside looking for clues to identify the perpetrators who tripped the alarm. We have a few minutes. What's up?"

"Ashley is being threatened via her phone." She inclined her head. "I suspected she was just contacted less than a minute ago. The background details are very private." She hoped he understood she would fill in the details later. Threats to people always ruled out keeping a secret.

JJ looped his hand on Ashley's arm. "Come on, Ash, let's go to my office and figure this out."

Jo stacked the meal remnants onto the tray and headed for the kitchen. She noticed JJ's office door was shut when Tommy stepped into the kitchen.

"Hey, Jo. Glad you're safe. How is Ashley?"

"She and JJ are having a private discussion. Can I make you a cup of coffee?"

He set his Stetson on the counter. "I know better than to turn down that offer."

She poured and made a cup of tea for herself.

"The culprits deduced that the PC is here. I suspect JJ will want to go after them now that they know where you live."

Jo laughed. "How will you trap them without the bait being here, Tommy?"

"You have a point."

"A short time ago, Ashley received a text from someone who is blackmailing her."

Tommy's expression soured. "Is this where you fill me in on why Ashley and Mike are fighting?"

Jo bristled. "She gave me private information about her college years. It may or may not be related to the poisoning and attack on Mike. I know you'll say this is police business, but she's making progress by allowing JJ to check her phone. Let's leave out the why issues for now."

JJ opened the door and signaled them to enter. Everyone took a seat, then JJ said, "Ashley's letting me download data from her phone. I will check with her cloud provider for additional data. Tommy, I believe we can trace the calls and texts backward to learn the true identity of who is squeezing her. With some good evidence, I think she'll voluntarily fill in the gaps. I feel we need to take it slow."

Ashley looked at the screen and read the message. Her eyes filled with tears of agony. "He's demanding I provide Mike's PC intact, otherwise either he or my son will be eliminated. What a mess. It's all my fault, though I still don't understand why." Another message arrived. Her face drained of color, her eyes appeared vacant as she read the screen. "I must not tell the federal agents or else."

CHAPTER 36

Should I Change?

JJ ushered Ashley into the living room, followed by Tommy. "These guys are in hiding, at least for now."

"My guys are patrolling the area. They'll alert me if they uncover anything," promised Tommy.

JJ and Ashley took seats next to one another but said nothing. "Jo, honey, would you mind getting some snacks?" He poured a finger of whiskey into a crystal glass and handed it to Ashley. "Drink this, Ash. Tommy, you want some too?" He held up the decanter.

"No, I'm ready for some of your coffee, Jo, if you could make a cup for me."

Jo offered a soft smile. "Sure thing. I'll be right back."

Ashley gently swirled the golden-brown liquid in the glass, watching it.

"Ash, let me borrow your phone again, please," JJ said.

She offered up the device with no expression before returning to her mindless activity of playing with the liquid contents.

JJ chuckled. "You've had a tough few days, Ash. The small amount of whiskey will help you relax, promise. Although I've reviewed your messages, I'd like to make a copy of all the contents."

She nodded.

"I'll be right back. Tommy is here if you need a refill. I shouldn't be too long."

JJ walked to his office and shut the door. Touching the keyboard caused all the screens to come to life, each showing different options. He quickly created a new folder labeled AH. Using a Bluetooth connection, he extracted all the data to that destination. "ICABOD, if the house camera's video captured any images of the men who attempted to break in, send a copy to the secure SharePoint Agent Andrews provided."

"I have already started running the facial recognition program on the images. There were two men with Asian features. Their mouths were covered. No distinctive characteristics appeared. Their clothing was grey," stated ICABOD.

"I want you to activate the microphones in the common rooms and record all the questions and answers," instructed JJ.

"Company! And I am invited?" said ICABOD with a bit of excited inflection. "Do I need to change from my lounge attire, losing the fuzzy house shoes? I could easily create my avatar in a period costume of a musketeer with a nicely plumed ostrich feather, if you want a conversation starter. No one is saying a word outside of this room."

JJ quietly laughed. "Thank you, I have it covered. Analyze the data in the folder of Ashley's mobile device. Extract as much history as you can from her cloud provider, especially if any of the messages were deleted and can be recovered. Triangulate the signal origins of calls and texts over the last four weeks, longer if the data is still available."

"It should not take too long. Do you want me to appear on your cell phone with my image when I complete my analysis?"

"I need to get some additional details to identify who is at the root of the problem and what their goal is. If you need more information, please feel free to text me. I need some answers." JJ stood to leave.

ICABOD announced, "JJ, the cell phone ID initiated its calls and text messages to Mrs. Hayes through multiple anonymizing servers to cloak their identity. I took the liberty of searching for other sources of call IDs not in her contact list, which suggests there may be multiple burner phones that have made contact. It makes sense that the perpetrator would believe this technique would obfuscate their identity. I have determined that the cell tower sources of the calls to Ms. Hayes originate in and around Fort Worth, Texas."

"Good work, ICABOD. What about identifying the purchaser or the stores that sold the mobile devices?"

"I used the burner phone ID to identify the store that sold it, but these types of units are almost always purchased for cash, with little or no ID required. Once the minutes are used, a new unit gets acquired via cash. These prepaid burner phones have unique identifiers, allowing people to make and receive calls. By law, the carrier maintains a record of each device in its database. There are no checks and balances to verify the legitimate user's name for the phone user. It will take some time to verify the aliases used to purchase the phones. No credit cards were used, but the mistake they might make is to use cryptocurrency rather than cash if the store accepts those methods of payment. If that occurs, then I can dig deeper to discover the owner of the crypto-wallet, JJ."

"Excellent."

JJ returned to the living room. Ash's glass was empty; she was munching on a muffin. He returned her phone. "Sorry for the delay. Early indications, based on cell tower triangulation signals, suggest that your stalker is in the vicinity of your home, the private airfield, and Granbury. The programs I fed the data into are still doing some analysis, which will take a while. Are you ready to answer a few more questions?"

Ashley nodded with a sad expression. "I wonder if that is why, several times, based on the content of the messages, I felt like I was being watched. Creepy as all get out!"

Tommy asked, "How far back do the call records go?"

JJ replied, "I set the parameters hoping to catch information up to four weeks back. Ash, you tried to block multiple numbers, but they were overridden at the carrier level, which means this guy is a talented hacker."

Ashley's eyes widened. "So, you believe me, JJ. I did try to block from the very first."

"Yes. Part of this thing feels like a vendetta of sorts. Can you provide more details for us?"

Ashley shared part of what she had told Jo, almost anxious to get it off her chest.

Chief Tommy finished up his phone call while getting a coffee refill from Jo's kitchen.

"Agreed, Major. My deputy will remain on guard while you and Andrews view the aircraft. We've got things under control here. JJ forwarded some additional data to Andrews' Dropbox, including the video footage of the attempted break-in here at his house. He has a program comparing the individuals to the hospital's footage from last evening. JJ said the hospital film showed no visible facial features. He is checking for other correlating points that would indicate the individuals are the same in both instances. Shall I assume you and Andrews will join us here at the Rodreguiz's after your inspection?"

After listening for a minute, Tommy replied, "Understood. We may have more information to share with you when you arrive."

CHAPTER 37

Open Book

JJ spotted the official-looking vehicle on the monitor and remotely opened the gate.

Andrews and the major parked next to Tommy's cruiser. They got out and stepped briskly towards the kitchen entrance.

JJ opened the door. "Good afternoon, gentlemen." He extended his hand to each man in turn. "Please come in. May I get you anything to drink or eat?"

Agent Andrews said, "I'd—"

Major Johnson interrupted. "You're very kind, JJ. We ate lunch after we reviewed the airplane parts and current engineering notes. We're here to visit with you and Tommy."

"Tommy is right behind me," Jo said, stepping into the kitchen with Ashley on her heels.

Tommy and JJ entered through the doorway at the far end. The men exchanged handshakes.

"JJ, I'm taking Ashley out to the pergola. We may stick our feet in the pool. If anyone has questions for us, please text me." Jo herded Ashley outside.

JJ led everyone to the dining room off the kitchen, where they found seats around the table.

JJ opened, "Agent, have you had time to share the information I placed into the Dropbox for your investigators?"

"Yes. Thank you for providing the data. I do not have any responses yet."

Tommy suggested, "Why don't you tell them what you've found so far with your analysis, JJ?"

Major Johnson withdrew a recorder and set it on the table. "Does anyone have an issue with my capturing the conversation?"

"No problem," they replied.

"Gentlemen, we verified Mrs. Hayes is being pressured by an unknown adversary to deliver Mike's briefcase. Text exchanges show the initial request was to provide the combination. I've traced the call identifiers to the macro-cell towers, through anonymizing servers used to cloak their call routing information. The culprit exploited burner phones with prepaid phone numbers. My program is mapping the signals from the macro towers in and around Fort Worth, Texas."

Interested, the major leaned forward and exclaimed, "Thorough detective work, JJ. You and your organization are as good as your dossier states."

"Thank you, Major." JJ grimaced. "Sadly, that's where the cleverness ends. Burner phones have unique identities to permit them to participate in any carrier network. They are used to help individuals hide in the shadows or avoid commitment to a telecommunications carrier. I can identify the device, its geo-location in proximity to the macro towers, and even the carrier they are registered with. I have no way of identifying the owner. Individuals typically pay cash for the units, allowing no corresponding data to the true owner."

"Your initiative is commendable. I am glad you're on our side. Working the messages and calls backwards to help frame a valid search area is key. The origin being close to Lockheed Martin means the individual has some ties to our organization. They certainly are aware of a valuable engineer and know he has family members." Johnson paused and glanced toward the agent. "Andrews, do you think it is possible we have other staff members being threatened? The military contracts are a mainstay of our business relationships."

"It is within the realm of possibilities, Major. I will have our team determine all the endpoints for transactions by the Call IDs JJ identified. I will have the team search back for six months as a start and match those results to all known mobile phones for Lockheed employees." Agent Andrews added, "During our review of the airplane, we found some liquid in a take-out cup. We have sent that to the lab for analysis."

"Good idea," said JJ. "I recall seeing that cup in the panoramic photos I filmed of the plane's interior. It had a cover, as I recall."

The major added, "We're hoping it might provide a link for the poison."

JJ felt relieved to be able to focus on Mike's condition and the events in Magnolia Bluff. Something niggled in the back of his mind when he heard an inbound chirp of a text. Reading the screen, he felt like he'd won a modest lottery jackpot.

"Gentlemen, one of my programs running an analysis has concluded and sent the results to my phone. While it's true that there is no mechanism to track cash purchases, cryptocurrency transactions are a different matter. We have the burner phone identities from the carrier host; thus, we have the costs. The program examined the aggregate expenses for five burner phones in the target zip codes to determine if anyone used a local ATM to convert cryptocurrency to cash within the timeframe of the estimated purchases. We have a hit. The total cash price, including taxes, matches a sum withdrawn from a cryptocurrency exchange known for its lax enforcement of Know Your Customer (KYC) rules. Even more interesting to me is that the cryptocurrency wallets used are identified as being under the control of the Lazarus group. In case you are unaware, they are from the Democratic People's Republic of Korea, with a reputation for hacking and money laundering.

Agent Andrews appeared dumbstruck for several seconds. "You're suggesting the next generation stealth code that Mr. Hayes' program manages is likely being targeted by people funded by the Democratic People's Republic of Korea. That's North Korea." Tommy marveled and blew a long, low whistle.

"Fairly circumstantial evidence," Major Johnson cautioned. "I don't see a smoking gun in your findings, sir."

JJ shrugged and grinned. "It's not perfect. However, individuals need verifiable credentials to log in to complete an ATM transaction. The underlying blockchain code traps that information, writing it to the transaction list. Here is the name that was used." JJ wrote a name on a piece of paper and pushed it across to the two men.

Andrews and the major looked at one another with expressions of disbelief. They turned and stared at JJ.

"By your responses, I gather you know who this is."

Jo observed her friend heading toward the brightly colored chairs closest to the pool. Ashley's footsteps, slow and hesitant, reminded her of someone walking the plank. The sun sinking toward the horizon hadn't diminished the hundred-degree heat of the August day, though the humidity was absent. Jo took out her cell, selecting the home application to power on the ceiling fans and launch her background jazz playlist. "There," Jo declared. "Air flow will keep us comfortable. Please let me know if you find the music too loud." She waved a hand toward the cabinet. "I have towels out here if you want to dip your feet."

"I'm numb. Thanks for getting me out here. I'm not sure I could face another round of questioning. Major Johnson clearly isn't my fan."

"I doubt he rose to his rank coloring anywhere outside the lines." She stood and asked, "Would you like some iced tea? I recall I have a pitcher in the refrigerator out here. I bet I have chips and salsa too."

Ashley winced. "I think that is a good idea. I need to stay alert in case the feds want another round of questions. Plus, I love your fresh, homemade salsa." She rubbed her forehead while Jo filled the tumblers. "I can appreciate that JJ wanted me to relax, but that whiskey was strong, especially on an empty stomach. It had a hint of pecan."

Jo set the snacks between them and handed Ashley the tea with a slice of lime. "Here's to better days and new beginnings."

Their glasses touched. Ashley said, "Telling Mike will finish ripping us apart. I'm not sure I'll survive."

Jo wanted to help her friend. Offer words of wisdom. Something. Anything. "I get that you don't want to face Mike and tell him everything. I know he loves you. Look at your life from his perspective, not from your deep-seated, self-imposed guilt. He might have a different perspective now from that of an idealistic college graduate at dinner with his folks."

Ashley softly chuckled with her eyes focused on the horizon Jo couldn't see. "You know how it starts, Jo. A girl wants to get noticed by the handsome, smart football jock, but with the herd of competition, it appeared like a bakery where you take a number and stand in line. I thought Mike was a nice guy. We had some great conversations during classes. Not a flirty kind of exchange, but like friends. He was a genuine guy. Everyone thought he'd be a good catch as the star running back for the Yellow Jackets. The college co-eds fawned over him. Even the female sportscasters seemed about to drool when they got to interview him."

"I've seen pictures of JJ with Mike when they were taking flying lessons as well as other times when they got together," Jo responded. "Both are attractive. I've often thought JJ was too brilliant and good-looking to want me. But that's not how it works when love is involved."

Ashley nodded. "Earning a spot on the cheer squad in my freshman year meant we had time outside of classes to get to know one another. Just as he devotes his time to work now, Mike studied as if his life depended on it. He also loved playing football, earning a starting position at running back in his sophomore year. He divided his time and recognized he didn't have time for any other commitments. One of the seniors on the team, who was on the second-string as an offensive guard, invited me to one of the frat parties. I fantasized that Mike might be there, see me with this guy, and get jealous. Up to that point, I'd lived a sheltered life. College parties were full of music, lots of people, and probably beer, which I have never been too fond of. Seemed like a fun way to meet other people.

"When I arrived at the party, he dutifully served me my first drink, like a gentleman, and introduced me around. It never occurred to me that I'd be used. Thankfully, one of the other cheerleaders, the one with good common sense, found me a few hours later. She helped me get dressed and walked me back to my dorm room. She begged me to go to the doctor. I was humiliated and so ashamed, I didn't go for rape counseling or medical treatment. I pretended the whole nightmare didn't happen. I missed my first cycle, which wasn't unusual, but when the second month showed no change, I panicked. A school doctor confirmed my fears.

"I begged my parents for some money to take advantage of what I led them to believe was a year-long exchange program. They were thrilled and proud of me. I found a place in Alabama where I could pursue remote studies online and access medical care, with adoption services. It seemed like a good idea. I felt too young and ill-equipped to be a mom."

"How awful for you, Ash. You were eighteen, nineteen, right?"

"I felt like a failure, even though the people who adopted Brett wanted him so much. I've never seen or spoken to him. His mother sends me pictures at milestone events. He's a good student. My folks wanted me to return to classes at Georgia Tech, which I did. Sadly, they died in a car accident not too long after I resumed school. It was rough for me, but at least they never knew how bad I was. I worked harder than I thought possible to get an education and be in the top one percent of my class. Mike said that my brain power was what he fell in love with first."

Jo quietly asked, "Didn't you tell the jerk about your situation?"

Ashley finished her tea, then implored, "Perhaps another sip of that pecan whiskey is in order after relating my horrific choices." Her eyes welled with moisture again.

"It's up to you," said Jo. "But I think you'd do better to get it out in the open. Stop beating yourself up, you're a grown woman now."

Ashley's shoulders slumped, resigned. She clenched the empty tumbler like a lifeline. "The guy laughed at me, claiming I couldn't prove it was his because I was too out of it. He was right. I don't remember a thing, other than waking up naked. He graduated during my trip abroad," she added with air quotes. "I never saw or heard from him again. I doubt he gave me a second thought in his string of conquests during college." She placed her hands over her eyes and blubbered. "I felt like a fool."

"Foolish, maybe, or simply manipulated," soothed Jo.

"When I returned to school, I never went to another party. I stayed on the cheer team but only attended well-chaperoned events." Ashley straightened with a pensive expression. "Then a slice of silver lining provided me hope. Mike was attentive when he returned for his graduate work. We met up in the library or the cafeteria fairly frequently. During the last semester of my senior year, we dated. We enjoyed hiking on weekends, visiting outdoor fairs, and dining at cheesy restaurants with patios. He worked as an intern at Lockheed during the summers. He liked that I was a Texas girl. He attended my graduation. We got married two weeks later. The big lumbering brute. It was more than I could ever have dreamed possible after all the trauma. I promised to love him and to make no more mistakes."

Jo smiled. "You guys do seem great together. I saw that the first time we met."

"Do you think JJ will find any information from my phone data?"

"I don't know for certain, but he is very good at tracing digital footprints." Resting her chin on the palm of her bent elbow on the table, she thoughtfully suggested, "Your stalker seems like he has a vendetta against Mike. You say you're protecting Mike and Brett, but are you protecting someone else? JJ needs the names of anyone, past or present, who might be behind this mess. I believe you are being manipulated, like you were when you were a co-ed. If the same guy is involved, you could turn the tables."

She whispered. "Or Mike could react. If Mike hunted Allen and hurt him, he'd end up in worse trouble." She covered her mouth. "Please don't tell anyone the monster's name, Jo."

CHAPTER 38

Once the Testing is Complete...

Two days later, JJ was surprised to learn that Mike's doctor was releasing him on the condition that he remain in the area for five days in case of issues. JJ was pleased to have him stay at the house, hoping Ashley and he might reconcile.

JJ arrived at nine in the morning outside the hospital entrance, moments before a nurse pushed a wheelchair holding his friend. JJ helped Mike get into his SUV, ensuring he was properly secured. He returned to the driver's seat, ready to head home.

Mike huffed a sigh of relief. "Geeze, JJ, I didn't think I'd ever get out. Thanks for getting me. I swear, another day spent in that bed would have driven me nuts. So, what's the current scoop?"

Before JJ put the car into drive, a hospital admin ran to the vehicle and knocked on the window. "Mr. Hayes, glad I caught you before you left. You left your briefcase in your room." She lifted it and passed it through the window.

Mike laughed. "OMG, of all the things to forget. JJ, I can't believe I wasn't holding it." He hugged the briefcase close.

"Thank you, ma'am," JJ called out the window. "Mike, I think you need some good rest, buddy."

Mike got excited. "JJ, I haven't had my favorite coffee in days. Do you have a local shop that can create a mocha coffee latte infused with dandelion extract?"

"Perhaps. On the square, we have a popular coffee shop. We can stop by and see if they can create your favorite beverage. No promises, though."

"Thanks for trying, buddy. You're the driver."

Putting the car into drive, JJ ran several relevant points through his mind. "Mike, how long have you liked this specific latte blend?"

Scrunching up his face thinking, he finally replied, "Maybe six months or a bit longer. That deli I took you to last week. The café's owners are a hardworking pair. They provided it as a free test one day when I was buying a sandwich. One sip and I was honestly hooked. I have even gone above and beyond to recommend the café's menu to everyone I know. The feedback to me has been, 'Thanks for the recommendation.' They offer something new once a month, which has been a win. People flock to the establishment on the day they add something to the menu."

"Who else knew you were here in Magnolia Bluff besides the major and the federal agent who are here?"

"Heck, JJ, I don't know. I told you where I was going. I never told anyone at work. Why?"

"When Jo called in your crash, we suspected it must be you. Local police realized it after we told them. They never released the name or names of the person or persons involved in the accident. Do you agree that only high-profile people got word of your crash?"

"It would seem so, JJ. What's your point?"

"Someone knew you were here, in a crash, and in the hospital. To me, that stinks of insider information."

JJ pulled up to the new coffee shop on the square. "Wait here," he said, then got out of the running car, leaving the air conditioning on. He returned in a scant fifteen minutes with a large cup of coffee. "Here you go, buddy."

Mike took the cup and sipped it through the top.

JJ watched Mike's expression dramatically change while he shifted the car into gear.

"OMG, JJ," he said, swallowing, holding back a threat of hurling the sip. "This tastes disgusting. It is flat and bitter."

"We may have to take a drive to Fort Worth for your special blend. Let's go home so Jo can feed you."

"Should I be scared?"

Mike said, "I'm hoping I'm not putting you and Jo out, camping with you. I don't want to drive to Fort Worth. Relaxing by your pool would be perfect. I don't think I'm required to answer any more questions. Are we going to find some time to finish the radar project?"

"Possibly, at some point. I want you to rest and recover. Besides, I think you have a priority more critical than the radar documentation."

"What in heaven's name could that be?" he said, eyeing his friend suspiciously.

"Mike, you need to man up and face your wife."

Mike bellowed, "What? You said she'd gone."

"I lied." He shrugged. "You need to stop your childish, cranial-rectal inversion and talk with her like an adult. Ash has something she's terrified to tell you. She loves you. Heck, you told me she's the love of your life. You owe it to your relationship to listen. Get your head on straight.

"On the other side of that discussion, we'll solve who your alleged assassins are working with to steal the stealth technology you and I crafted. We're at the end of the final quarter in this competition. Look, buddy, I'm gonna throw a long bomb to end the attacks on my two best friends. So, suck it up, buttercup. Listen to her story and your heart."

Hidden Keys

JJ slowly pulled the Porsche up next to Ash's rental near the pergola. He exited and went to the passenger side, hoping Mike would be cooperative in speaking with Ashley. Mike wouldn't look at his friend while shuffling like a man of ninety. JJ was insistent.

Jo poked her head out and around the edge of the garden where she was working. Moments later, Ashley's head appeared. Both wiped their hands clean, with dust filling the air in front of them. They walked towards their husbands, Jo beaming and Ash with a reticent smile. Though the mid-morning weather was bright and cheery, everyone radiated anxiety for different reasons.

Mike snarled, "I thought you'd be home by now. It's been two days."

Ashley angrily glared at Jo, then announced, "I would have been, except someone hid my rental vehicle's keys."

Jo comically raised her head away from the scene in a mock attempt to feign innocence. JJ chuckled.

Mike suddenly laughed like a maniac, staring intently at Ashley. "You ended up with a rental car. That's hysterical. I didn't want you to lose the keys, so I put them under your pillow. I figured when you discovered they were missing, you would lie down to think on it."

Ashley covered her face. "You must be kidding." Then she giggled. "Wow." She marched closer and quietly said, "I deserve your wrath, but honestly, I was trying to protect you. I've kept secrets I should have shared before we married."

Mike's eyes misted. "Oh, Ash, I've been poisoned, crashed my plane, and I'm being hunted. I'm at the epicenter of a national defense program under investigation. The last thing I want is to lose you. Can we go inside and talk? JJ thinks it will help my cranial-rectal inversion problem."

Ashley almost chuckled, then reached for his hand. Together they went into the house.

Jo frowned. "You could have waited until my free garden labor finished."

JJ stomped his feet at attention and saluted her. "I, of course, volunteer to help with the garden. I'll even cook dinner later."

In a flash, JJ's innocent look disappeared. "We'll need to get cleaned up afterwards, right?"

Leaning against the headboard, Mike caressed Ashley's arm, pulling her a bit closer. "I'm so glad you finally decided to tell me, honey. I'm sorry you felt I wouldn't understand. Tell me his name and I'll kick his butt from wherever I find him to next summer."

Ashley sighed. "It happened a long time ago. I can't change it, and neither can you. I've not thought about him or how he took advantage of me at all until this jerk on the phone mentioned my son. I have no plans to see Brett. Although you should be aware that he could come looking for me. I permitted his parents to provide the info if he asks. I have to believe he's had a good life with loving folks."

"I think I understand how tough it's been for you. You made the only choice you could at the time. I will never regret having fallen in love with you. I'd do anything for us to stay connected, honey."

"I tried to protect you and made a mess of everything."

"My work is important to our nation's military. Don't forget, whoever has been pestering you is probably the one who tried to hack my work account. I'm sorry I put you at risk." Mike stared into her eyes. "I love you, sweetheart. Together we'll make *US* work."

"I agree. No one can hurt me with you by my side. I won't make this mistake again."

"How about I show you how much I care?"

Ashley angled for a kiss filled with passion.

CHAPTER 40

Subtle Tweaks

Early in the afternoon, JJ completed the final adjustments to the home video monitoring system and conducted a few tests. The new design had to accurately record external movement along the fence lines and structures, including roofs. Satisfied with the results of the various scenarios, he breathed a sigh of relief. "There. No one and nothing that moves can approach without being picked up."

Noting the fading light, JJ placed a call to his favorite police chief. "Tommy, I've re-rigged the cameras like we discussed. Do you want the images forwarded to your phone as well in case we get rushed?"

"If you can do it easily, sure. Will the messaging be the full video or a single snapshot?"

"Good question. Single images transfer faster. I am targeting updates every thirty seconds to highlight any intruder's progress. The video will remain intact on my system."

"Sounds good, JJ. What about when there's no full moon? Don't forget, country living contains more shadows than city life."

"I considered the darkness factor. To solve this, I increased the sensitivity levels of all my external sensors to trigger at the slightest movement. Then I utilize various night vision technologies."

"Wow, is this like military grade?"

"It's similar to what soldiers leverage for image intensification, thermal imaging, and augmented reality. The results are stunning."

He snorted. "I guess you'll need to forego skinny dipping in your pool with Jo for a while."

"A little personal, my friend." JJ laughed. "We'll wear our swimsuits, at least until these guys are apprehended. Once the culprits are in custody, I'll cancel the program that automatically sends info to your phone."

"Have Mike and Ashley been made aware of our plan, JJ?"

"Not yet. But I suspect they'll be willing to act as high-value bait to the intruders, with the briefcase not containing a laptop. If our fish strike soon, you'll see it in your messages. I want you to loop in the feds staying at the Flower B&B. Lily was more than happy to have the business, though she questioned their professions."

Tommy laughed uproariously. "Lily will feel important when she figures it out."

"Agreed. I expect a strike tonight. Time is not their friend. We're armed and safe."

"I'll remain close."

"Thanks, Tommy. Good night."

CHAPTER 41

Playing Cards

JJ and Mike sipped their espresso, designed to keep them alert. JJ angled his phone to view the display easily if the program alerted him to an intruder.

Jo entered the kitchen carrying her weapon to refill the tea pitcher and check on the guys. She quietly asked, "Ash is anxiously pacing in our room. Any sign yet?"

"Nothing at this point. Tommy doesn't feel they left the area. I don't think they have any other option than to try for the laptop."

"What time do you think they will attack? How much movement do we need to have inside so they know we're still up?" she asked, biting her lip.

"I can stay active in front of the windows to keep them interested," offered Mike.

Successive texts with scrambled video appeared on the phone display. "Return to the safe room. Now! Lock it up. Damn! They're using infrared beams on each camera to ruin the pictures we wanted for evidence. At this rate, I won't have photos of the assailants. The distorted images are advertising their approach." He turned, stunned to find his wife frozen in place, staring at the phone screen. "Honey, did you hear me? You better…"

Suddenly, the kitchen exploded from a flashbang designed to permit quick access. JJ jumped. Fearing potential disorientation from the blast, he pushed Jo toward the safe room. He caught sight of his friend shaking his head. "Mike, can you hear me?"

"Yeah, I'll be fine."

"Two hooded guys, inbound, Mike. If they're the ones from the crash site, they'll hit fast." JJ pulled Mike next to him to block access to the hallway where Jo escaped.

JJ watched the first assailant rush Mike, hitting him in the gut. Mike huffed, then caught the edge of the table to balance.

Though JJ worried about Mike's strength and size working against him in the close combat battle, he focused on his assailant shifting slightly to the right. The man barely missed slamming into him, but kept his balance. They squared off.

JJ taunted, "Are you game for a re-match, my Kung Fu friend? How's the head after using it to stop the door?"

JJ knew from the way the guy moved the fight wouldn't be a slam dunk. The opponent pressed forward with a flurry of strikes, but JJ was trained to win. He deflected and parried, using his body as a shield, searching for an opening. The opponent overextended on a punch, leaving his torso exposed. JJ pivoted, shifting his weight, delivering a swift, sharp kick to the opponent's side. Momentarily stunned, the wiry man stumbled back. JJ closed the distance with his hands moving in a blur of calculated strikes. He delivered a jab to the man's face, followed by a swift elbow strike.

The man groaned, his momentum coming to a halt. He tried to regain control with a jab that missed. He was too weak to make a meaningful strike. JJ spotted an opening for a final move. "Thank you for the spirited combat." He grinned. "Consider our contest over," he said, then completed the perfect move. One he'd practiced countless times. The man crumpled to the floor, down but not out.

Abruptly, JJ relaxed his stance and stood upright, before offering a slight bow.

The man looked over his shoulder as Jo used his head to sound her signature *klong* using her weaponized cast-iron skillet.

Mike hollered, "JJ, can you help me get this fast-moving ninja hamster?"

JJ rushed to assist Mike in subduing the second attacker. Both of the invaders were trussed with zip-ties in seconds. Jo's victim remained out cold.

JJ, breathing hard, called Tommy. "I've got a pair for this round."

"On my way. I'll turn them over to the feds. Is everyone okay?"

"Yes. We're good. Jo got one of them."

Tommy twisted the key on the cell door, then went to his office. He carefully set his Stetson onto the hat hook before dropping into his chair. With a sigh of satisfaction and a slight smile on his face, he placed the call, enabling the speaker.

The serious authoritarian voice answered, "This is Major Johnson."

"Good evening, Major. This is Chief Jager. I have two suspects in custody in my Magnolia Bluff jail. I figured you or Agent Andrews would like to speak with them."

"Good news, Chief. Have you identified them as the two who were at the hospital?"

"Correct. Mr. Rodreguiz provided the videos from his home surveillance system showing the break-in. I have matched one of them to the image from the patient's room video. My deputy also made a positive ID for the other one who brought his coffee. Mr. Rodreguiz, his wife, and Mr. Hayes were responsible for containing the pair until I arrived. I transported them to my jail in the town square."

"Mrs. Rodreguiz wasn't injured, was she? And what about Mrs. Hayes, you didn't mention her."

"Mrs. Hayes is fine and wasn't directly involved with the fight inside the home. Mrs. Rodreguiz made her contribution as the Frying Pan Queen and sustained no injuries."

Major Johnson chuckled. "I'm guessing there's a story behind that. Perhaps you and I can discuss it sometime."

"Anytime, sir."

"The security team will arrive by midday tomorrow to take them off your hands, if that is acceptable to you. It would be helpful if you turned over any evidence to them. You've been more than helpful, Chief. Everything you have contributed to this investigation will be in my report. I thank you."

CHAPTER 42

Confused

Two military police escorted Kamal into Major Johnson's outer office within the Lockheed Martin facility. Having undergone a modernization effort in the not-too-distant past, the walls were bright with portraits of various commanders and aircraft manufactured by Lockheed Martin. An American flag and an Air Force flag were positioned in either corner, flanking the assistant's workspace.

Kamal looked around for Drake, who usually sat at the desk. He nervously asked, "What's up? Is there something wrong? Does someone need a password reset?" Neither of the armed men responded, their faces holding serious expressions.

One of the escorts stood behind Kamal, while the other knocked on the inner door on the side.

"Enter," the commanding voice insisted.

Opening the door, the escort gestured for Kamal to proceed inside. Kamal noticed the two men at a worktable, cattycorner from the massive desk, which appeared to be organized as it always was when he came to these offices. An imposing portrait of the current president was on the wall behind the enormous leather chair. The same style of flags graced the area to either side, along with some greenery planted in large brown ceramic pots.

Major Johnson stood. "Gentlemen, you can wait in the other room. I will call if I need you." He shifted his steel-grey eyes to the guest and gestured to the open chair. "Please, take a seat."

"Good day, Major," Kamal began as he sat. "How may I be of assistance? Drake usually calls when you have an IT issue to give me a heads-up."

"Today is a little different, son," replied the major.

His tone increased Kamal's trepidation and confusion. Even so, he decided to wait. He placed his hands in his lap to hide his shaking fingers.

"Kamal, you know me as I've had this office for some time. Drake is running errands. I'm not certain if you know Agent Andrews, a member of the FBI I've requested help from." He inclined his head to his right.

Andrews turned his expressionless face in acknowledgment but said nothing.

Kamal swallowed the fear that settled like bile in his churning stomach.

"We're going to ask you some questions," Johnson continued. "I expect you to answer to the best of your knowledge."

"Yes, sir," agreed Kamal with a nod, hoping this would be resolved quickly as he had no idea why he was involved.

"We are investigating the attempted theft of our top-secret stealth technology, which we suspect might be part of a plan to sell it to a foreign power. Our capability is a matter of national security. Arrest and prosecution of those involved will be executed to the fullest extent of the law. Do you understand the gravity of the situation?"

"Sir, I understand national security, but I don't know how I can help you," Kamal replied in a shaky voice.

Ignoring the comment, Johnson looked at his tablet and continued, "The records indicate you've been employed in the IT department at Lockheed Martin for a little more than six months. You passed your security clearance for hiring purposes without issue. You have worked with many employees in this location. By all indications and monthly checkpoints, you have performed your duties in an above-satisfactory manner. I need you to tell us everything you know about Mike Hayes and his current project."

Stunned, Kamal's breathing accelerated. Sweat blossomed on his neck, working its way down his back. He tried to clear his throat, yet faltered. "He's…he's a nice, dedicated guy. He works long hours but is pleasant and polite when we talk. I can't fathom that Mr. Hayes would be party to stealing defense technology to sell."

Smirking, the major stated, "I agree, he's not. But we're here to discuss your involvement."

Kamal flinched like he'd been slapped with a heavy, wet towel. "You can't be serious. I worked hard to become a naturalized citizen. I love my adopted country. I was thrilled to get hired for this position at Lockheed Martin. I love flying, but I could never be a pilot. I have an aptitude for technology, so IT is a good fit for me. Here, I get to see some of the most magnificent machines. I would never—"

"I want to know why you've been helping deliver food and lots of coffee to Mr. Hayes from the little deli across the street."

Confused, Kamal cautiously reported, "I did it as a favor to the two men who are trying to earn a spot in America. I understand they are on a work visa and studying to become citizens; they shared this with me one time. Four months ago, Mike—er, Mr. Hayes, told everyone around his work area that the guys were struggling to make a living and wanted to live the American dream. The breakfast and lunch menus are delicious, so other staff members were happy to purchase something from the deli. The pair appreciated his efforts on their behalf by creating a wild coffee concoction he enjoyed daily. If Mr. Hayes missed going there, they asked me several times to bring it to him, sometimes with a food item they insisted Mike relished. If he missed a day or two, as he did when his system was hacked, they provided me with a container to bring back to the office, the day he returned to work. I asked why Mr. Hayes was receiving ongoing special treatment, but they only smiled and bowed. Somebody told me it was because—"

"Did you know the coffee being delivered to Mr. Hayes was poisoned? If they loved him so much for how he had helped them, then why would they poison his daily coffee?"

Following a rapid heart-dropping sensation, Kamal gulped. "P-p-poisoned?" He closed his eyes. "That can't be."

The major added, "This is where the story doesn't seem to work. You like Mr. Hayes. The deli owners reportedly like Mr. Hayes. Yet, somehow, poisoned coffee is in his hands daily. It is confusing that people who liked Mr. Hayes would do this."

After a few moments of near-murderous silence, Andrews volunteered, "Gosh, it's almost lunch time. What say we go grab a bite to eat at your favorite deli? You can introduce us to… hmm, what are their names?"

Kamal, struggling to comprehend the statements made by these two men, robotically replied, "Mal-chin and Jun."

Andrews thumbed through his notepad. He stopped at a page, appearing to read the contents, and smiled. Closing the notebook, his eyes returned to Kamal. "You're right. Mal-chin and Jun, we discovered they are Korean nationals."

Mike stared numbly out the window, repeating to JJ, "My coffee was poisoned. The major called me this morning. Why would the deli-boys serve me arsenic after all my word-of-mouth advertising for their business? I enjoy helping hard-working individuals who are trying to make a living in the best possible places. If these guys are the actual source of the poisoning, I want to know why."

"Mike, there are several possible explanations," offered JJ. "Usually, the answer is not what you expect. In my experience, it is someone pushing buttons of someone else to get what they want. Let's see what they come back with."

CHAPTER 43

Nice Try

Major Johnson entered the deli through the door, with Agent Andrews escorting Kamal. Mal-chin's welcome fell silent as the two MPs methodically cleared the establishment of customers. Jun strode through the swinging kitchen door, then stopped seeing the MPs guarding outside the entrance to prevent customers from entering. The two owners huddled behind the counter, frozen in place. Kamal nervously fidgeted, not making eye contact with the owners.

"Mal-chin and Jun, my name is Major Johnson. I work at Lockheed Martin with Kamal, here, and another employee, Mike Hayes, whom I believe you know."

Mal-chin replied, "Yes, I am Mal-chin. Thank you for coming to our deli. How may we serve you?"

Without changing his serious expression, Johnson said, "I was told you are the owners of this deli. That's quite an accomplishment after arriving in America less than a year ago." He glanced at his notepad and modified, "Sorry, more like six months ago. I am interested in how and why you chose this location so close to the airbases in this area."

Mal-chin looked at his friend and swallowed as fear etched across his face. "Suh, we had not much money, but we are willing to work hard. We were shown places where we could connect with a sponsor." He took a breath and slowly continued, "We saw opportunities in many cities, each more expensive than this location. We thought this location was better than a big city. Our sponsor agreed and co-signed for the lease and equipment needed to open the doors. We achieved early success with help from locals like Mr. Hayes. We are indebted to our sponsor for having this business."

"I see. How did you come to know such a generous sponsor? Is this person a relative or friend of the family?" asked Johnson.

Straightening and sounding more in control, Mal-chin replied, "Suh, the lunch crowd you sent away is creating a problem. We need customers daily to meet our payment requirements. Why are we being interrogated? Are we being arrested?"

Andrews stepped closer to the narrow counter barely separating him from the two men, and demanded, "We want to know how come you located a nice deli business close to several military installations. Then, why did you get close to one important project manager at a major manufacturer? So chummy that you make certain Mr. Hayes received a special daily coffee laced with poison."

Kamal shrugged at the owners.

The major held a clear bag containing a disposable cup. "Our engineer purchased a latte to go a week ago. This cup and its residue contents were matched to the one recovered from Mr. Hayes' crash-landed airplane, which tested positive for arsenic. Kamal here stated that he often delivered these special lattes as a favor to you. You even went so far as to deliver his final coffee in time for his last flight."

"Mr. Hayes crashed," whimpered Jun.

"Yes. And I want to know why you were poisoning him with your coffee."

Jun's tears filled his eyes. "We were ordered to. They'll kill our families if we don't."

Mal-chin backhanded Jun. "Quiet. They won't believe us. They all think we lie."

Jun nodded and quietly sobbed.

"Did Kamal know you were poisoning our engineer?" he demanded with a commanding tone.

Mal-chin slowly rolled his head back and forth. His shoulders slumped dejectedly. "No, he was being used. We cannot leave our business often if we want to make our weekly payments on time."

Kamal closed his eyes and drew a ragged, relieved breath.

Andrews interjected, "Is the benefactor who helped you establish this deli, the same one who demanded the daily poisoning of Mr. Hayes? Was anyone else getting your special lattes?"

"Only Mr. Hayes. We are two Koreans trying to make a living in America, so we can send for our families," insisted Mal-chin, his chin jutting out nearly defiantly. "You don't know how difficult it is to make ends meet and save. We work around the clock."

Major Johnson nodded sympathetically before setting his briefcase on the counter and releasing the latches. He retrieved a folder and withdrew two photographs. He flipped them over and pushed them toward the men.

The stunned expressions of both men spoke volumes.

The major calmly stated, "Your story might have worked if we didn't have excellent intelligence services. Our resources had no trouble uncovering these pictures of you in your military uniforms. The North Korean Special Operations Force is the branch in which you serve. The insignias and medals identify you as cyber warfare specialists."

Both men slowly closed their eyes, groaning in unison.

Andrews, obviously at the end of his patience, demanded, "The name of your sponsor or handler, NOW."

Last night, frustrated at the lack of additional information gathered from Mal-chin and Jun, Agent Andrews had the pair transported to the local jail. They were charged with conspiracy, espionage, and immigration violations. Their hearing was scheduled for this morning at the U.S. District Court for the Northern District of Texas. Agent Andrews was waiting for the data from Mal-chin's cell phone.

Meanwhile, he headed to Major Johnson's office to update him on the current status of the suspects. Upon arrival, Drake was on the phone. He waved the agent through to his boss's office.

"Good morning, Major. Our illegal immigrants will appear before the district judge this morning. The charges are such that the prosecutor has requested that no bail be offered. Data downloads from the phone will be shared on the secure Dropbox when the team finishes the extraction."

"Excellent, Andrews," said the major with a frown. "I hoped we could get the name of the handler, but since they had not met in person, that does make it problematic. Kamal will arrive soon to see if he can provide any more thoughts on this mess."

"I am glad Lockheed's overall vetting process for new hires is thorough. Kamal appears to be a hardworking individual who wants to uncover the truth. Everything on this guy checks out. I would like to see if—"

Major Johnson's intercom interrupted the conversation. "Sir, Kamal, from our IT department, is here and says he has an appointment."

"Yes, Drake, send him in, please."

Kamal appeared confident as he strode into the room, nodding to each of the gentlemen. "Major, I arrived as soon as I finished with your request," he said with a wry smile. "I found a couple of interesting entries in the access logs. Three of the transactions I confirmed were recorded as using my ID, but I did not make them." He handed over the copies of the data logs and a thumb drive.

"Let's take a seat at my table and review these in detail, Kamal."

The two men looked at the paper copies for several minutes.

"How do you know these logins aren't yours?" asked the major.

"Sir, I was taught to secure my equipment before leaving the building. It is always locked in my IT-assigned space before I go. This includes lunch off-property. The cabinet I use is behind a keypad that must be altered every Monday morning. To complete any Lockheed Martin virtual private network or VPN login, I'd be assigned an imaged laptop to run the proper protocols from outside the facility." Kamal traced the digital journey of the entry point with his finger. "Additionally, look at where the trail leads after the login."

"Who in the building has that digital location address?"

Kamal rifled through to the last page in the stack of procedures. "The person who works with that IP address is Mike Hayes, sir."

"So, the trail after login goes to his on-site network storage space, then leaves."

"Yes, but the time inside there varies from two to five minutes." Kamal grinned. "Gentlemen, after this third attempt—" his finger indicated the spot— "my manager disabled Mr. Hayes' login because he noticed something was wrong. The originating address of the login was not assigned to any staff member. Our recently optimized AI-enhanced security defense program locked Mr. Hayes' account. I was told to lock Mike's PC as a precaution. When I informed him, he got mad. I believe you can verify the time back to these timestamped reports of Mr. Hayes taking some leave."

Andrews was unconvinced. "If it wasn't you, how the hell did your credentials get grabbed for the remote access?"

Kamal nodded. "That bothered me as well, sir. The badges we carry have a snippet of the security protocol and our user IDs embedded in them. A determined hacker could use near-field communications to copy the information without alerting the target. It's akin to contactless credit card hacking, called skimming. It can be accomplished several feet from the target and is increasingly prevalent."

"Are you suggesting someone with an understanding of this facility's badge-in process targeted you for the silent lift of your credentials?" asked Major Johnson, appearing slightly shaken.

"I am, sir."

Andrews shook his head. "Then…this person used your user ID to go on a shopping spree inside our defense network." He rubbed his chin, concerned. "Who would understand the security protocol well enough to want to frame you, while trying to pirate our latest stealth technology?"

The major mused, "In my experience, it's usually someone you know with an axe to grind. That narrows the field of suspects. Andrews, I need details of employees who have left employment here within the last six months. From this list, Kamal, you must identify individuals who would have had access to the high-security details. Everything we've seen on Hayes demonstrates that no one outside of work would have a frosty fricking clue of what he's working on."

Agent Andrews nodded and placed the call to the head of Human Resources.

CHAPTER 44

Biscuits and Gossip

The morning was barely underway as Lily Greenly smiled with the finishing touches of her watering effort. She announced to the riotous flowers she showered, "Okay, plants, do that flora and fauna thing that keeps people coming to my Flower Bed & Breakfast for heavenly getaways and great home-style cooking."

Her teenage helper, Renata, hollered from the kitchen, "Lily, the food caravan arrived early. Need help, please."

Lily coiled the hose, hiding it in the colorful ceramic pot, and wiped her hands dry on her apron. She scooted into the kitchen through the back door. "Now, child, there's no need to fret about the folks coming in to eat. We cook on demand. Start them off with coffee and juice. Easy, right?" Last month, they celebrated the teen's first anniversary of working part-time, but she didn't like facing the public side. "Do you want to take the orders, or would you rather I do?"

Renata's Hispanic features were usually masked, but her grasp of the obvious, shown by rolling her eyes, meant Lily's questions sounded sarcastic. "Ms. Lily," she deadpanned, "if we don't cook in advance, why is my morning assignment when I arrive to fry the bacon, sausage, and hash browns before our customers get here? We have two vats of coffee being warmed with burners. Juice is next to them on the sideboard in the dining room. The biscuits are ready to come out of the oven."

Lily studied Renata for a moment and then giggled for a few seconds. "Why, Renata, I think you've adopted my smart-ass attitude. I remember when you first started, you only said, 'yes, ma'am.'" Lily sighed heavily. "You're gonna make a great woman." Lily partially covered her mouth like doing a side whisper in a play, "Probably by the middle of next week unless I miss my guess."

Renata smirked.

"I'll check on our customer to see if someone wants a couple of scoops of sarcasm on the side," said Lily. No one was waiting in the foyer, but a thirty-something gentleman with broad shoulders, wearing nice jeans, a western shirt, and polished cowboy boots, entered. He stood a moment inspecting the interior. Then inhaled the aromas and grinned with pleasure.

"Excuse me, young man, may I help you?" She bent her head to catch his eyes, realizing he was slightly taller than Tommy, one of her regular customers. "Hon, they grow 'em big where you come from. I'm Lily."

With a slight bow of his head, the man said, "Nice to meet you, ma'am. My name is Hank. They tell me that the two best places in Magnolia Bluff to feed a hungry boy breakfast are either Harry's Diner or Lily's Flower B&B. I was also told that if you want local hometown gossip and chatter, Flower is the preferred destination. Is this true?"

Lily playfully swatted his arm. "Don't just stand there with your stomach growling, Hank, mountain man. What your nose told you is only a part of the story here. Let's get you settled in so I can put some meat on your bones."

She led him to the dining area, where a few of the B&B guests had grabbed beverages and tried to catch her eye to place their orders. She handed Hank a menu after he took a table in the corner. It seemed he was a watcher as the seat he selected had a view of diners and foot traffic. Lily placed a coffee carafe and a cup on his table. She walked to the adjacent table to take their order. Turning toward Hank, he appeared pleased with his sip of coffee, licking his lips. He smiled with the menu in hand, indicating he had decided what he wanted to eat.

"Mister Mountain Man, what brings you to our fair town? Have you heard juicy things?"

"I fancy myself a writer, ma'am. Small towns seem to have unique goings-on that make for great stories. I heard last week that some bumpkin landed his plane in a field rather than on the runway at the airport. I figured it was a crop duster flown by someone with a hangover. Is that true?"

Lily laughed and winked. "How about I get your breakfast order started before I regale you with small-town tales?"

"I'd like a healthy slab of bacon and sausage, along with a half-dozen scrambled eggs. Don't forget the biscuits and gravy." He grinned.

Lily's eyes twinkled as she dashed off to take another order before assembling the plates.

Jo flumped down on the patio chair, feeling dejected. Ashley glanced her way but said nothing.

"Harrumph," groused Jo. "I don't get it, Ash. Lily at the Flower B&B has these flowers growing riotously with gorgeous blooms. In my yard, they resemble weeds. I have no idea what I'm doing wrong." She folded her arms over her chest, then added a frown.

"Jo, you don't live here year-round. I know you said the neighbor boy acts as your caretaker while you are in Brazil or traveling. I've heard that plants never behave the same when you've a substitute gardener covering for you. I know if I'm not out every day coaching my plants, they get mad. These few plants appear unhappy at the very least."

Jo huffed. "I'm going to go see Lily and ask her. You can come with me. Just don't give her too much information about what's been happening between the four of us, because it'll immediately be on the internet under the section labeled, *Lily said*."

Ashley smiled. "Great idea. It'd be good to get away from the house for a while. I'd like to see the town square and meet the folks who live here. Mike is going stir crazy complying with the doctor's orders to stay local. I am hoping JJ will keep him distracted while they finish the program's documentation."

Jo cautioned, "Those are the types of details we don't want to share with Lily, if we see her."

"I understand, Jo. Let's get ready. You might take a couple of pictures to show her." She clapped her hands, engaged in the idea. "Let's tell Mike and JJ so they won't worry."

Jo pouted. "I know what they are going to say...*argh, not all the bad guys are accounted for, so please stay here*."

Ashley smirked. "They'll fret over anything. We'll be fine. What could go wrong?"

Jo decided to dig up one of the victims from the garden. She placed it into a bright orange bucket and then loaded it into the back of Ashley's rental. "Let's get cleaned up, Ash, and take a ride to Flower. Afterwards, we can get an ice cream on the square if you want."

"You don't have to ask me twice." Ashley danced into the house.

Jo paused at JJ's office. The guys were in the process of reviewing something. "Honey, I have a problem with some of the plants in our garden. I dug one up to take to Lily for her evaluation. We're going to head over to Flower; the late breakfast and early lunch crowd will be thinning by the time we arrive. Then we plan to loop the square and grab an ice cream."

"I will worry since we haven't identified all the players in this mess." A few moments later, he nodded hesitantly. "However, I doubt you will be accosted in broad daylight. Text me when you get there. Which vehicle are you taking?"

"Ashley's, since the plant is in a bucket. I know you don't like dirt in the Porsche." She grinned. She rushed over and kissed his cheek. "Thanks, we wanted a diversion. It looks like you both are finishing up."

"Have fun. We'll fix supper on the barbecue later. Any preferences?"

"Whatever you guys want."

Ashley leaned into the doorway and smiled as she wiggled her fingers goodbye.

"Be careful, you two," added Mike.

"What could possibly happen?" replied Ashley with a dismissive wave of her hand.

CHAPTER 45

Too Much Information

Jo directed Ashley to the best place to park in front of the Flower B&B. She met Ashley at the back hatch. The rear opened, revealing her garden problem. She carefully retrieved the bucket holding the sad, almost flowering plant.

Ashley stuffed the keys into her purse after positioning the strap over her head. The bag rested on her hip. "Do you need help?"

"No, I have it. It's so pathetic," she complained, turning toward the entrance. Catching sight of the abundant flowers growing, she groaned, "See? See what she does. It's not fair. I've done everything Lily's done. Hers are thriving, but mine appear to be on death row. It's not right."

Grinning, Ashley replied, "I agree. Her flowers are vibrant, with delightfully subtle scents. I think you might be exaggerating a bit, though. Only four of your plants look sick. The rest are stunning."

"What if the ones that aren't so well infect the others? That's my worry." Jo stomped toward the porch stairs of the entrance. "Come on, Ash, I'll introduce you. Lily's a peach. She'll understand why I'm worried."

Jo spotted Lily clearing a table. She led Ashley through the foyer and smiled at well-fed patrons they passed. "Doesn't it smell delicious?"

"Definitely," agreed Ashley. "Maybe we should have a snack here and skip the ice cream?"

Jo chuckled and steered them toward an open table. She hefted the bucket onto one of the chairs. She sat in a seat to the left, facing Lily, who was speaking to a customer. "It looks like she's almost done with the customer. If you'll watch Oscar the plant, I'll grab a coffee for you and juice for me from the sideboard."

"Won't she think we're being rude to help ourselves? I don't want to disturb her customers. We can wait until she's free."

"Oh, Lily won't mind. She loves me and JJ."

Jo observed how Lily broke off her dialogue and rushed to the table when she stood to get their beverages.

"Hi, sweetie. Sit. What are you ladies up to this morning? Breakfast is almost over, but you know we can rustle something up for you." She eyed the lady with Jo and added, "Hi, I'm Lily. You're a pretty thing. How do you know Jo?"

"Hi, Lily. I'm Ashley. My husband, Mike, and I are visiting JJ and Jo for a few days from Pecan."

"That is some pretty country near Granbury. I've not been in a while, but their town square is almost as pretty as ours." Spotting the bucket, her expression shifted to disapproval. "Jo, hon, what's with the pot of dirt and weeds?"

Jo wanted to burst into tears, but restrained herself. "Oh, Lily, I've done everything you told me to make my garden look like yours. I think I have a black thumb, not green like yours. Help," she implored with big eyes glistening.

Lily studied Jo through a squinted eye. "Are you asking me to diagnose this plant right here and now?" Moving her hands and pulling items from her apron pocket, she added, "Jo, I don't have a biological lab in my pocket or the kitchen. If you think I'm gonna taste the soil to see what minerals are missing, try again. As cute as your orange bucket is, I don't think it belongs in my dining room, do you?"

Jo blushed, embarrassed at the scene she unwittingly created.

Before Jo could comment, Lily continued, "I've got breakfast guests needing food and gossip. I can't wait to hear yours." Lily laughed. "What can I get started for you ladies to eat?"

Jo, finding her manners missing, grimaced. "My good friend, Ashley, got tired of me grousing about the poor gardening I'm doing. She wanted to meet you. After seeing your flowers, she agreed, you're the expert. I wish she had reminded me to use my manners before barging in here. My apologies. I'll take Oscar outside and think of ways to improve my social skills."

Lily laughed uproariously. "Jo Rodreguiz. You and Ashley tell me what you'd like to eat." She reached over and plucked the handle of the bucket, lifting it. "Oscar, huh? I'll take him out the back through the kitchen. I'll bring you coffee, juice, and a plate of biscuits. Let me take care of my guests. Renata can begin the cleanup." She giggled as she walked away. "Oscar, I'm not sure if there are enough prayers for me to say to save you."

Jo glanced at the large man in the corner, who seemed to be suppressing a smile. Mortified, she clapped her head. "I'll never live this down."

Ashley reached over and patted her arm. "At least no one is laughing, except Lily." Then she snorted.

They both quietly hooted.

Tommy removed his Stetson, setting it on the only space on his file-covered desktop. He raised his eyebrows, recognizing the caller ID. "Good day, Major Johnson, this is Chief Jager."

"Chief, you're on speaker phone with Agent Andrews and me. We've arrested two suspects in Fort Worth in connection with the poisoning of Mike Hayes. Unfortunately, neither of these men matches the person from the hospital videos. It seems like we have at least a team of four people of Asian descent involved. The individuals we have detained admitted to being involved in the coffee delivery process. However, they both swear to never having met their handler, who had the poison delivered and provided instructions over cell phone conversations. They indicated the voice sounded masculine and more mechanical than natural. Andrews and I have reason to suspect a former employee may be behind some of the activity. To that end, we conducted cross-referencing with digital forensics and identified three potential persons of interest who left Lockheed within the last six months. Each had different reasons for leaving. We located two that we are bringing in for questioning. The last known address of the third was a dead end."

Andrews added, "With four individuals in custody connected to this mess, we suspect he is seeking other ways of fulfilling his agenda. It seems plausible he might take a more hands-on approach to getting stealth technology. We have no evidence to support this, just a gut instinct."

"Agent Andrews," said Tommy, "I've found more often than not that gut instinct can certainly help. Mr. Hayes, per doctor's orders, is to remain in Magnolia Bluff for another two days. Who should I be on the lookout for? Can you send me a picture and stats on the man?"

"Check your Dropbox for our secure transmission," said Johnson. "The suspect in question has the background to commit the cyberattacks we uncovered. You'll see the details in the documentation. He's a big guy, an ex-college football lineman, named Henry A. DeSoto. If he is spotted, don't spook him. We want to question him."

"Copy that, Major. Have you alerted JJ Rodriguez and Mike Hayes with these details, or should I?"

"We are setting up a conference call with them, but wanted to make you aware first, Chief."

Tommy accessed the Dropbox files on his computer, displaying the pictures on his screen. "I appreciate the heads up, gentlemen. This DeSoto fellow is a big boy, standing at six feet three inches. So he should be easy to spot." Tommy chuckled. "They do say the bigger they are, the harder they fall."

They all snickered and disconnected the call.

CHAPTER 46

Small Town Gossip

Lily chuckled as she took Oscar out through the kitchen door into the back yard where she placed the bucket on the cement step by her utility cabinet. She opened the doors, selecting the items needed. Methodically, she added some coffee grounds, a scoop of standard-mix fertilizer, a cup of water, then covered the soil with peat moss to retain the moisture.

Traipsing back into the kitchen, she washed her hands before returning to the dining area. Smiling, she picked up the cash from the table of one of her regulars. She noticed the girls finished their coffee. The plate between them was empty, so she approached. "Jo, Ashley, I have Oscar outside with his treatment in the works. Jo, why don't you show Ashley the entire garden while I finish up with my last guest?"

"Thank you for being so sweet, Lily." Jo rose and added a short hug. "Ashley, you've got to see some of the flowers in the back area. You won't believe they're real when you first spot them."

Ashley grinned. "I'm in. Lily, your coffee was superb. We need to come back for breakfast in the morning with our guys." She linked her arm with Jo's and they headed out through the kitchen.

Lily moved toward her last guest with a smile on her face.

The man looked up, matching her smile. "It seems, Miss Lily, you have great powers of healing that drive people to seek you out. In addition to providing a perfect breakfast, you're a plant doctor. Remarkable. Maybe I should do my story on you."

Lily chuckled, feeling the warmth of a blush creep up her neck. "You'd be surprised by what people bring me to help with, young man. Now tell me about your need for gossip for your magazine short story."

"I was hoping to get the inside scoop on the plane that landed several miles short of the runway. I want to interview the folks who found him in his plane, nose down in a field."

"You seem to know as much as I do. If you're hoping to get to visit the crash site or the plane, the police chief has it still cordoned off. Even the nosy neighbors can't get up close."

"What a shame."

"One of the two ladies who brought the plant for doctoring, Jo, lives adjacent to that location. She and her husband were the first responders."

"No kidding." He pulled a small pad from his pocket, scribbling a note. "Give Miss Jo this. I'll let her decide if she wants to call me and provide an exclusive interview."

"I will, Hank," she said, slipping the message into her apron pocket. "Are you ready to settle your check?"

The man rose and handed her a fifty. "Will this cover your memorable breakfast?"

"Let me get you some change."

"No need, it was worth every penny. Good luck with the plant recovery efforts."

The man sauntered out the front door, vanishing from her sight. She gathered the dishes and brought them into the kitchen. He had been a bit too generous. Hearing a vehicle, she presumed was his pulling out from the front, Lily filed his generosity away in her mind.

Jo enjoyed sharing the beautiful gardens, situated behind the B&B. "Ash, don't you love how the pathways weave through the flowers and the whimsical artwork scattered about?"

"It's genius. I love my garden, so I captured a few photos to see if I can incorporate some similar ideas."

"Jo, Ashley," called Lily, "are you girls still around?"

Jo tugged her friend's arm as she replied, "Sorry, Lily. We'll be right there." Seconds later, they made the turn at the side of the gardens and headed toward Oscar's bucket. "We got side-tracked looking at the metal artwork you've added since I was last here."

"I sponsored the Senior Art Class and purchased a few of their creations. Their colors and movement in the wind are lots of fun," Lily clarified. "Glad you like them."

"Where did you get them. I think we'd both like to add a few to our gardens."

"Certainly. Ann, your neighbor, made several of them. You might want to ask her if she has any left." Lily cocked her head. "I'm surprised she didn't let you know. Ah, well. Let's talk about Oscar, child."

Jo looked at her feet and did a side step. "I promise, I've been doing everything you told me to. I'm terrified all my plants will die."

Lily patted her arm. "They're plants, sweetie. I can provide more starters. I added some extras to the soil. I'd like to see how it does for a couple of days. If it improves, then I can give you some to add to your place, and I can also show you how to apply it if needed. I'd like to see what percentage of the garden is affected. Poor Oscar does appear sad. How many more square feet of plants look like him?"

"Four," replied Jo, not daring to face Lily with her failure.

Ash giggled and hip bumped her friend.

"Four feet square of an entire row, four feet wide. Yikes, that's a lot. Are they all together or scattered throughout the entire space?"

Jo caught Ashley giving her the evil eye. She cleared her throat. "No, Lily, four, as in four plants. They are in scattered places. This one was the easiest for me to dig out."

Lily appeared dumbstruck. "Jo, I know you worry, but some plants won't make it no matter what you do. Four out of the three hundred starters we planted isn't a problem in my book. I can give you four starters to take home, or we can wait and see how Oscar does." She laughed, unable to gain control. The silliness continued until the other two joined the merriment.

Catching her breath, Jo said, "I'm sorry to panic. But I did want to show Ash your place. And, she wanted out of the house."

"Ashley, how long have you known my girl here? I've known her going on four years, but this is a whole new side to her."

"We met almost six years ago when my husband, Mike, and I were married. Mike and JJ have known each other for almost eighteen years, right, Jo?"

"I think so. They got their pilot licenses at the same time," she clarified.

Lily smacked her thigh and pulled out the note. "My last guest today is a writer for some magazine. He said he's in town to write a story on small-town gossip. He wanted to speak to you and JJ about the plane crash."

"Oh!" She scanned the note. "I'll let JJ know when we get home. Thanks, Lily. I'll come back in a couple of days to check on Oscar, if you don't call me first."

"No problem. I need to get in there and help Renata finish up so she can get home. Where are you two troublemakers headed now?"

"Ice cream," said Ashley. "I've heard the place on the square makes it the old-fashioned way."

"Sounds like fun. Nice to meet you. You're welcome to breakfast tomorrow as well. I want to meet your man," said Lily, hugging her. Turning to Jo, she added, "You too. Your face appears a little fuller."

Jo blushed, slightly ashamed at not telling Lily about the baby. She promised herself to tell JJ they needed to return soon and tell her together. "Really? I did have two of your biscuits. They're irresistible." She embraced Lily. "We're going to walk around to Ash's SUV, which is parked out front. Talk soon."

Stopping to admire another cluster of blooms, Ashley said, "Jo, Lily's plants should be the envy of anyone trying to grow a garden. Sheesh, this is more of an arboretum than a bed and breakfast."

"That's why I brought you to see this place."

They entered the vehicle on their respective sides, closed their doors, and clicked their seatbelts into place. Ashley started the engine, hitting the air conditioning full blast.

Pulling out of the driveway, Jo remarked, "Chief Jager's here. Do you want to stop and say hi to him?"

Ashley stared at her buddy as she sarcastically replied, "I think I'll pass. I don't feel like being grilled again."

"He stood by you."

"Yes, yes, he did, and I'm grateful, but I'm ready for ice cream. Now, left or right, ma'am?"

"Turn right, Ash. Head down five blocks and take a left. We'll park by the library and walk over," Jo suggested.

Three blocks later, Jo felt the pressure from the barrel of the gun at her temple and froze.

The deep voice ordered, "Keep heading straight, Miss Ashley, I believe that's your name. Don't turn around or stop the vehicle. If you do, I'll hurt your bestie."

"Don't you dare hurt her," Ashley pleaded.

"Do what he says, Ash," said Jo with a confidence she didn't feel. She thought of the man's voice. It resembled the actor Sam Elliot's but with a wad of glue in his mouth. He didn't want to be recognized, so one or both of them must know him.

CHAPTER 47

Clash of the Players

Entering the kitchen, Lily said, "Sorry I took so long, Renata."

"No problem, Miss Lily," the teen replied. "I have everything done. Can I walk over to the ice cream place and meet some friends? I'll call Ann to pick me up there."

Lily looked around, pleased with the sparkling counters and the hum of the dishwasher. "It looks great."

"I even cleaned all the tables and the sideboard. We had a good crowd today."

"I agree." She pulled the fifty-dollar bill from her pocket. "Here, this is yours for showing initiative. Now scoot."

"Guau! Gracias, Miss Lily," Renata exclaimed, slipping into Spanish.

Starting a new pot of coffee, Lily decided to do some chores. She took off her apron, adding it to the pile of laundry. Then she rounded up the soiled napkins, towels, and other washables. Grabbing the basket, she lugged it to the commercial washing machine. It would be a solid accomplishment to finish the folding before setting the tables for dinner. Then she'd check to see if any new guests were arriving later. Finished with her chores in the utility room, she headed out the swinging door, almost hitting Tommy.

He grinned. "Lily, any coffee left?"

"Tommy Jager, if you aren't a sight for sore eyes. Of course, I've got coffee for you. Pick a seat. I'll bring you something fresh."

A couple of minutes later, she returned, setting a steaming cup next to him. She noticed that Tommy had pulled off his Stetson, placing it beside him. "I saw Jo and her friend Ashley when I pulled in." He sipped his coffee with appreciation. "Good brew, thanks. Did they have lunch here?"

Lily raised her eyebrows with a surprised look. "No, Jo had a sick plant and asked for help." She eyed his hat. "You only take your hat off for two things. I know you're not here for the first thing, so it must be for information."

Tommy suppressed a smirk. "I can't give you all the details, but I'd be grateful if you would keep a lookout for a person of interest. I have reason to believe he's headed into town. Please do not disclose my request to anyone. If you learn something, please let me know. No one can know you helped me. He's a large man, taller than I am. He's supposed to be built like a football lineman. So, hefty too."

Lily studied Tommy for a moment, then pulled out her cell phone. She pressed the button on her security app to access the video from today. Selecting the zone for the dining room, she played with fast forward until the mountain man entered. Turning the phone toward him, she hit play and paused once the man was in the frame. "Sort of like this, Tommy?"

Tommy raised his eyes with an expression of admiration and surprise. "Exactly like this." He shook his head in disbelief. "When did you see him last?"

"You just missed him. I knew there was something off about him. After Jo and Ashley arrived with their plant, they had a quick snack before I shooed them outdoors through the kitchen.

Then, all he wanted to talk about was the plane crash and its location. He wrote a note for me to hand to Jo."

"Do you have a video feed from the exterior that might show him getting into a vehicle?"

She thumbed through the app and pulled up the feed from the front camera, thankful that JJ had installed her security system last year. Turning the video toward Tommy, she hit play again, but didn't see anything specific.

"Can you send me all your video feeds to my email, Lily? I want to get out an APB."

Lily noticed his frown of annoyance as he furrowed his brow.

"Where's the note?"

"I gave it to Jo," Lily said, panic rising in her chest. "He paid for lunch with a fifty-dollar bill."

"Where is it? I might get a print."

"I gave it to Renata, who was on her way to the town square. Sorry."

Tommy reached over and squeezed her arm. "No worries. Tell me again why I don't have you on the police payroll doing detective work?"

"Do you think he'll bother the girls?"

"Let me get this information on the airways. Call me if he returns."

CHAPTER 48

Somewhere to Meet

"Pull into the deserted parking lot coming up on the right," the man demanded, keeping the weapon trained on Jo.

Jo's cell sounded with an incoming call.

"Lift your phone and show me the screen," he stated.

"It's my husband. I was supposed to check in when we headed to the ice cream store. He'll be worried if I don't answer, or at least reply."

"Pull over and park, Miss Ashley. Keep your eyes facing forward and your mouth shut," he said, feeling in total control. "Miss Jo, I want you to text your husband the following text. I will watch every keystroke. Don't make any deviations."

Jo nodded and held up her phone so she could type as he spoke. Ashley whimpered.

"Be quiet. This is your last warning, Miss Ashley," he snarled. The barrel tapped against Jo's head, and she flinched, but remained silent. "What do you call your husband?"

"JJ."

"All the time?"

"Yes."

"Fine. Type, JJ, I am busy with Ashley and can't speak now. I'll let you know when we are finished and headed home."

Jo tilted the screen to show him.

"Good. Do you think he will respond to this?"

Jo read the screen. "No."

"Press Send." He prodded Ashley with the revolver on her temple, making her jump. "I didn't say you could move. Where is your husband?"

"I don't know," Ash said with fear in her tone. "Probably with JJ."

"Do you think he'd trade you and your friend for his laptop?"

"I don't know," she whined.

Jo quietly said, "I bet he would. Why do you want his laptop?"

"That is none of your concern, little lady. Miss Ashley, start up the engine and head toward the first right turn."

"No one uses that road anymore," said Jo.

"Good to know," he said. "Drive nice and slow."

Tommy rushed to his squad car and called in the information on the vehicle, along with the suspect's details. He told them to issue a countywide APB. Completing that chore, he called JJ. "Hey, I have some bad information. Can I send it to your Dropbox from my phone?"

JJ said, "Yes. Use the number 40621 as a message code. The SMS transmission is secure to that number. Does it have to do with Mike's case?"

"Yep."

"Let me pull you into this conference call with the major and Agent Andrews. He's briefing us on the latest he has," said JJ. "He filled in a missing piece with Mike by identifying an ex-employee named Henry A. DeSoto. Mike told us the guy was dismissed for cause. He worked in the IT department."

JJ conferenced Tommy into the call, then pulled up the video feeds.

"Thanks, JJ. Gentlemen, this suspect showed up at the Flower B&B and had a late breakfast. The owner, Lily, captured a video of him in the dining room and parking lot. He introduced himself to Lily as Hank, without providing a last name. I issued an APB on his vehicle."

Mike interjected, "I forgot he preferred going by Hank. Hell, I don't recall much of anything about him from college."

"That's great news," said Agent Andrews. "I'll send some men to assist. The team should arrive within the hour."

"Thanks. I appreciate the support," said Tommy. "Lily said he questioned her about the plane crash and where it was located. She told him he had to get permission from me to access it because it was still roped off." He took a deep breath before he continued. "Jo and Ashley showed up at Lily's asking for plant help. Lily directed them outside, but the suspect heard the girls talking. He later asked Lily about them as well while they were out back."

JJ groused, "Are you saying he saw the girls? Did he leave with them?"

"No, look at the video. It shows him leaving in his vehicle."

"Crap, Tommy. I kept running the video forward, looking for when the girls were leaving. He must have returned on foot. The tape shows he slipped into the back of Ashley's rental. The girls got into the vehicle a while later, but it doesn't appear they saw him because they were busy talking." JJ smacked the table with his hand. "Let me call her to see if she picks up the call. I should be able to get a signal on her location." JJ called Jo's cell, and it rolled to voicemail. "No, no, no. Call me back, honey," he pleaded.

"Did you get a location signal? My deputies are out in force, if you can tell me where to send them."

"Andrews, get your teams in the area now," insisted the major.

"On it, sir."

"I've got the location and am tracking the coordinates. I'll push the journey visual to all your cell—. Wait, I just received a text from her. The text came from her phone. But I don't think she typed it. The content is not like anything she'd usually say. He better not have hurt her or Ashley. Mike, please connect to this bridge from your cell phone. We're going to head toward her location."

"JJ, you're not the law," stated Tommy firmly.

"You're right. But I am the husband. I will find her."

"You need to stay right there, cowboy," insisted Tommy. "If you have a way to identify her location, then I suspect you can also see if she's moving?"

"I can. That's how I plan to intercept her position."

"That's a poor idea, and you know it," echoed Andrews. "You can direct a great deal from your location. I can convey it to my team."

JJ slapped the table, then stood and started pacing. "Tommy, I can't sit here and do nothing."

"I agree, but I've known you to have lots of digital tricks up your sleeve," soothed Tommy. "What else can you do to get us additional information? I wish we had eyes on them or a drone."

"I don't have a drone here, but I do have some thoughts. I have a special program on Jo's phone. It might give us more." JJ took a breath. "I'll stay here for the time being."

"Come and sit, JJ," Mike suggested. "Let's work on a plan before we react. That approach has never worked for us."

CHAPTER 49

Careful What You Wish For

Jo's mind raced to review their options as DeSoto directed Ashley toward an undeveloped area. Spotting a familiar landmark, she recalled it was reasonably close to Flower B&B. Traffic rarely traveled on this part of the roadway unless someone was lost.

Ashley stuttered, "Are you the person who's been blackmailing with texts and calls?"

"I guess you're smarter than I thought." He snorted, then pushed the barrel of his revolver into her neck.

Ashley grimaced. Jo prayed her friend would remain calm.

"Pull up close to that SUV parked near the corner and stop." Ashley complied without a word.

"Put the vehicle in park. Pull out your cell phone. Carefully, MISS Ash Ley. Don't try anything, or your friend here will be first. You don't want another failure, do you?" he snickered. "When I finish your instructions, you will call your husband. You're to tell him you will be there shortly to pick up his laptop. When you have it, you will return here immediately. No speeding. No, trying to get attention from anyone you pass either way. Do you understand?"

She nodded with a sniffle.

"Put a pin drop on your location so you won't get lost returning."

She pushed the keypad and showed him.

Jo hoped JJ would be able to do something. Frustrated, she flexed her fingers, cataloguing what she knew. Through her peripheral vision, he seemed like a large man, but she couldn't identify him. Not only was he masking his voice, but he also wore a hoodie. Half his face was hidden behind a bandana.

He nodded. "Good. Suck it up, buttercup. You're going to drive alone to Jo's house to pick up the PC and bring it back to me here. You fail to do that, Miss Jo dies. I will hunt you down and make you pay. If you bring the police back, Miss Jo dies. Plus, the police you bring die. Then I'll find you."

Jo noticed Ashley's fingers shaking on the steering wheel. She said a silent prayer to give her friend strength. *What a mess* echoed through her mind. The guy was so hateful.

He stated, "Bring me the PC with no extra trouble. This ends today. Call him, now!"

Ashley was shaking so much that Jo worried she might not be able to comply.

Ashley fumbled with her phone for a few seconds, then she sucked in a deep breath. The tones indicated she'd placed a call. The ringing meant it was on speaker. Jo sensed the feigned cheerful tone when Ashley said, "Hey, Mike. It's been a busy day with Jo. I'm going to arrive at the house in a little bit. I must get your laptop. Meet me at the kitchen door with it, please. I'll deliver it, then return with Jo. No questions or wasted time; no police, please."

"Yes, Ashley, I understand."

Disconnecting the call, she drew a ragged breath. "Do I go now?"

"No," DeSoto barked. "Roll down all the windows."

The revolver stabbed Jo's neck again, making her tremble.

Warm air burst into the cab. The back door opened on her side, then hers opened, too.

"Miss Jo, get out, and stand still," he demanded. "Don't turn around. When I tell you to go, you will close the door, look straight ahead, and walk toward the other vehicle. Let yourself into the passenger side and close the door. If you try to run, Miss Ashley is dead. Do you understand?"

Jo whispered, "Yes." She wondered if she'd have enough time before he got there to call JJ or maybe text.

Loudly enough for Jo to hear, he said. "Ashley, repeat your instructions."

Ashley managed an unsteady response, "I must go to Jo's house and return with Mike's PC. No police. No extra discussion."

"Correct. You have nine minutes to get there and nine minutes to get back. Any longer and you will find a Miss Jo corpse."

JJ scowled from his mounting fury. He quickly typed into his laptop chat window, thankful no one else could see.

> ICABOD, continue listening mode. Update the location information as it changes and transmit it to everyone.

> Program continuing. Location static, JJ. Tommy is close to the target, but he told his team to stay hidden.

> Add a timer to the conference call screen so we can track Ashley's travel in seconds.

> Done.

After hearing Ashley's statement, everyone stared into their respective screens.

Mike shifted in his chair. "I can't fathom how scared she must be. What more can we do, JJ?"

"I need to get the laptop ready to go."

The major asked, "Mike, you and JJ have already uploaded all the RadHalCaT to the facility Dropbox. Wipe the drive and give him the PC."

JJ countered, "I think that's a mistake, Major. A potential lost opportunity. Your notes indicated that the hacker had previously accessed portions of Mike's program files. I think it would be better to leave the code intact, with perhaps some amazing modifications designed especially for him. He's smart enough to check it before releasing the women. I want him to feel success in his belly before we flip the table and he hurls. I owe him big time for threatening my wife and the wife of my best friend. He may have unwittingly opened the whole can of Whoop Ass, but he gets it all. If he thinks it's solid, he'll upload it without any delays, which is exactly what I want."

Andrews excitedly shouted, visibly angry on the screen. "Are you insane? Those robbing bastards can't have—"

The major touched Andrews, who paused his tirade.

"JJ," said Major Johnson, "what kind of surprise do you have in mind?"

Grinning, JJ announced, "I'm going to simulate a low-level reboot of Mike's PC, with the addition of a poisonous code my team built for a Russian blackmailer from last year." Texting a quick note to ICABOD, he closed the text box and shared his screen. "As this reboot is done, the poisonous code is disguised to run in the background alongside the RadHalCaT application. As soon as it is recompiled for Korean and/or Chinese systems, it will programmatically propagate in maximum digital damage mode." He stopped sharing the screen and sent a text.

> ICABOD, did you finish compiling
> the modification to the laptop?

> Yes, JJ. It is done. Anything else?

Keep track of Jo.

The major grinned. "I like your idea. There is no way they will be able to use the stealth application?"

"Correct. The changes are completed. It is ready to go, sir." JJ smiled mischievously, sensing a surge of confidence at having a solid plan to interrupt the evil scheme. "Gentlemen, let's listen in on the one-way conversation from Jo's phone. Mike, you had better be standing outside to hand your PC to Ashley. Based on the screen time, she should arrive in under three minutes. Do not tell her anything that will worry her more than I suspect she already is."

"I won't. But I'm going to hug her and whisper I love her," Mike promised.

JJ nodded in agreement. "Tommy, this is going to be the toughest on you. Are you close enough to intercede if needed, but hidden so he doesn't react?"

"We're good, JJ. My guys are spread out to intercept him, no matter what direction he takes out of town. We have eyes on the vehicle. I can see Jo sitting on one side. She looks as stoic as ever."

"Thanks. Once he has the laptop, I believe he'll let the girls go. He doesn't want a statewide manhunt. However, I don't think Ashley will be able to drive back, so can a deputy transport her car? Or Mike and I will head that way?"

"No problem, JJ," replied Tommy.

"Gentlemen," JJ began with a serious expression, "if he looks like he's going to hurt them, or if we hear anything from Jo's phone that makes me think he will injure them, I will activate a sequence on her phone. It will give you roughly six minutes to reach them, Tommy."

Mike questioned, "What the hell are you planning with my wife, JJ?"

Both the men in Fort Worth leaned forward, seeming interested in the response.

"It's a sound program that will force all of them to grab their ears. It will keep him from pulling any trigger. No permanent damage, Mike. Would I hurt, Jo? Please make certain you cuff him first and save the laptop. If he can't upload it, perhaps I can determine a way to do that."

"My team understands," replied Tommy.

"If he does as I expect, his next move will be to get somewhere to upload the data to his buyers. He wants a payday, I suspect. This is exactly what we need him to do."

Tommy pushed back his hat, stared into his screen, and sighed, "I'm glad you're on our side."

JJ chuckled. "Once the buyers get the impossible code infecting their systems, they will extract revenge on DeSoto by cutting him into pieces before killing him."

CHAPTER 50

How Was Your Day?

In the side mirror, Jo observed Ashley pulling in behind the vehicle. The engine went quiet. Ashley exited with the PC in her hand, holding it over her head. A few feet from the car, she came to a stop.

DeSoto growled, "Open your door. Remain seated, but motion for her to approach. As she is near your door, remind her to look straight ahead. I would hate to kill you both."

Jo did as he requested. Ashley headed toward her side of the vehicle, now carrying the laptop beside her.

"Keep your eyes focused right, Ashley," said Jo.

Ashley handed over the device, left her hand extended.

Jo passed the laptop to the man. "We've done everything you've asked. I want to get out now."

"No. Not yet. This feels too easy. Both of you wait right where you are. I need to verify that this machine contains the missing code I need to complete the package. If it doesn't, you're both dead."

It seemed like an eternity to boot up the machine. The man replied with a giddy voice as he announced, "Ha! It's all there. Come to papa." He shut down the machine and ordered, "Give me both your phones. I wouldn't want you to get brave and call the cops."

Jo passed them over without a word.

"Get into that rental of hers. Sit there for thirty minutes," he ordered. "I need to find an open Wi-Fi café to complete the upload. There should be a gas station with a restaurant on the highway."

Jo got out and gently closed the door, not wanting to spook the jerk. She glanced everywhere to see if JJ was in sight. Not sensing him, she looped her arm through Ashley's. "Let's take one step at a time. We don't want to cause him to get nervous."

As his vehicle started up, Jo stepped onto the curb and continued moving toward the rental vehicle. Ashley's steps faltered. "You did well to get there and return. Real good, my friend. However, I think you should pass me the keys."

"Oh, Jo, do you think Mike will be mad about his laptop?"

"JJ would have thought of something. Don't worry."

Ashley nodded. "Mike said he loved me and hugged me. When I told him everything but the guy's name at your house, I thought we might be okay. I wasn't convinced until I saw him. I won't hide much from him anymore. And, not for long, that's for sure."

"Great idea. Once you and I get some food along with a short nap, you can do that." The vehicle pulled away. "We're going to make it because of your bravery, my friend."

Ashley appeared pale as they reached the passenger door. Jo helped her in and secured the seatbelt. "Thanks, I'm thirsty. We'll swing by Lily's for some water. It's close."

Ashley closed her eyes and sighed. "Good. Are you feeling all right?"

"I am now." Chuckling, Jo scooted to the other side and entered. She started the vehicle and turned on the air conditioning.

Checking the mirrors to see if it was enough time to risk heading out, she spotted an ambulance pulling up behind them.

Jo grumbled, "I hope you and Mike will return when it's a little less thrilling in Magnolia Bluff. The rescue team arrived behind us. I bet we can get water."

"We'll return. How else will our babies get to play together?" Ashley giggled. "I couldn't let you have all the fun."

Jo turned her head, seeing that Ashley had her eyes closed, but a sly smile. "Does Mike know?"

Her friend shook her head.

"Well," Jo snickered, "I won't tell until you say to."

A knock on the window startled her. She turned. Her face burst into a smile when she saw Tommy. She rolled down the window.

"How was the ice cream, Jo?"

"We didn't get any. But we sure could use some water."

"Hey guys," Tommy shouted to the EMT team, "bring a couple of bottles of water with you. I think these ladies can sit in their vehicle while you check them."

Jo provided a grateful yet weary grin. "I want to borrow your phone and call JJ."

Tommy handed her his cell. "You are already connected, Jo. Please don't hang up."

She nodded, "Hi, honey. We're both fine. He's masking his voice and is wearing a bandana. We're tired and thirsty now that the adrenaline is ebbing. The EMTs are going to examine us. I don't feel like driving, though."

"I'm so glad you're safe. Thank you for doing everything right. Tommy, if the EMTs say they're good to go, can you get one of your deputies to bring them home?"

"No problem, JJ. I need to get on the road to find this guy, but I'll have Deputy Mars bring them back."

Jo added, "JJ, he has both Ashley's and my phone, along with the laptop."

JJ let loose a low whistle. "Well done, sweetheart. Tommy, we're tracking him. He's heading down the main highway."

CHAPTER 51

Things Going My Way

JJ looked forward to purchasing a new phone and case for Jo. He chuckled while everyone in the video meeting listened to Hank cautioning himself. "Dude, don't go so fast that the police decide to pull you over for a ticket. You're nearly home free. No one knows any of the details about what you're driving. Get onto the Interstate, find a good-sized truck stop with Wi-Fi, and gas up."

The voice coming over Jo's phone sounded different. JJ scrunched his face, wondering why the change.

"Based on his direction, I think I know where he's headed. I'll get two guys to that location asap," said Tommy.

Andrews appeared nervous. A thumbs-up signal appeared from JJ. "He's likely looking for a spot. There is faint road noise coming across the channel."

"I have a car following at a discrete distance," offered Tommy.

Twenty minutes later, Hank mumbled again. "I thought there was one not too far down this road. Yep, there it is." The volume of the voice increased, "It's time for my payday."

"He has no idea," promised a grinning Andrews.

JJ reported, "The triangulation on the location of Jo's phone shows it stopped inside the Georgetown city limits. There's a large fueling station. During my search of the establishment, I noticed that it has a fairly extensive menu in a dining area, offers showers,

225

provides internet access, and fuel. Based on the phone's geo-location, as soon as he boots up the PC, I can easily pinpoint the Wi-Fi location. I disabled the need to enter a password, so he'll connect immediately. He'll locate his designated secure network before he transfers the code. Are your men in place, Tommy?"

"Sure are."

Andrews anxiously asked, "How much time do we have? I've got men closing in on the location. They're about eighteen minutes out. Tommy, where are you?"

Tommy responded, "JJ, I'm following your directions. I'll have my vehicle parked close to the entrance in five minutes; it's unmarked, so he won't get jumpy. A pair of my guys are inside incognito, having coffee in a rear booth. They're aware he is armed with at least one handgun, from what Jo said. When my men checked in a few minutes ago, they said it's between normal meal crowds, according to their waitress, which means the foot traffic will mostly consist of in-and-out folks. Andrews, remind your team the man is dangerous."

JJ added, "He'll be focused on getting logged in to the network, then to their assigned secure site to complete the transfer of files. His situational awareness will likely be minimized due to the limited foot traffic. It's going to take him some time. I wouldn't be surprised if he orders something to eat, because he won't be able to establish a direct connection to a country like North Korea or China. I would expect his target to be a secure Dropbox. He will call them to retrieve the data after all the files are loaded. We need to have patience while he delivers our surprise package."

Tommy cautioned, "JJ, I don't want to give him too much time because his situational awareness might awaken while he is sipping coffee, waiting for the call back."

"Tommy, your team inside is a great wild card. I am adding them to this call. I accessed his IP address and the Wi-Fi header information; I will be able to alert everyone when the data stream upload is complete. Then you and Andrews can do your thing. From my side, we don't care if they speak to him or not."

Major Johnson asked, "Won't his contact be suspicious if DeSoto doesn't answer? At the very least, DeSoto needs to speak to them to demand his funds and provide payment instructions, unless that arrangement was already in place. We don't have any evidence on that, though Andrews has received a judge's signature to access his bank records."

JJ considered the concerns for a few heartbeats, then his fingers flew across his keyboard.

ICABOD, I need a synthesized voice for Hank A. DeSoto. I want to impersonate him when the North Koreans call him back.

Anticipating the need, JJ. It is available for your use.

JJ was pleased. "Gentlemen, I have a synthetic DeSoto voice we can use during the call. I will let you know when the upload is complete."

Tommy pulled his unmarked vehicle into the truck stop and parked behind a couple of supply trucks near the back entrance. He inserted his earbuds and slipped his phone into his uniform shirt pocket before he added his Stetson. "Hey, guys, I've arrived." He sauntered around the building. "I'm going to enter through the side door like my guys suggested."

The chief opened the entry, walking into the cooled air and country music. The organized shelves were stacked with everything a traveler could need, along with a host of Texas-themed souvenirs. Locally made jerky sat at the front, along with rows of candy, a few hanging baskets of fresh fruit, and two walls of coolers containing a range of beverages, from water to beer and wine. Gigantic restroom signs were in the corner between them. He headed toward the expansive dining room filled with fifteen or so booths. He was relieved to see most were empty.

Suddenly, Deputy Stevens' voice boomed in his earbud. "Tommy, the food here is excellent. Everyone has piping hot eats. I like it not being too crowded, we can hear ourselves think."

"DeSoto made his connection to the Wi-Fi and is linking to his target endpoint. It should be two or three minutes before he starts uploading. He will likely be watching the screen while drinking his coffee," JJ interjected. "I like your way of providing us the details, Stevens. I suspect it looks like you and your table-mate are having a conversation."

Stevens added, "You bet." He chuckled. "I'm so hungry. I want to order a sandwich like the one that guy got a minute ago, Tommy. It has a bun that looks to be nearly a foot long, filled with a mess of meat and vegetables. You need both hands to enjoy that baby."

JJ added, "Data transmission is underway. We've pinpointed the location of the server receiving the information. I'm sending it to your team, Andrews."

Tommy headed to the counter, glancing around the dining area. He saw his men, with Stevens's back toward the door. The pair appeared immersed in conversation. A couple of booths down, two teens were on their phones, laughing. Their target was sitting at the table in the back corner.

"May I help you, officer?" said a seasoned waitress with a no-nonsense tone.

"Yes, ma'am. It's been a quiet day. I'm nearly off my shift." He tilted his hat back a touch. "I want a coffee to go, please. Black and room for cream." He smiled at her. From the corner of his eye, he noticed their target in the corner looked up for a second. He must have decided he wasn't being threatened by a cop ordering coffee. The man was large, even when seated. His big hands were wrapped around the long Italian-style bun. He took a massive bite as his eyes focused on the screen. "I'd like a piece of that peach pie to go, too," Tommy said to the waitress.

"Sure thing. It won't be too long. I need to start a new pot of coffee."

The teens approached the cash register area.

"No worries, you take your time. Do you mind if I grab a seat while I wait?"

"Of course, help yourself. We aren't busy, as you can see." Her hands waved out to the empty booths as she replied. She laughed and went to attend to the paying customers.

Tommy relaxed his stance and turned his head away while he quietly said, "I can get to him in seconds. We have him boxed in perfectly."

Andrews hastily added, "My men are ready to enter. They have secured the parking lot, so no one else will be able to enter. You taking a seat with him is a good distraction. However, I'd like my team to arrest him due to the federal charges. We are indebted to you and for the presence of your team if there is an issue."

JJ announced, "Tommy, the upload is complete."

Grinning, Tommy sauntered over and plopped down across from DeSoto. "You know, Hank, Lily's gonna be most indignant when she hears she didn't feed you enough at breakfast."

DeSoto slammed the laptop lid. He quickly reached toward his side.

"Stop!" Tommy insisted with his gun leveled at the man. "Put your hands flat on the table."

Andrew's two agents rushed to either side of him, one with his weapon drawn, the other relieved the suspect of his gun.

"You're under arrest, Henry DeSoto," the agent stated, helping the man stand.

Tommy grinned as they read him his rights and an extensive list of charges. DeSoto's arms were pulled back and cuffed. Tommy reached over and removed the phones from the top pockets of his shirt, smirking.

Red with anger, DeSoto lashed out, but Tommy confidently rapped him atop his head with his semi-auto 9mm Glock, abruptly ending the useless tirade. The two agents struggled to usher the uncooperative former lineman to their vehicle. Stevens and Tommy's other deputy made the assist to get the suspect to the unmarked federal transport. Tommy tipped his hat to the waitress. "I'll be right back, ma'am."

The agents ignored the protesting suspect and shut the door. Tommy stated, "One bad guy loaded. The feds have his weapons, cell phone, and laptop. All we need is…"

Andrew's agent handed over DeSoto's cell phone, alive with an incoming call to Tommy. "JJ, the call is here, let me step to the side to answer it. I'll shift my earbuds to my mobile phone speaker, and you can work your magic."

Executing the plan flawlessly, in DeSoto's voice, JJ arranged for the payment transfer to go to DeSoto's bank account, which he had the caller verbally verify for security purposes. The call disconnected after a simple *Thank you.*

CHAPTER 52

No Kidding

JJ looked across the faces of those on the conference bridge. Tommy had reconnected with his screen from his patrol car, making him almost jealous as he popped a bite of peach pie into his mouth.

"Gentlemen, I'm sure we will have further details on this later, but I'd like to wrap up this call as my wife and Ashley are in the driveway almost to the house. I believe we can agree that today was a good one for our country."

Andrews said, "I'll feel better once we hear that the surprise package has detonated. Then we can celebrate the capture and await the prosecution of Henry Allen DeSoto."

The major nodded. "Agreed." Then he stated, "I'm certain, based on your well-placed code, we'll get the results over the airways and pass them along. With that said, JJ, I hope you realize the lives your actions have saved. That technology in the wrong hands could have compromised our military power. I thank you. Don't be surprised if you hear additional comments of gratitude from higher-ups, as I suspect you will."

JJ chuckled. "Go ahead and get that bubbly when we disconnect, Agent Andrews. My team has just received this communiqué from the Chinese warfare specialists. The Chinese have disabled all communications and digital connections from DPRK because of what may be a computer virus that has crippled the North Korean military systems. Oh dear." JJ raised his hand to his face and added a cheeky grin. "It appears that some of their weapon systems have begun to self-destruct. The Chinese military is on high alert."

The major guffawed for a moment. "We'll need to confirm through our normal channels, but thanks for the heads-up, Mr. Rodreguiz."

Mike and JJ disconnected the call. They stood and turned to find Jo looking confused, facing a stunned Ashley.

Ashley mumbled, "Oh my God, Henry Allen DeSoto?"

Ashley shook her head and placed one hand out to avoid an embrace from Mike. "I want everyone to sit. I want to share the truth I've withheld for far too long. I believed I could outrun a horrible past, yet it almost got us killed."

Jo said, "We're not having a long conversation without food and beverage, Ash. Give JJ and me a few minutes to put together something we can easily eat."

Ashley wanted to thank her friend as she pulled JJ along to help her. Not looking at Mike, she took a seat and folded her hands.

Jo carried in a plate with fruit, cheeses, and meats in one hand and a basket of bread and rolls in the other, which she set in the center of the table. JJ added glasses, plates, and silverware, which Mike distributed to each place before taking his seat.

JJ announced, "If we are getting all the backstory, then I believe we each need our favorite adult beverage so we can cheer the good guys and boo the bad."

"I'd prefer tea, JJ," said Ashley in an even voice.

Focusing on her, he provided a glass of tea. "In my digging for background information, I uncovered the leverage Hank had over you, Ash. He was not only threatening Mike's life, but also the child you gave up for adoption, your first year in college."

Ashley's eyes filled, but she inhaled to grab at the last of her composure. "It was him. He told me his name was Allen. He invited me to a frat party where he put something in my wine. I suspect it was what they call a roofie. Then he raped me and left me naked on one of the beds. I was stupid for not reporting it. I could only have the baby and find what I hoped would be good parents. I was so ashamed."

Mike's mouth gaped wide with astonishment. Ashley looked away.

JJ continued, "The Lockheed security people first believed it was Mike running a covert operation selling national secrets. They dug further and found DeSoto was the shady one. The irony of the situation was that Mike helped DeSoto get a job at Lockheed by using their common college background as a lever, even though Mike didn't remember knowing the guy in college. His education checked out, though his grades were nowhere near as good as yours, Mike. I suspect he was jealous of your success. He was only made second-string on the football team, too." JJ cleared his throat and continued, "DeSoto worked in the IT department, gaining visibility into who was assigned to which project. He discovered what program Mike was responsible for and decided to win for a change. From there, I believe he worked on a plan to sell the information to the Chinese, who used the DPRK as their intermediary for communication and data exchange. He stayed employed long enough to learn how the security process worked. I found evidence of unexplained fund transfers. I suspect the money was intended to facilitate the placement of the four operatives to support his plan to capture the next generation of stealth code. The two in the deli slowly poisoned him. I believe the guys at the crash site intended to copy the code from the laptop and then return it to the briefcase. Thankfully, the plan backfired."

"I'm so glad you survived," Ashley said, while she looked at Mike. He returned her gaze with warmth in his eyes. His hand slid on top of hers.

"The poison in your drink was to help soften you up. You were going to be blamed, but they didn't count on me showing up to gum up their plan. The attack at the hospital came next, followed by the raid on our house. When all that failed, DeSoto decided to take matters into his own hands." JJ turned and reached for Jo. "I am sorry that I didn't foresee you getting caught in the middle. I'm beyond grateful you weren't hurt. More than I can tell you, sweetheart, especially when you are carrying our baby."

Mike stuttered, "Jo, you're pregnant? Wow! Congratulations, you guys." Mike struggled. "Ashley, I want to know—"

Fearing the worst, Ashley proclaimed, "I've had to live with this awful secret, always afraid. When this voice threatened you and a son I've never met, I couldn't even tell you. All he wanted was the combination to the briefcase. I refused to give him any correct information, but his calls and texts scared me so badly that I couldn't. Please forgive me, Mike." She lay her head on her folded arms, emotionally exhausted.

After a few moments, Mike brightly stated, "I think I'll have that drink now. Sweetheart, may I get you something too? Would you like your favorite?"

The pressure lifted from her with his affectionate tone. Forgiveness seemed within arm's reach. Ashley giggled, "No, honey. I can't have any liquor for the same reason Jo isn't drinking. I hope you'll be pleased knowing you and I are going to be parents."

Jo slid her hand into JJ's. "I want us to make sure that these new lives get to grow up together. They can be best friends like Mike and JJ."

The Flight Enigma

If you have read some of our other stories in the Magnolia Bluff Crime Chronicles, were you surprised by the international espionage aspect of this story?

Did you enjoy the Jo and JJ characters, and if so, why?

What do you feel is the strongest theme for this story?

Who did you feel was the most believable character in the mystery?

Would you have preferred more details on a particular character? If so, which one? (Note: Because we'd love to tell their backstories.)

What was your most significant ah-ha moment in the story?

Did you feel the evil characters received fair treatment?

Which of the other books in the Magnolia Bluff Crime Chronicles have you enjoyed? We are on the 4th season, going strong.

Did you find the threads viable and fun to untangle?

Would you like to see more of Jo and JJ?

Do stories about international espionage in small towns cause you concern?

Did you laugh about Oscar and his wilting?

Is there anything in the story you wish we had left out?

What one thing do you feel we could have done to make this story more enjoyable?

Please let us know your thoughts in your reviews or invite us to your book club meetings via *Authors@EnigmaSeries.com*

Thank you for taking the time with *The Flight Enigma*. Read on.

The Women Who Cried Through the Storm

Richard Schwindt

"That it will never come again
is what makes life sweet."
Emily Dickinson

PART 1
Sunday evening, late summer

In the still verdant glory of late summer, I was looking at a Taoist poem in a small book drawn from the shelf in my office. On the cusp of retirement, I considered what was being left behind, and what remained.

I had my family—no small thing, a flower garden eked from clay, and memories, some good, and some horrific.

Many therapists don't retire at all. They shuffle into their dotage, clinging to those intense and introspective one-hour increments with hurting and confused people.

I should be happy in my accomplishments—those I have helped, but I wanted more.

Kate stood at the door with her arm out, something in her hand.

"Chris, it's for you."

I placed the book back on the shelf. My phone had been left in the kitchen. Kate answered, and brought it to me. She sounded angry.

I took the device while she ostentatiously drank from a large glass of chardonnay, then disappeared up the stairs.

"Hello."

"Christopher, it's Sonia Parker."

"Hello, Sonia, nice to hear from you."

"Is Kate okay?"

"She's fine, thanks." This was a lie. Even the sound of Sonia's voice made Kate's blood pressure rise.

"I need you to help me with something."

"Is Les alright?"

"Les is fine. It's my son, Michael."

"Michael?" I glanced up the stairs.

My name is Chris Allard. I am a social worker and psycho-therapist, based in Toronto. Seventy-two years old, I am married to Kate, father to Roxane and Angela, grandfather to Liam and Ruth.

I am too old to be seduced by anyone, though if that were ever to happen, it would be Sonia Parker.

Cool, brilliant, and strikingly beautiful, Sonia had been appearing at irregular intervals in my life since I had become an adult.

I looked out at the gloaming; amber light reflecting on the maple trees, as remembered emotions washed over me. Though still summer, some of the leaves showed crimson and gold at the margins.

Many years ago; weeks before Kate and I were to be married, my late mother, Dr. Marie-Giselle Allard, had appeared at our home in Scarborough on a Monday night, accompanied by a stunning young woman.

Blonde, cool and seemingly aloof, she looked at the world through intense ice-blue eyes.

"This is Sonia Parker," mom said with customary insouciance, "one of my interns. Sonia, this is my son Christopher. He may or may not turn into a good therapist."

Both of us looked awkwardly around while she carried on. My mother, one of the great psychoanalysts of her generation, did not, in the modern parlance, have a filter.

"I have a paper to complete tonight for the psychoanalytic institute, so Christopher will be taking Sonia to dinner. He is about to be married to the beautiful Katrin' Michalchuk, and she is to marry the handsome Lester Kurelek, so I anticipate no unfortunate erotic occurrences."

My mom really talked like that. And by the time our car was headed downtown, Sonia and I were both so embarrassed we could barely look at each other.

"Christopher, are you there?"

Shaken out of memory lane, I replied. "Yes, sorry Sonia," then told another lie. "I was thinking of Les."

"Christopher, in a way, that's why I'm calling. When Les returned from Ukraine, I was terrified. It was like someone else had come back in his body. I felt abandoned, and turned to some-one trustworthy to deliver the therapy he needed. You gave me my husband back."

Her voice resonated emotion. Dr. Sonia Parker, from her leafy domicile in Ann Arbor Michigan, one of the five most cited psychoanalysts in North America, was referred to by friends and colleagues as "Mrs. Spock" for her apparent emotional control.

I knew better. Lester Kurelek, intuitive and emotional, a brilliant painter and portraitist, understood this in his outwardly dispassionate wife. In a way, it helped him trust me more as a therapist.

As a sniper in Ukraine, Les had come face to face with the darkness inside, and among the many changes that conferred on him was an appreciation of men who had engaged with their own demons.

My wife, on the other hand, wouldn't trust Sonia with a grocery list. Kate knew my weakness. She too was intelligent and beautiful, as well as loyal to a fault. When I betrayed her many years ago by sleeping with a client, she had been wounded to her heart.

"What's up with Michael?" I asked. I had heard his name of course. He was a psychologist, employed by a small liberal arts college somewhere in Texas. From the little I had heard, he much resembled, and was much beloved by his parents. He was married, and they had a baby girl.

"He's not himself. I can tell."

From a psychotherapist of her caliber, this was a remarkably vague description. Again, her emotions interfered. But she had already become aware of how it sounded. "I think he may be having dissociative episodes."

"What kind of dissociative episodes?"

"I'm not sure. He sounds different to me on the phone. And his wife says he has become withdrawn and forgetful. Sue's a lovely girl and I trust her judgement. But they have a baby in the house that needs a fully engaged father."

I glanced again up the stairs. We had recently repainted the railing an odd shade of green. It was Kate's selection and offensive to the eye, but I more wanted to see if she was eavesdropping.

"Could he call me and arrange an appointment? As I'm sure you know, things have been winding down with Les. I will be retired in six months, but could probably see Michael with minimal conflict."

A pause followed.

"Sonia, does he know you are calling?"

"No."

So that was it. A worried mom calling about her son; a common scenario, except in this case the mom was a psychoanalyst, and the son an adult psychologist.

"You must know how that sounds."

"I want you to have dinner with him tomorrow night, and report back to me. I will pay your hourly rate of course."

"Sonia, listen to yourself. I would have to violate a half dozen clinical boundaries before the first bite." I realized my voice was raised and, again, glanced upstairs.

"Christopher, I wouldn't ask if it wasn't important. Yes, I know how this sounds."

"Am I supposed to fly to Texas, then buy him a steak fried chicken and a Lone Star?"

"I think it's chicken fried steak. And no, of course not. If his plane is on time, he's just arrived in Toronto for a conference. He'll be staying at the Delta hotel downtown. He thinks he's having dinner tomorrow with an old friend of mine - his father's therapist."

"You've already arranged everything."

"Yes."

"Fine, how about this? I go to dinner with Michael and get to meet your son. We will have a few drinks, a good dinner, and I will check to see if he is okay with me calling you afterwards."

I paused. There was one more thing. "There's going to be no payment. I'll share some impressions if there is anything to share."

One notable characteristic of the Kurelek/Parkers was their generosity. Not only had Les several times tried to pay more than my fee, but I once had to return a sketch he had sent me of a Hickory tree in his back yard.

"It's just a graphite sketch," he said, "on a phone pad."

"Yes, a sketch I could sell for a thousand bucks online tomorrow. Stop it! I can't believe your wife never explained therapeutic boundaries to you."

"Alright, from now on you only get your hourly fee and the charm of my personality."

"That's all I need."

"Christopher. I took the liberty of providing Michael with your number. He'll call you after his day is done. Are you there?"

Once more I had been jolted from my memories.

"Sonia, as you know, we all dissociate. Right now, talking to you—hearing your voice—I'm dissociating. Maybe Michael has a lot on his mind."

"Of course he does. I know that. There are some things that have happened… if he wants to tell you… it might be best heard from him. Christopher, I would not ask anyone else to do this. You know I trust you… Michael is my only child."

Saying no was off the table.

"Christopher, I have taken the liberty of making a reservation for two at a Japanese restaurant on Bay Street. Is that acceptable?"

"Sure, I love Japanese food."

"You will hear from Michael tomorrow."

Kate, after eavesdropping

That woman makes him crazy. He told me about their first meeting, and I am sure he regrets it, but there is more to the story. I have only met Sonia a few times when she and her husband came to town to see Marie-Giselle. The cool blonde genius of Chris's fevered imagination. I wasn't impressed. Another academic who deleted her feeling side.

What an over emotive Parisian like Marie-Giselle saw in her, I don't know. Maybe those in thrall to their emotions can only wonder at the those who are not.

As to her son, I'm going on Google to get his story. Lester, the husband; he's okay. Lovely man, brilliant artist, crazy handsome; looks like Paul Gross. Maybe the son is more like him.

Downtown Toronto on a Monday night

Michael had called mid-afternoon and invited me out for dinner. We agreed to meet at the Saint Andrew subway station, grab a drink, and proceed to the restaurant.

The day had been hot and humid, as Toronto can be during the summer months. Even in the bustle and clatter of downtown, a strange stillness hung in the air.

I don't think it's intentional, but Michael Kurelek leaves a hell of a first impression. Just his size alone, on an athletic frame, let alone the movie star looks and big smile.

"Christopher Allard, so great to meet you at last! My mom has told me all about you."

I laughed. He had a distinct American accent, though not one I would have associated with Texas. And I doubted his mom had told him everything.

"Nice to meet you too. By the way, only my late mother, and your mom ever called me Christopher. Chris is great."

"Sure thing, Chris. Call me Mike."

I found a small pub on John Street, leaving time to hike over to the restaurant for our reservation.

Inside, we occupied a booth and ordered shots of rye.

Conversation came easy. Both of us were therapists and, as it happened, on the same philosophic wavelength when it came to things like family therapy, eclecticism and hypnotherapy.

"What does your mother think of family therapy?" I asked.

"She thinks family therapists are clinical showboats who wouldn't know a transference experience from a chicken sandwich."

I laughed. "My mother would have said exactly that, but with a strong Parisienne accent."

After a pint of beer and another shot, we departed for the restaurant. As we approached the towers and evening shadows of Bay Street, walking through the crowds of bankers and other habitués of Canada's financial heart, I reminded myself that I would never keep up with my younger companion's thirst for strong drink.

Or keep up with him at all. He kept having to slow down in order to accommodate his older companion. And because I was the one who knew the way.

Once seated in the quiet restaurant, nipping at some sake, Mike came to the point. "Chris, I know my mom well enough to know this is a set-up. She wants to know how I am doing, doesn't she?"

"Mike, I was going to explain all of this. Yes, she did call me, and she is worried about you. But she also knows I won't share anything from our conversation without your permission."

Mike picked up the menu. "If you are okay with it, I wouldn't mind telling you about some recent experiences. You've done so much for my dad." He put the menu down again. "I know we've never met before today, but I need to get some stuff out."

"I'm in, Mike. Let's enjoy dinner, and then I know a quiet place where we can have a nightcap and talk."

The Library Bar, at the Royal York hotel

"Am I keeping you up too late?" Mike asked.

"I'm good; no sessions scheduled until one tomorrow." After filling ourselves with high end Sushi, we sat in a lovely old-school bar in the hotel, sipping on expensive scotch. The chairs were plush and comfy, the atmosphere warm and intimate.

"My mom said I was having dissociative spells, didn't she?"

I nodded.

"I have, but it's gone further than she thinks.

"I've been having blackouts, even when I'm not drinking. Finding myself at the other end of town for no reason. Twice, I found myself standing outside a house rented by a student."

I sat listening, clinical instincts activated, even though I needed to remind myself that Mike Kurelek was not my client. Still, I wanted to help him elaborate.

"How long has this been going on?"

His eyes moved in and out of focus, as if he were working on not dissociating now. The first thing that crossed my mind was that he'd experienced some kind of trauma.

Then it occurred to me that accidentally triggering dissociative anger in a bar, with a guy Kureleks' size might not be a brilliant idea.

He seemed to anticipate me. "Sue - my wife, she's seen more of this than anyone. There's no rage or rampage, or even irritability. She would say I just disappear mentally, and sometimes physically."

He remembered my question. "It started when Butch died."

"Butch?"

"My neighbor's coon hound. One morning in May, I stepped out to go to work, and found him."

"Were you close to this dog?" I had learned many things over a long career, and one of them was classifying the death of a pet as a serious bereavement.

"He saved my life while I was boar hunting. Sue and I saved his life on several occasions."

Swirling the glass around, I took another sip. His body language made it obvious that he was deeply affected.

"He lay on our doorstep. Butch had come to us before when he was injured, and I guess he thought…"

Mike paused to compose himself, took a few breaths, and continued. "When I realized what had happened, I scooped him into my arms. Sue came to the door and began to sob. Sonia heard her and began to cry. I took his body next door to his owner— my friend Jack—and soon he was sobbing too."

"And you, Mike? What were you doing?"

"Consoling my wife, my baby daughter, and my best friend."

"You weren't sobbing?"

"I couldn't. I can't. I'm the one who has to hold it together."

I didn't reply. I didn't have to. He knew what he was saying.

"What do you know about Magnolia Bluff, Chris?"

"Just that it's somewhere in Texas. At some point your dad said you live there. I hear the fishing is good."

Mike's eyes widened. "Is that all my dad told you about it? Good place to fish?" He shook his head in apparent disbelief. "You didn't google me, did you?"

"No."

"You can't share anything my dad has said. I know. But something to understand is there have been violent deaths in Magnolia Bluff, and I have been affected by them, and helped solve a few." Once more he looked on the cusp of dissociating.

"You can't imagine what it's like being a therapist in a small town, and trying to solve a murder at the same time."

"I don't have to, but I see you didn't Google me either."

"What does that mean?"

I wanted to keep him on track, and he had said something that couldn't be allowed to slip away. "You said that you had gone to the apartment of a student while dissociated."

Before he could respond, an attractive young server appeared and slipped a folded piece of paper beside Mike's glass, smiled in his direction, then left.

"What's that about?"

He didn't even glance at the paper. "It's an invitation. It will have her name, phone number and the time she gets off work."

I could hear the change in his tone.

"This sort of thing has been happening to me since I was fifteen. Did it ever happen to you?"

I shook my head. Definitely not. "I'm fortunate. I'm married to a wonderful woman."

I had another memory. "Actually, something like this did happen once a long time ago, and I made a stupid mistake."

"I'm sorry," he said. "I'm married to a wonderful woman too. I would never cheat on her, but…" He stopped mid-sentence and pushed the note under a serviette, then help up his hand. "See, I'm wearing my wedding ring. Chris, women have actually done this in front of Sue."

"That's terrible. What did she do?"

Mike chuckled, and temporarily returned to Texas. "No assault charges were pressed. Sheriff Blanton told the ladies in question that he didn't prosecute girlie slaps, and they ought to have more respect for another women's property."

"Sheriff Blanton sounds like quite a character."

"You have no idea."

"I still want to know about the student you mentioned."

"Sure." Mike waved for more drinks. "Her name is Meredith. She's a student from California. We had a big problem at the college last year, and she helped me solve it. She has a very high IQ, kind of like you."

"Me?"

"My mom says your IQ is twenty points higher than the next social worker in line."

"That's not a high bar."

Realizing that I had just slagged my profession, I added: "Your mom has never liked social workers much." But I was not deterred. "What is it with this Meredith? Are you attracted to her?"

"No. Well, maybe. Chris, she's a student. She's twenty-one for God's sake."

"Is she a client?"

"No, I knew it would be unwise."

"Then you are attracted to her."

"I can't be."

"Of course you can. The problem is that you can't admit it."

He looked up and glared, but only for a moment.

"Mike, you had to support your family and friend when the dog died. You should be faithful to your wife. But you can't deny your emotional foundation. This dissociation business. It sounds like a trauma response to me. Has there been more?"

He took a sip of his new drink. "Yes, quite a bit more."

"Push too much crap inside, and that crap finds its way out. I think we both know you need to find a therapist of your own to take a deep dive into these issues."

He took a last swallow of his drink. "You interested in the job?"

"I've put my clients—your dad knows this—on retirement watch, and provided six months notice. I think you might need someone ongoing. It wouldn't be fair to you for me to start, and then leave."

Mike laughed. "I feel better, Chris. It always helps to get something off your chest."

"That good, but it's not therapy."

"Maybe if we meet for drinks again, I could tell you about the time I shot an arrow through the spine of a serial killer."

"Wow." I took one last appreciative drink of the scotch in my glass. "I could tell you about the time I brained a murderous bureaucrat with a large rock."

"Really?"

"Yeah."

We were still laughing as we rose from the table.

Mike laid a row of US bills on the table. He had covered dinner too. "You want the note from the pretty server, Chris?"

For a moment I was tempted. How much fun would it be to leave it somewhere Kate could find it? But it was time to go. "I'm good, Mike. Let's head out."

Kate

Chris came in drunk, of course. And kind of stirred up. So, there was no good time to tell him what I had found out about Michael Kurelek, and the crime-ridden madhouse known as Magnolia Bluff, Texas. I didn't want to ruin his mood, but to be honest, I hope this is the last we have heard of Michael Kurelek and his murderous little town.

UNDERGROUND AUTHORS AND THE MAGNOLIA BLUFF CRIME CHRONICLES

AN AUTHORS CO-OP

The late Caleb Pirtle III organized the Underground Authors in mid-2020. The purpose was to harness the collective reach of a dozen authors to promote each other's books.

Fortunately, writers like to write. It didn't take long for the group to come up with the idea to create a member collection of short stories with a central theme to aid the joint marketing efforts.

Beyond the Sea: Stories from the Underground was published in April 2021. (Pick up a copy from Amazon) with the publication of the story collection, the co-op began calling itself the Underground Authors.

Little did the authors realize that with the publication of *Beyond the Sea* things were about to change and change in a way they couldn't even imagine.

MAGNOLIA BLUFF

In May 2021, following an online writers conference, CW Hawes proposed that the Underground Authors write a multi-author series. After a flurry of emails, the group sketched out the broad picture of the town, the important landmarks, and the main characters writers would use in his or her books. Magnolia Bluff Crime Chronicles was born.

The series revolves around the goings-on in the small, fictional Texas Hill Country town of Magnolia Bluff. Each author chronicles our small town's lives, loves, and deaths. There are a dozen different perspectives on life in Magnolia Bluff, Texas—a beautiful little place on the shore of Burnet Reservoir, where murder waits in the wings.

We are now in our fourth year. Magnolia Bluff has taken on a life of its own. For the writers and readers, the town has become a real place.

We are amazed at the incredible reception the series has received. It's exciting to know that we have something a little bit unique in the world of crime fiction.

We invite you to sit back and enjoy this chapter in the ongoing saga that is Magnolia Bluff. If this is your first visit, you are in for a delightful treat. And if you're a return visitor, you know what to expect: humor, suspense, and people you care about.

All the best, and be sure to look behind you.

Breakfield works for a high-tech manufacturer as a solution architect, functioning in hybrid data/telecom environments. He is a long-time technology geek who enjoys writing, studying World War II history, traveling, and cultural exchanges. Charles loves wine tastings, cooking, and Harley riding, often inserting these incidents into the stories. As a child, he moved often because of his father's military career, which even helps him with the various character perspectives he brings to life in the series. He continues to teach Burkey humor.

Burkey is a business architect who builds customer solutions on a good technology foundation. She has written many technology and white papers, but finds the freedom of writing fiction a lot more fun. As a child, she helped to lead the kids with exciting new adventures built on make-believe characters, was a Girl Scout until high school, and contributed to the community as a young member of a Head Start program. Rox enjoys family, learning, listening to people, traveling, outdoor activities, sewing, cooking, and thinking about diversifying the series.

Breakfield and Burkey started authoring non-fiction papers and books, but it wasn't as fun as writing fictional stories. They found it interesting to use the aspects of technology that people are incorporating into their daily lives more and more often. This was a perfect way to create good guy/bad guy stories with elements of travel to the various places they have visited either professionally or personally, humor, romance, intrigue, suspense, and a spirited way to remember people who have crossed paths with them. They love to talk about their stories with private and public book readings. Burkey also conducts regular interviews for Texas authors, which she finds interesting. Her first interview was, wait for it, Breakfield. You can often find them at local book fairs or other family-oriented events.

The primary series is based on a family organization called R-Group. They spawned a subgroup containing the original characters, as the Cyber Assassins Technology Services (CATS) team. The authors have ideas for continuing the series in both tracks. They track the more than 150 characters on a spreadsheet, with a hidden avenue for the future coined *The Enigma Chronicles,* tagged in portions of the stories. Fan reviews frequently suggest that these would make good television or movie stories, so the possibilities appear endless, just like their ideas for new stories.

They have book video trailers for each of the stories, which can be viewed on YouTube, Amazon's Authors page, or on their website, www.EnigmaSeries.com. Their website is routinely updated with new interviews, answers to readers' questions, book trailers, and contests. You may also find it fascinating to check out the fun acronyms they create for the stories summarized on their website. Reach out to them at *Authors@EnigmaSeries.com, Twitter@EnigmaSeries,* or *Facebook@TheEnigmaSeries.*

Please provide a fair and honest review on amazon and any other places you post reviews – We appreciate the feedback.

MAGNOLIA BLUFF CRIME CHRONICLES SEASON 1

MAGNOLIA BLUFF CRIME CHRONICLES: SEASON 2

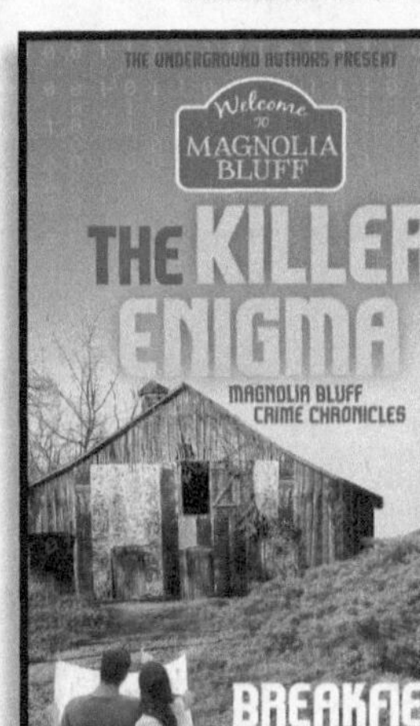

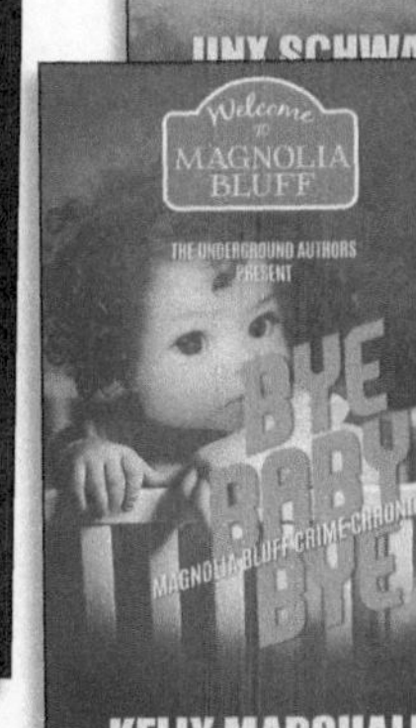

MEN LYING DEAD IN A FIELD

MAGNOLIA BLUFF CRIME CHRONICLES: SEASON 3

MAGNOLIA BLUFF CRIME CHRONICLES: SEASON 4

We would greatly appreciate
if you would take a few minutes
and provide a review of this work
on Amazon, Goodreads
and any of your other favorite places.

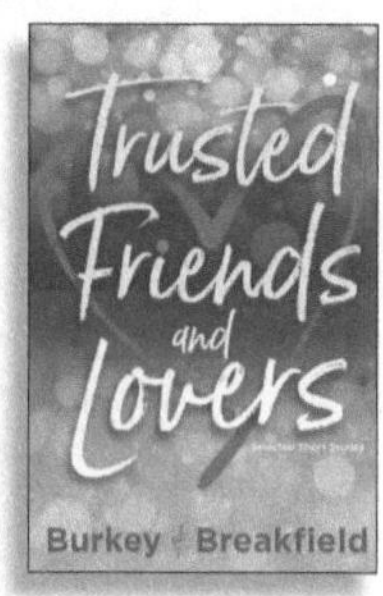